GENEALOGY
OF MURDER

GENEALOGY OF MURDER

A DEB RALSTON MYSTERY

Lee Martin

ST. MARTIN'S PRESS ✹ NEW YORK

Library of Congress Cataloging-in-Publication Data
Martin, Lee, 1943–
     Genealogy of murder   /   Lee Martin. —1st ed.
        p.   cm.
     "A Deb Ralston mystery."
     ISBN 0-312-13975-6
     1. Ralston, Deb (Fictitious character)—Fiction.   2. Women
detectives—Texas—Fort Worth—Fiction.   3. Policewomen—Texas—Fort
Worth—Fiction.   4. Fort Worth (Tex.)—Fiction.   I. Title.
PS3563.A7249G46   1996
813'.54–dc20   95-43881
                                                                        CIP

10 9 8 7 6 5 4 3 2

This one is especially for Katherine Marcella, who gave me a corpse and an idea.

Special thanks to the LDS Church Historian's Office for looking up names and dates for me.

If there is actually an organization called the Daughters of the American Flag, I apologize most abjectly. Mine was an independent invention. I did not, however, invent the religious prejudice displayed in the membership form, which is the reason I did not accept several different people's friendly and well-meaning invitations to join the DAR. Although the clause does not apply to me, it hits a good many of my friends.

The experiment discussed in this book is actually in progress in several places in the United States, but to the best of my knowledge Fort Worth is not one of those places.

Genealogy
of Murder

$\mathcal{P}\,r\,o\,l\,o\,g\,u\,e$

. . . .

"I'VE GOT AN extra corpse," my son-in-law Olead Baker said over the phone, his voice crackling with anxiety.

That was the second thing he said. I only half heard the first, because I was busy looking at the computer screen. I ought to be, but am not, ashamed to admit to having become slightly addicted to computer games, particularly odd and complicated forms of solitaire.

"Huh?" I said, and clicked the mouse. I went on clicking the mouse, absently, while I half-listened to Olead.

Looking at the computer screen was what I was doing that glorious Saturday morning, when I was scheduled to work but had taken comp time on the grounds that I had housework to do. Now I had a load of clothes in the washer, a load of clothes in the dryer, and a load of dishes in the dishwasher, and how much could I be expected to do at once for cryin' out loud when I didn't know what time Harry, our son Cameron, and our ward Lori would swoop back down on me? I had been called out about 2 A.M. on something that looked like something but turned out to be nothing, and the rest of the family, trying hard not to wake me, had breakfasted on Cheerios and left for the library. It had been after ten before I crawled out of bed, found Harry's note taped to the front of the refrigerator, helped myself to Cheerios, started on the housework, and turned on the computer.

I was still playing with it when my son-in-law Olead Baker

called me and said diffidently, "Deb? I think I've got a problem."

"What sort of problem?" I asked resignedly. Actually Olead is not given either to having problems or to calling me to solve them, but I really, really wanted to use my day off for *me* just for a change.

"I've got an extra corpse."

So, as I've mentioned, I answered, "Huh?" and mouse-clicked a few more times before I fully registered what he said.

"Would you like to run that by me again?" I asked then.

"Okay, you know that experiment I'm working with?" He sounded somewhat calmer now that he knew I was really listening.

"Yes," I said.

He started to go on, and then interrupted himself. " 'Scuse me, I've got to get that other line."

Obviously he did; I had twice heard that little click that means call-waiting on the other person's line. The phone went temporarily dead, and I sat and held it.

He left me plenty of time to think. Yes, I was very familiar with what he was working on, though so far I had managed to avoid accepting his frequent and affectionate invitations to visit it.

Olead is a medical student—come to think of it, he is now an intern, but he is still going back and forth between the school and the hospital where he is interning. The county medical examiner's office is in the same block of buildings as the medical school, and the two organizations jointly are involved with an experiment the various pieces of which are being conducted in various places across the country. The whole idea, even to me and I'm quite used to corpses, is rather grisly.

But it's in answer to a real need: Too much of what we think we know about how corpses decompose is based either on anecdotal evidence or on evidence that comes from areas with climates different from our own. Accordingly, medical schools and/or medical examiners' offices in several different areas—Virginia, where the concept began and where it's warm and very humid; Texas, where it's hot and pretty humid; Arizona, where it's hot and dry; Oregon, where it's cool and humid; and Alaska, in an area that's cold and dry—are all involved with the same large-scale experiment. In each area, it involves a large chunk of land away from smelling distance of anybody who's not involved with the experiment. A compound is then created by fencing around and over with chicken-wire threaded with slats on the sides, so as to cut down visibility from the outside and make sure nothing larger than a sparrow or a small rat can get in or out (after all, nobody would want part of that experiment being dropped on somebody's lawn by a bored crow). There is, of course, no slatting on the top, as the sun needs to reach the compound, but few people will fly over in a helicopter anyway.

Then there's a charged razor-wire fence around the chicken-wire fence, with a passive burglar alarm and an active burglar alarm both wired in, so that even if the electrical current is somehow shut off, at least one alarm will be triggered if a wire is cut. It should not be necessary to protect decaying corpses with charged fences, razor wire, and burglar alarms. But in the real world, it is necessary: They could be stolen for assorted reasons by anybody from teen gang members or frat rats out on a lark to Satanists, Santería cult followers, and the like.

Inside the fence, assorted cadavers have been strewn around. Some are in the sun; some are in the shade. Some are clothed; some are not. Some are lying in the open; others are in closed vehicles or buildings; some of the buildings are air-conditioned and some are not. Some of the cadavers have been buried in shallow, coffinless graves, others are in deep, unlined, coffinless graves, and still others are in deep, plain wood coffins, the kind a murderer might cobble up in a hurry if he was pretty handy with tools.

The unburied cadavers are checked twice a day; the others are checked far more seldom because, of course, unburying a corpse interrupts the natural process so that a separate corpse is required for each period of time to be tested.

All this takes a lot of cadavers, which are hard to get. A few people, either from generosity or from the fear that their relatives couldn't afford to bury them, leave their bodies to medical schools, but most schools need more cadavers than they're getting. No, burking is not under consideration; not only is it illegal, but furthermore normally buried bodies are embalmed, which abrogates the purpose of the experiment, and anybody producing a still-warm corpse, as Burke and Hare did in Edinburgh when grave-robbing got too difficult, would also have to produce a death certificate and answer a *lot* of questions.

But from what Olead had said, it appeared that nobody had stolen a body; nobody had tried to get paid for producing one that was too recently, and too suspiciously, deceased. No, what seemed to have turned up was an extra corpse, which, I had a hunch, probably meant I wasn't going to play any more computer games today *or* be home hussifrying around when the rest of the family arrived. I moused up to the top left corner and closed my program.

Olead finished his other phone call and resumed talking to me.

"The darnedest thing," he went on earnestly. "Deb, it's this old guy, nice haircut, shaved, clean, kind of—uh, portly—looks like he might've been a doctor or a lawyer or something, and he's just lying here out in the open—"

"Where are you?" I interrupted, trying to subdue the unrighteous wish that it would turn out to be one of several defense lawyers whose murders I have frequently, despite the fact that my other son-in-law *is* a lawyer, told people I would be delighted to work.

"Well, I'm still out here at the compound."

"Then who was the other call? I thought you must be in an office."

"No, I'm just out here at the compound." He was more nervous than I had realized; Olead is not in the habit of repeating himself. "That was Professor Lindstrom; he wanted to know what was keeping me."

"Did you tell him?"

"Well, no, I said I'd explain later."

. . . . .

"Enough with the 'well,' " I said, and he chuckled nervously. "Did you call nine-one-one?"

"I wanted to talk to you first. I mean, what's the emergency? He's sure not going anywhere. And this one would land on your desk anyway, most likely. Deb, this is really strange. There's two dead rats near the body."

He now had all parts of my attention that he didn't already have. Those two dead rats could mean several things, and I wasn't too crazy about the implications of any of them, because the fact is that human flesh is normally perfectly nutritious rat food. Human flesh that seemingly poisoned rats . . . well. Who could help but wonder how that corpse had gotten to be a corpse?

I could think of a lot of possibilities. But I couldn't do anything about those possibilities until I got there. And he was probably right that this one would land on my desk anyway.

"This Professor Lindstrom," I said. "Is he the one in charge of the experiment?"

"Yes, why?"

"Because you'd better call him, tell him what's going on, and ask if another cadaver has been put in the compound without you knowing it. I know you ought to be told"—I forestalled his interruption—"but that doesn't always mean you will be. So find out. Then call me right back."

"Okay," he said, and hung up. He called back about three minutes later. "No new cadaver. And Professor Lindstrom is fit to be tied. He told me he'll be right out here."

"Glorious," I said. "Tell him to stay away from the body—police orders." Then I sighed, not audibly, and went on: "I'll call Captain Millner. Stay at the compound and wait for me. And be sure to—"

"Keep Professor Lindstrom away from the body. And myself too. Right. I know."

$\mathcal{O} n \varepsilon$

. . . .

I DO NOT work homicides—officially. The Homicide Unit, to which I briefly belonged before being put into the Major Case Unit, officially works homicides. The Major Case Unit officially works complicated cases that fit into no other category, including, usually, that of homicide. The theory behind the Major Case Unit is one person, one case, and that one person stays with that one case until it's cleared. Of course, it rarely works that way.

Every now and then, in Homicide or in any other unit, there's a case so weird, so kinky, that no matter where it ought to belong theoretically, it winds up being dropped into the lap of the Major Case Unit. All too often those weird, kinky cases—especially if they're homicides—seem to land in my lap.

As did this one, because Captain Millner reasoned, as I knew perfectly well he would regardless of the fact that I was supposed to be off work that day, that since my son-in-law had found the corpse (whether or not it was murder, and those rats certainly suggested it was) I should have some unique ability to pick his brain and find out what was in there even if he didn't know himself. In vain did I point out that Olead had nothing to do with the case—he'd just found the body.

But I took some fiendish delight in the fact that Captain Millner decided, as he sometimes decides, that he'd better go have a look for himself. I knew what he was going to find there, and I knew that he knew too and that he wouldn't dream of going out there if his curiosity weren't much stronger than his stomach. I never faint or throw up at crime scenes. Captain Millner doesn't faint, but he has been known once or twice in his life to throw up.

Even in November, which this was, the stench of one decaying human body is recognized instantly even by somebody who has never smelled anything of the sort before. I've heard it described as sweetish, but I don't know why. I don't find it sweet, or bitter, or sour, or—to mention the last of the four basic tastes that everybody is supposed to have—even salty. I can't describe it, but like everybody else who's ever smelled it, I can't forget it. It's as if some instinct deep inside us warns us that this is what we will all come to.

The stench of thirty-four decaying human bodies is not really that much worse than the stench of one, and even at best there is nothing about it to remind one of lavender and lilacs. All the same I stood stoically in the middle of it not because it wasn't disturbing—it was very disturbing—but because I knew perfectly well that after I'd stayed in the compound for about five minutes I'd no longer be able to smell it, whereas Captain Millner, who was running in and out with his face purple and his handkerchief over his mouth and nose, wasn't giving his olfactory nerves the chance to go numb.

Olead, who reasoned the way I reasoned (probably because he had been with the experiment since its inception and had learned the hard way, which was the same way I learned), was standing with me about five feet away from the worst corpse, watching Millner with a rather puzzled expression. I should mention that Captain Millner stands six foot two and looks more like the movies' idea of a fine, upstanding, superior officer than any other cop I've ever seen; he is well past sixty now, though he has made no warning rattles about retiring, and his dignity is usually the most noticeable thing about him. He does not look like somebody who would be totally grossed out by anything. But in the middle of the compound gateway, the little puddle of what had once been his lunch, which he had scuffed dirt over with the toe of his shoe, testified to the condition of his stomach and/or nerves in this matter.

To his credit, I will add that he was still here. And I will also admit that the first autopsy I attended I spent almost the entire time sitting on the floor because I did not trust my legs to hold me up and the medical examiner's assistant was using the only chair. (Captain Millner, who had nobly escorted me to said autopsy, had gone out the door with his hand over his mouth about three minutes before I sat down).

By now it was a little past noon. Olead had arrived to check the compound about 10 A.M.; the extra corpse had been over in the back left corner so he hadn't found it immediately. The compound had last been checked about twelve hours earlier, and the corpse hadn't been there then. No, Olead hadn't checked it that time, but Professor Lindstrom, who was talking with Olead when I arrived, gave me the name and phone number of the medical student who had—one Tara Larsen—and I'd called her myself, using the phone at the compound. She told me she had painstakingly compared the present condition of each corpse to her notes of the condition of each corpse when she last checked it two days earlier, made carefully detailed notes of all changes, taken photographs where applicable (the kind of photographs that go on a computer disk, not the kind I would take), and gone home and entered all the changes on her computer's hard disk and immediately backed up that file on a floppy before going to sleep. There had been no extra bodies and no dead rats, and yes, she would have noticed. (I might add that she had no classes on Saturday and was not delighted to be awakened by a ringing telephone.)

Professor Lindstrom told me that normally, at night, the compound is in darkness, but when someone arrives after dark to check conditions, that person flips a switch and the entire area is flooded with light the way a tennis court is at night. That was something I could check. Although there were no houses in the immediate vicinity, I could see a high-rise apartment structure about a quarter of a mile away, with the backs—the bedroom sides, probably—of about forty apartments toward the compound. Maybe somebody in that complex had noticed that the lights at the compound were turned on twice last night. Maybe somebody could remember about what time after eleven the lights were turned on.

And maybe not, and maybe whoever put the corpse in here hadn't turned on the lights at all; for that matter, they could very well have come over here this morning, before Olead arrived. Of course that assumed that the perp knew the schedule, but most likely anybody who knew the compound existed knew the schedule or knew how to get it.

We were still waiting for Ident; there had been several major burglaries Friday night and Ident had calls stacked up, though Irene had promised to rush right over as soon as she could break free. And we were still waiting for somebody from the medical examiner's office; the chief examiner and one of the other examiners were off duty, having worked late Friday night and expecting to work late Saturday night, and couldn't be reached by telephone. The one who remained—I didn't know who that was—was at a shooting on the south side. An investigator from the ME's office was en route, but of course he would wait for Irene.

In the meantime, we'd all had a good look at the corpse. It was lying face up, with legs together pointing toward the west, arms loosely at its sides. It could have been properly laid out for burial, except for the location and the lack of coffin and clothing. Olead, after seeing it and realizing that it didn't belong here, had avoided getting near it, so any footprints or other trace evidence would still be intact, and there was no use calling a transport team until after Ident and the ME were through.

There wasn't the slightest question as to whether this corpse was dead. Rigor mortis had come and gone; I guessed from what I could see that he'd been dead about two and a half days, and Professor Lindstrom, who knows far more about the human body than I will ever learn, guessed the same. But somebody had partially attended to the body: The usual slack position of the jaw was gone

. . . . .

9

and the mouth was completely closed, and the eyes, which normally are half to fully opened, also were closed. Or had been closed; one of them still was. The other, along with its eyelid, had been nibbled on by some small carnivore, probably one of the rats, as had the nose, most of which was gone. (In just the twelve or so hours it had been here? I wondered, and asked Olead. "Yeah," he said, "that happens.")

But still, it seemed to have been attended to at one time, and that attention was part of the reason it looked laid out for burial.

And I could see what Olead meant about the person who'd once inhabited this corpse. But even that was odd. . . . The skin was pinkish, rather than the grayish shade I'd expect to find by now, and the huge, deep purple splotches I'd expect to find visible (visible at least to somebody lying on the ground, which I had done for about one minute to check that very thing) on the back where the blood had pooled when the heart stopped beating were not present. In the middle of those huge purple splotches should be yellow-white, sometimes wrinkled, areas marking the actual contact points between the body and the ground, but if the postmortem staining wasn't there, probably those marks weren't either.

If the staining had been present, as it ought to be, it would have told me whether the body was lying now in the same position it had been lying in for the first two or three hours after death. It would not tell me whether the body's location had changed without its position being changed. Almost certainly it had, because it had become a body far too long ago for neither Olead nor Tara Larsen to have noticed it before. But once the blood pools in the lower part of the body it congeals, and then it remains in the same places even if the body is moved, even if the body's position is changed (which is barely possible, because postmortem lividity is usually almost, if not totally, complete before rigor mortis sets in).

So where the hell was the staining? This body had been dead long enough for rigor mortis to come and go—at least twenty-four hours, probably closer to forty-eight to sixty—so why was no staining visible? Unless he'd bled dry—but if he had I couldn't see a sign of a wound, at least not without turning him over, and I obviously couldn't do that until Irene was through with her work.

I was staring, now, at the face, the hands. I had the feeling that in life, this portly man—he had once been heavier, wrinkles and loose skin proclaimed, and he must have lost weight recently—had had a very ruddy complexion. His almost-white hair was neatly, even elegantly, cut, and his face was carefully shaved. His fingernails were painstakingly manicured and buffed to a natural shine. His hands, what I could see of them without risking damage to trace evidence, were chubby and unworked. He was totally naked (and circumcised, for whatever that was worth—probably nothing), lying on his back on the ground, and there was a long scar, purply fresh, down the middle of his chest. But I could visualize him before he lost that weight, could see him in a gray suit, an elegant necktie with a neat tie tack. The necktie was maroon and the tie tack was small and gold, with some sort of monogram or other small device on it. His handshake had been strong but not obnoxious, and his hands were firm and rather cool. . . .

No, dammit, I wasn't imagining things, I *had* seen this man somewhere, dressed like that. I *had* shaken hands with him sometime. But where? Not church. I'd recognize somebody from church more easily than this even if I didn't know his name. Not a lawyer. I would recognize somebody in the prosecutor's office. A defense attorney I might halfway recognize but I probably wouldn't have shaken hands with him, and I had no reason to be in contact with any other attorney except of course my son-in-law Don Howell, husband of my oldest daughter, Vicky. A banker? A car salesman? Where had I encountered him? I went on mentally running through categories of people with whom I would shake hands.

"What is it, Deb?" Usually a question like that would have come from Captain Millner, who's more familiar with my facial expressions than I am in view of the fact that I spend a minimum of time using a mirror. But Captain Millner had desisted his running in and out and was now standing about forty feet away, at the compound gate, talking with Irene. The question came from Olead.

"I know him," I said.

"Then—?"

"I know him but I don't know him." That would be incomprehensible, probably, to anybody who didn't know me, but not only does my son-in-law know me, furthermore he is preparing to become a psychiatrist, and he's read a lot of books on how the human mind functions.

He just nodded. "You'll think of it."

"I wish I was as sure of that as you are," I answered.

That was when the ME's van rolled up outside, moving a little too fast for a gravel road and shooting up a stream of gravel behind the tires as the driver braked and the van skidded. Dr. Andrew Habib bounded out, followed a little more decorously by his investigator Richard Olsen.

This does not mean that Andrew Habib, or for that matter Richard Olsen, was oblivious to the smells of long-dead humanity. Far from it. I once knew Habib to conduct an autopsy—only he calls it a postmortem examination because he insists, incorrectly, that autopsy means surgery on oneself—while wearing a gas mask when we had a particularly obnoxious corpse wash up on the banks of the Trinity River.

But smell be damned, Andrew Habib likes weird cases.

Irene Loukas, now head of Ident, had arrived before anybody from the ME's office. After talking with Captain Millner for a while, she had fussed and fiddled with cameras, photographing the corpse from all angles, including an extreme close-up showing just the face, and crawled around on the ground looking for footprints and so forth, but it had been three weeks since the last rain, and the ground was dry and hard. She wound up contenting herself with collecting dirt samples in case a suspect—suspected of improperly discarding a corpse, if nothing else—was ever developed and

. . . . .

turned out to have dirt in his shoes. Then, of course, she'd joined us to wait for the ME. She was hesitant even to go wait outside with Captain Millner, because that might compromise the reputation she was working toward of toughest chief of identification in Texas, but finally she went to talk with him anyway. That, as I said, is where she was when Habib finally showed up, and she could walk off with Richard Olsen in earnest conversation, probably about what she had done already so he wouldn't need to.

Habib looked at the body. "It's dead," he announced, and looked at his watch, because the death certificate would give the time at which the body was pronounced dead—not that Professor Lindstrom couldn't have said the same thing some time earlier. Then he looked at the rats. He reached for one of them, glanced at Irene, and pulled his hand back.

"You through with it?" Irene asked. Of course she was referring to the corpse, not the rat.

"No," Habib said, "but you can have it for now. And I want that rat as soon as you're through taking pictures."

"I'm through taking pictures, but I'm not through collecting evidence. I'll tell you when you can have the rat." Then, wearing thick plastic surgical gloves, she lifted the leaden hand and turned it with some effort: Even after rigor mortis passes, it's hard to move that stiff dead weight. "All right, Uncle George, let's see if we can find out who you are."

"Uncle George?" I asked. "Why Uncle George?"

"Why not Uncle George?" That was unanswerable; we had to call him something, and John Doe is so unimaginative. "Deb, there are more gloves in my kit," she said. "Get them and help me, would you?"

I did not ask where the other Ident officers were. Obviously they were either off duty or busy, and my knowing which, and where they were busy, would add nothing to the situation.

Also, I did not ask what she was doing. I knew. With assistance from Richard Olsen and me and ultimately from Dr. Habib as well—this corpse was heavy—she was trying to get fingerprints.

The hands were clean and well cared for, but the fingerprint ridges were so thin and delicate, and the fingertips themselves were so wrinkled, both from premortem age and weight loss and from postmortem shriveling and beginning decomposition, that no matter how carefully all of us worked, the fingerprints were illegible. I could see that at a glance, and I didn't have to look at Irene to see that she was steaming.

"Look at it this way," I murmured, "he probably wouldn't ever have been fingerprinted anyway."

"Armed forces," she muttered back.

That was true. He looked the right age to have caught the end of World War II. But if so, would the prints still be on record? Was there any reason for them to be?

Well, that was immaterial, because we didn't have fingerprints anyway and we weren't going to have them. In a more decayed corpse, when the epidermis is gone, it is often possible to get fingerprints from the dermis layer of the skin, but obviously that wouldn't be the case here, and we couldn't very well let the body continue to decay until we reached that point.

"Recent severe illness," Dr. Habib said. "Probably febrile." I didn't have to ask for a translation to know that meant the victim had had fever; I've been around enough physicians to have learned at least a little of their language. "Pretty obvious what was wrong with him to start with, but as for cause of death—damn, he's pink—but if it was CO, what killed the rats?" I sorted out the parts of that reasoning he hadn't mentioned—namely, the fact that carbon monoxide poisoning turns the entire body a deep rosy red—as he looked questioningly at Irene.

She nodded, and he picked up the rat and—so help me—smelled its breath, or smelled where its breath would have been if it had still been breathing and not as stiff as if it had been taxidermied. Then, with a startled look on his face, he muttered, "Well, that answers that." He handed the rat to Professor Lindstrom, who had come back from the gate.

. . . . .

Lindstrom, after a quick whiff, looked equally startled, and then he and Habib looked back at the body and, almost in unison, nodded. "So *that's* going to be at least a partial cause of death," Habib said, as both of them stared at the corpse's chest.

Irene, following the direction of their gaze, nodded. I don't know if I nodded, but that fresh, long scar up the midline of the chest would say something to just about anybody. The problem was, I wasn't sure exactly *what* it was saying to either the physicians or Irene. Dr. Habib and Professor Lindstrom know more about the human body than Irene and I do, but she knows more about crime-scene evidence than the two of them together do, and I at least like to think I have a good bit of knowledge about homicide.

Which is what it looked like to me, but the doctors seemed to have ruled it out provisionally. "What is it?" I asked, goaded beyond endurance.

Habib glanced at me. "Oh, it's been embalmed, of course," he said.

"What do you mean 'of course'?" I demanded.

"Well, the color—there's dye in embalming fluid, so the body looks more natural. And lividity's gone; embalming fluid washes that out. And this little feller here"—he shook the rat—"didn't know embalming fluid's poison. I guess the body still smelled like food to him."

I practically had to shut my mouth with my hands before I could ask, "What's an embalmed body doing out here?"

"Now, I guess that's what you'll have to find out, isn't it?" Habib replied.

I looked at the miserably small heap of collected evidence—all properly packaged, initialed by both Irene and me, logged into Irene's notebook. "Out of that?" I asked sourly.

"Out of that," Habib said.

Apparently we had all there was. No prints. Oh, Irene would try again in the morgue, of course, and she might even call somebody from Dallas or even up from the state lab in Austin to see what they could do, but it was about 99 percent sure we weren't going to get

· · · · ·

fingerprints, because if they tried the next step—which is injecting formaldehyde or saline solution or even liquid paraffin into the fingertips in hopes of plumping them out to get rid of the wrinkles— the fragile skin would probably tear.

Still with the plastic gloves on her hand, Irene pushed open the mouth. If you can't get prints, the next best place to look is at the teeth—dental records are about as good as fingerprints when you're identifying a corpse, providing you can find dental records.

But they weren't going to help, either. His gums were as bare as those of a newborn baby.

Wonderful. Here we were, about two o'clock on Saturday afternoon, with an unidentified—but embalmed—corpse with unusable fingerprints and no teeth.

Irene looked up. The two physicians looked at each other.

"Cause of death?" Irene asked. Of course she knew we weren't going to get a firm cause of death until the autopsy, but often a skilled physician, especially one who's dealt with a lot of corpses found late, can make a good guess. And judging from the tenor of their conversation, they had already made that guess.

The two physicians looked at each other again. "Myocardial infarction?" Habib ventured.

Professor Lindstrom nodded. "That would be my guess. Second attack, probably." He glanced again at the corpse. "Or maybe third. Looks like he had bypass surgery after the first one and then he lost some weight, but it was too late for the weight loss to do any good. Chances are the transplants filled back up and the second bypass failed. That happens sometimes."

That sent me back to staring at the corpse. I'd seen the fresh scar. I hadn't noticed the old one that both doctors seemed to see. Looking for it carefully, I still didn't see it as the two doctors went on talking.

"Often," Habib agreed. "Too damn often. People won't change their diet and exercise patterns even if their lives depend on it." He looked at me. "But listen, Deb, don't go writing that into a report.

We're *guessing*. Wait for a firm cause of death."

"I always do, don't I?"

"Yeah, but you tell other people what I guessed. That's why I don't like to guess." He leaned over suddenly, looking more closely at the corpse's right leg, and then he sort of nodded at Professor Lindstrom. "Have a look at this," he said.

Lindstrom leaned over too. "I'll be damned," he said. He felt carefully around the corpse's upper thigh, lower abdomen, adjacent to the groin, where, now that they were examining it, I too could see some swelling and very slight purpling. To me, at least, it looked to be antemortem rather than postmortem. "That's recent," Lindstrom said.

"That's damned recent," Habib agreed. "But more than two weeks."

"Right," Lindstrom said, "because the bruising's gone. Not over four weeks, I shouldn't think. Probably not over about three weeks."

"Okay, Deb," Habib said to me, "we're still guessing, but most likely he's had at least one, probably two, maybe three or more, heart attacks, with surgery, probably bypass surgery, following at least two of them. He was in some hospital sometime in the last month for an angiogram and maybe a balloon angioplasty. He had some internal bleeding afterwards, in the upper thigh and lower abdomen. That's real common. The body reabsorbed most of the blood, but he was left with a gigantic hematoma. That's this. Looks like most of it has gone, but if he'd lived two or three months afterwards it would have all reabsorbed. So, say, most likely about three weeks ago, but an outside range of ten days to two months, because I don't know how much of it embalming would get rid of. Some, I'm sure, but as you can see, not all. As for the cause of death, well, I'll tell you for sure when I know for sure. But my guess is myocardial infarction. Heart attack, to you."

I hate it when he translates the obvious for me. Of course sometimes I need a translation, but when I do I can ask for it.

.   .   .   .   .

"Then what in the hell is it doing out here?" Irene demanded explosively. By "it" she meant the body, not the hematoma, of course.

Nobody had any guesses about that, any more than anybody had any guesses about anything else.

This seemed an appropriate time for what happened next: The transport team arrived to remove the body to the morgue.

The corpse, the medical examiner, and Captain Millner all departed, leaving Olead and Professor Lindstrom from the school and Irene and me from the police department.

Irene and I began to prowl around the outside of the compound, with Olead trailing after us. "Do you need me?" Professor Lindstrom called from the gate. "Because I've got a—"

"You're fine," Irene said, her eyes fixed on the ground.

"What?"

"I think anything else we need we can get from Olead," I interpreted.

What else happened at the compound? The three of us practically crawled around the entire place, in and out, looking at the ground, looking at the fence. At the end of that time Irene and I were both certain nobody had climbed over or dug under the compound fence, not that we thought anybody had, especially carrying a large, heavy corpse, considering that the compound was covered and that the fence was buried deeply enough in the ground, at a slant, to keep the most determined of animals larger than rodents (which for the purposes of this experiment are considered part of the natural process) from getting in or out of the compound. We examined the gate and the locks with considerable care. The locks were very good ones, and there was no sign that anybody had picked the lock or forced the gate. The burglar alarms were intact and looked untouched.

That left only one apparently possible answer.

Somebody had entered the compound with a key.

"But that doesn't make sense," Olead said. "I'm sure there are several keys, but the only ones available to anybody but the profes-

sors are the ones the students use, and you have to sign them in and
out."

" 'You' meaning the students?" Irene asked sarcastically. "*I*
would not be able to sign one out? Or would I?"

Olead is not too old to blush. He blushed. "Yeah," he said. "I
mean no. You would not be able to sign one out."

"How many of those keys are there?" I asked.

"Two," he said. "I've got one in my pocket, and the other was
hanging in the office when I got mine this morning. Tara had
signed hers in and out last night, and I signed mine out this morning."

"Let me see it," I said.

He handed it over. It was one of those institutional keys stamped
DO NOT COPY. Of course that did not prove it had not been copied,
but most locksmiths will refuse to copy such a key. In fact, most
locksmiths don't even carry the blanks for a key like that.

"Where is it kept?" I asked.

"In Professor Lindstrom's office in the school." He gave the
room number.

"How many people can get into Professor Lindstrom's office?"
Irene demanded.

"Professor Lindstrom. Tara. Me. A couple of other students and
interns. Probably the head of the department."

"Who else?"

"Nobody, so far as I know."

"Then who cleans the office?" That was the next question I was
going to ask, but I wouldn't have put it as sarcastically as Irene did.

"Irene," I said, "you should be aware that this young man is the
father of most of my grandchildren."

"Goodie," Irene said. "But I still need to know—"

"What I mean is, would you stop biting his head off? He's on our
side." Olead was looking back and forth between the two of us, his
mouth open, obviously still trying to get his own chance to say
something.

"I didn't know I was biting his head off."

. . . . .

19

"Then you don't listen to yourself very well."

"I've got a toothache," Irene muttered.

You've always got a toothache, I thought. Irene is a very tough cop in most respects. But for some reason it would probably take a shrink to figure out, she's scared to death of dentists.

"I know, I've always got a toothache," she added. "I'm working on it. Really. Okay, sorry. But—"

"What I was trying to say," Olead put in, "is, you think the cleaning people have a key, but they don't. Professor Lindstrom has a lot of confidential stuff in that office. The cleaning crew gets into his office only when he's there to let them in, and that usually happens only about once a week. The rest of the time he just sets his trash can out in the hall for them to empty—and even then not everything goes in his trash can. He's got a burn bag, and when it gets full he personally watches while it's incinerated. And his office hasn't got a regular college-issue lock on the door; it's got a superspecial dead bolt with a metal door and a metal door frame. Better than the locks on my house."

That didn't say much to Irene. But it did to me. Olead is one of the world's few real financial geniuses, the kind of people who can turn small money into big money without spending forty-eight hours a day on the job and losing their soul in the process. There's no telling how much money he could make if he wanted to work at it, which he doesn't. He just plays at it in his spare time, as he's done since he was about fourteen, and last he mentioned it he was up to about eight million dollars. And anybody with that kind of money has to keep the possibility of kidnapping in mind. My grandchildren—that set of them, anyway—are well protected.

"Okay," I said, "can you get me the names and addresses of the other students who have the key?"

"The list is in my office," Olead said. "Is it okay if I call it to you later?"

That was okay with me, and Irene didn't particularly care.

By the time I got through calling every funeral home in the

. . . . .

Yellow Pages to find out who was missing a corpse, finding that nobody was, and then recording my report for Millie to type later, four copies of the best photographs lay on my desk. Toothache or not, Irene was her usual efficient self. Ordinarily I would immediately have rushed copies to the television stations and to the newspaper. But Captain Millner came in while I was tape-recording and said, "Don't release photos to the press yet. I want to work on an idea of my own first."

"Do you need me tomorrow?"

"Aren't you off tomorrow?"

"I thought I was off today."

"That was comp time," he said.

Anyone who's on comp time can be called back in. For that matter, so can anybody who has a scheduled day off and anybody who's on vacation, if they're still in town. But the problem, to my mind, was that I had about six weeks' worth of comp time saved up, because every time I tried to use any of it Captain Millner told me that of course I had every right to use my comp time but today wasn't a good day.

He probably noticed my expression, because he added, "No, take tomorrow. And Monday."

Such generosity. Those were my scheduled days off.

"Maybe even Tuesday," he added. "Call me Monday sometime and ask."

I would do that. But I wouldn't hold my breath for him to okay it.

"And you've got a vacation day Wednesday, don't you?"

"Yes, I do," I said. Untrue to form for a vacation day, I about three-quarters of the way wished he'd cancel it. That would give me an excuse for not doing something I didn't really want to do anyway.

After telling me again to leave the pictures on his desk because he was working on something and would get them to the news media himself if we needed to, Captain Millner departed.

. . . . .

I do not know what he was working on. Whatever it was, and my guess is it involved calling a lot of hospitals to see if any cardiologists recognized their patient or their work, it didn't get us an identification, which is probably why he never told me exactly what it was he tried. But he also didn't take the photos to the television stations and newspapers. Actually, with computers, it would probably be possible to replace the missing nose and eyelid visually, but there would be no way of being certain that the computer-replaced nose looked exactly like the one the rats had eaten.

I went home and started cleaning house as fast as I could, to the extent that the whole family, at least those who still live with me (my husband, Harry, who is partially disabled from a helicopter crash; our son Cameron, who is four; and Lori, who is the girlfriend of our son Hal, who is now serving a Mormon mission in Nevada), pitched in to help me, and it was as clean as we can get it—without the assistance of my hyperactive mother, anyway—by the time we went to bed.

Sunday I went to church and then went home and made the kind of delicious, high-fat, high-cholesterol, Sunday dinner southerners are famous for, and even cleaned up after it—with Lori's help, of course—before declaring myself pooped and going and reading in bed until *Star Trek* came on television. I did not turn the computer on at all during the daytime, because I was trying to prove something to myself. What, I am still not quite sure.

I would like to say I received not a single work-related telephone call on Sunday, but that would not be true. Andrew Habib called to say that the rats had died of eating embalming fluid and no other poison, the corpse had died of a myocardial infarction and nothing else, and the veins and arteries around his heart, which had already been replaced at least once, were just about clogged solid, particularly a left descending something-or-other (which I was darned if I was going to ask him to explain—it had something to do with getting blood from the heart's chambers to the heart's muscles).

And still nobody knew who he was. No area funeral homes were

. . . . .

missing a body, and by now every funeral home in the Dallas–Fort Worth metro area had been called. There were no suspicious holes in any cemetery in the area. No area hospitals recognized him. No area cardiac surgeons recognized their work on him, though Millner admitted he hadn't reached very many cardiac surgeons, it being Sunday.

Irene Loukas called to tell me she managed to get one usable print from Uncle George, but it was not in our system and it was not on AFIS—that's the computerized Automated Fingerprint Identification System that links Texas and several other states—and she was going to fax the print to the FBI and ask them to check.

Prior to the advent of AFIS, there was absolutely no way to check any single fingerprint through the millions of fingerprint cards in the FBI files. Now, with AFIS, the FBI can run several hundred checks in one night, so that long-dreamed-of nationwide overnight fingerprint check was now nearing reality. But I didn't have to tell Irene that my gut feeling was that Uncle George wasn't in anybody's fingerprint files. She had the same gut feeling, which did not stop her from trying everything she could.

But other than those two calls, I peacefully spent the day with the family, not even succumbing to the siren lure of the computer until about 9 P.M., after Cameron was asleep, Harry was glued to his computer screen, and Lori was in her room doing last-minute homework. Effectively I didn't have any family to spend the remainder of the day with. Then I just turned it on to play FreeCell, an odd form of solitaire to which I lately had become addicted.

I wasn't going to use the computer on Monday either, unless I decided to play computer games, but I got bored after everybody else left.

Early Monday morning I did the housewife bit, of course, making a *real* breakfast, which nobody in the family was able to finish, as we are all used to cereal or muffins except on Saturday and Sunday, and getting Harry off to work and Lori and Cameron off to school (preschool, in Cameron's case) on time. Then I turned around to

· · · · ·

start on the housework, but we had done most of it on Saturday, and all I had to do was run the vacuum and put a couple of loads into the washing machine.

I looked at the computer.

The computer looked at me.

The heck with that. This was my day off and I was darned if I'd be enslaved by a machine. I picked up the phone and telephoned Matilda Greenwood, who is less and less interested in being Sister Eagle Feather these days, and said, "Is it okay if I come and visit you?"

"I wish you would," she said instantly, "because I've got something really weird going on."

I would say I don't know why everybody wants to dump really weird stuff on me, but I can't honestly say that, because I do know. It's because I've gotten pretty good at figuring out weird things. But I hoped Matilda's "something really weird" wouldn't include crime.

It took me about twenty minutes to get to her house, or rather, her apartment, which was over a small spiritualist "church" that she had founded because she was both a psychologist—I'd seen her credentials—and, according to herself, a trance medium. She'd thought, seven years ago when she started the church, that she could help old people who would be horrified at the thought of going to a real counselor but would gladly accept help from—and hand out money to—any phony who came along and promised to help them. Deciding to replace the phonies with her real, competent, caring self, she'd put out a wooden sign with the palm of a hand on it, painted red with all the lines palm readers use painted black, and over it in big letters she'd had painted the name she'd decided to go by: SISTER EAGLE FATHER, COMANCHE PRINCESS.

But the whole thing hadn't worked out as she'd hoped, mainly because she is far too decent to go to the lengths the phonies go to in keeping their gulls happy, and I'd had a hunch for the last couple of years that her Sister Eagle Feather identity was on its last legs and

· · · · ·

24

she was about to return to her real self, a Comanche (but not princess) psychologist.

Her problem, as I saw it, was in raising the money to make the change. As Sister Eagle Feather she lived, as I said, in an apartment over her alleged church. The frame building badly needed repainting, the outside stairs up to her apartment were so rickety they'd probably have been condemned if anybody had ever checked out the building officially, and, as usual, her car was gone, probably in the shop. She supplemented her income as a psychic with her income as a ghostwriter, or maybe it was the other way around—I never was quite sure. She'd managed over the years to pick up a few real psychological clients, whom she always saw at their homes, but there weren't enough of them to help much with finances.

I went up the stairs as gingerly as I usually do, clutching the banister's handrail as if it would help me although in fact if I started to fall it would probably help me along, and knocked on the door.

"That you, Deb?" she called. "Come on in."

I did, not pointing out that if it had been someone else she might have had a problem or two; I've given up warning her about unlocked doors because she ignores all my warnings.

Matilda was still sitting at her computer. She was writing books for clients on a Commodore 128 and I was playing computer games on a Tandy 486; if I had any decency I'd offer to swap computers with her except that I knew she'd just get mad, the same way she did the time Olead diffidently offered to set up a real office for her.

She stood up now. "I'm glad you're here," she said, and crawled out from behind the computer, knocking over only one stack of paper, which had been lying in the lid of a computer-paper box on the coffee table, in the process. As she picked the paper back up an orange marmalade cat delightedly leaped into the box, curled up with its head against one end of the box and its tail hanging out the other, closed its eyes, and began to purr. She shrugged. "Should have known I couldn't steal his bed for long without him getting

. . . . .

mad." She put the paper on the edge of a shelf. "I'm drinking Red Zinger today. Want some?"

The tea is excellent hot, and even better cold. "Sure," I said without asking which condition it was in.

This time it was hot. We sat down at the forty-year-old yellow Formica kitchen table to drink the tea and nosh on cookies. "I'm going nuts," she told me, brushing her hair back from her face with her left hand.

"What's wrong?"

"Oh, I don't want to burden you with my trouble," she said, "but—well, you might know what to do."

"Maybe," I said cautiously. I've found Matilda to be an extremely practical woman. If she didn't know what to do, there wasn't much chance I would either, unless it did involve a crime.

She gestured back toward the papers piled around the part of the living room she called her office. "It's this client," she said.

"Psychological—"

She shook her head. "Writing." She picked up her mug, gulped a little of the tea, and set it back down. "You know how I work— I give them a binding estimate based on how complex the work looks, half down before I start, one-fourth on delivery of the first draft, one-fourth on acceptance. Every now and then somebody stiffs me for the last fourth, but not real often. But I *never* start working without the half down."

She grimaced, drank some more tea, and added, "I wish. Usually I don't. But this guy—Marvin Tutwiler, he's a genealogist—was so convincing. He was having a cash-flow problem, he'd have the money real soon, no problem—and the job looked good and I needed the money. I always need the money. You know that."

I nodded. She really does. And I am probably the only one to know that, from the meager income she does have, she gives away more than she should to people she feels need it more than she does. I'd found it out by accident, never mind how, and I wasn't going to mention it now and embarrass her.

· · · · ·

26

"So I went on and started on it," she continued, "and I kept calling him, and he never was there but he'd always call back and say he was going to come in and pay me. You know, that gonna gonna? And finally Thursday he called me instead of me calling him for the first time since I got started and said he had the money coming, he'd pick it up that night and he'd come in and pay me Friday morning absolutely."

"And he didn't."

"No." She drained the cup, stood up, wandered over to the counter, poured the last tea from the two-quart Pyrex cup she used as a teapot, put five more teabags in it, and turned on the gas fire under the kettle. "No, he didn't." She sat back down at the table. "I called his house I don't know how many times from Friday through Sunday without getting any answer, I mean, not even an answering machine. I called again just before you called me and talked to his wife—Dora, her name is—and she told me she didn't know where he was. Well, you know what?"

"You don't believe that."

"Got it in one. I don't believe that. And—my car is on the blink again. I thought, if you wouldn't mind too much, would you drive me over there? And maybe, uh, we could pick up some groceries on the way, because what I usually do is, I walk to the store and then take a taxi back—"

"I wish you wouldn't do that," I interposed, knowing exactly how far the nearest grocery store was from her house. "Why don't you call me? You know I'd be glad—"

"The walk doesn't hurt me," she interrupted in turn.

"The taxi fare does."

She grinned at me and shrugged gracefully. "Anyway, today you're here. So if we could—"

"Sure," I said. "I'm on my own today anyway. One whole glorious day off."

"And you had to come waste it on my problems."

"Better that than wasting it on my own. Other people's problems are always easier to solve, because then I don't have to live with the consequences."

"Ri-i-i-ight, Deb," Matilda drawled at me.

We both laughed then, and she went into her mousetrap of a bedroom to change clothes.

$\mathcal{T} w o$

. . . .

THE TUTWILER HOUSE was red brick and rather small, but astonishingly neat, especially for the part of town it was in, which wasn't the greatest. The front yard was solid St. Augustine grass, which takes more work and a lot more water than Bermuda grass, and it was mowed a little shorter than St. Augustine actually likes to be mowed. The ends of the broad, coarse leaves looked chewed, but the color remained brilliant green despite the lateness of the year, and the lawn was swept of every fallen leaf. The front sidewalk was tidily edged, and the swept concrete walk to the front door was thickly bordered with grape hyacinths, though of course this time of year all that was apparent was the closely planted spears of foliage. A white picket fence, looking freshly painted until I realized it was white vinyl rather than wood, separated the front yard from the back. There was a carport, not a garage, with a dark blue late-model Chrysler backed into it.

"He ought to be able to pay me, if he can afford to drive a Chrysler," Matilda remarked cynically as we got out of the car.

This was not police business. I stood back and let Matilda knock on the door.

The woman who came to the door was about my height and age, slim, with graying brown hair in a vaguely Hillary Clinton cut, an extremely hassled look on her face, and a broom in her hand. "Come in, come in," she said crossly. "I suppose you're more of them?"

"More of what?" Matilda asked blankly as we followed her into an almost too-neat maple-and-blue-floral-chintz living room.

"Police. They said some more would be coming." She closed the door with a vicious crunch rather than a slam. "But I never expected one that looked like *you*." She was eyeing Matilda, and I could see no reason for the hostility of her expression. Even out of buckskin and beads, which she wears only for ceremonial occasions, Matilda's appearance is unusually striking. Today she was wearing a mostly maroon batik skirt, a maroon long-sleeved shell, and brown boots, with her glossy black hair in two thick braids swinging well below her shoulder blades.

Matilda, more puzzled than annoyed, looked at me.

"Well, I am," I admitted lamely. "A police officer, I mean. But that's not why I'm here. I'm just with Ms. Greenwood."

"And you're Ms. Greenwood? So why are you here?" Her expression, as she glared at Matilda, darkened into far more hostility than would be called for by any situation I could think of.

"I'm hunting Mr. Tutwiler," Matilda said.

"I suppose you're another one of his girlfriends? And you brought the *police* with you? Don't you think that's a bit uncalled for? Do you think I'm hiding him under the bed or something? Well, I'm not. You called me this morning, didn't you? Well, as I told you over the phone, I'm sure *I* wouldn't know where he is." Dora's voice was emphatic, and she punctuated her words with vigorous swings of the broom in her hand. "I'd have told you if I did. But dearie, you better get used to that. Not knowing where he is, I mean, and him showing up, or not showing up, hours after he's said he'd get there. He's an awful liar. But I suppose you haven't figured that out yet."

Matilda cleared her throat. "No, I'm not one of his girlfriends," she said. "I'm a writer. I've been working on a project for him."

"Then I suppose he owes you money."

"Well, yes—"

"You'll get none of it from *me*. So you might as well go on about your business. You and the police too." She stalked back to the door and pushed it open.

Psychologists are not noted for easy dissuadability. Neither are Comanches. "Look, can we start over?" Matilda said. "My name is Matilda Greenwood, and when Mr. Tutwiler contracted for me to write this book for him, he gave this address and phone number as where I could reach him."

"Oh, so *you're* the one who's left all those messages on my answering machine. No, Ms. Greenwood, he doesn't live here and he hasn't lived here for the last four months, ever since I threw him out on his little shell-pink ear and filed for divorce. Now if you will excuse me—"

"Your answering machine wasn't even on this weekend."

"I know it wasn't. I turned it off. I'm tired of getting messages for that—that—" Evidently words failed her, but her hands on the broom gripped so tightly that her knuckles turned pasty yellow. "Especially since he quit picking them up. But you've left plenty of messages before. Now will you please *leave*—"

"Mrs. Tutwiler—"

"*Please* don't call me that," Mrs. Tutwiler said. "It's Gaines. Dora Gaines. I'm taking my other name back legally just as soon as the divorce is final." She had her hand on the door, holding it open, just waiting for us to leave so that she could slam it.

"Ms. Gaines—"

"*Mrs.* Gaines. I'm—I was—I was a widow."

"Mrs. Gaines, I really have to talk with you," Matilda said loudly. "Could we please sit down a minute? And anyway, why were you expecting police?"

Mrs. Gaines released the door, which closed with the soft swoosh of a pneumatic tube door-closer. She sat down, rather limply, on the couch and dropped the broom, which clattered to the floor. "Do either one of you know how to clean up fingerprint powder?" she asked, her tone suddenly weary rather than brisk.

. . . . .

"I think I can help you with that," I answered. "Did you have a burglary?"

She nodded. "I've been gone to Padre Island for a week, my married daughter and son-in-law, they live in Corpus Christi and they wanted me to go with them camping on South Padre Island and so I did and we had a *wonderful* time, so peaceful this time of year with most of the crowds gone, and then when I got back—oh, you wouldn't believe the mess! Glass broken in the back bedroom, everything pulled every which way, all the books out of the shelves. . . ." She began to cry. Her voice muffled behind her hands, she went on, "And then the police came, and they told me I couldn't clean anything up until the crime-scene people got here and I had to wait *three hours* for that and now there's fingerprint powder everywhere, and I don't know what to do about it—they didn't get much of anything, only two fingerprints they said, they just made that horrible mess. . . ."

Matilda is better at making soothing noises than I am. She did so, as I stood uneasily just inside the now-closed door. After a while Mrs. Gaines reached for Kleenex, blew her nose loudly, and said, "They say there's no fool like an old fool. Well, I didn't know I was old enough to be a fool, but I'd been so lonesome since Howard died, and when he—Marvin—proposed to me I just fell like a ton of bricks. He seemed so nice, then. I mean he didn't even want to *do it* without he was married. He's a Mormon, you know. Mostly he marries other Mormons. Not all at once, of course, they don't do that anymore, but he marries a lot of women one at a time. I didn't find that out until later. He doesn't screw women till he marries them. But boy does he screw them then."

Her sudden descent into coarseness made the multiple meanings of the word *screw* quite apparent. Here Matilda glanced at me, and I felt myself blushing. Like most people who are religious, I am acutely embarrassed when a member of my religion misbehaves, especially in the name of religion.

"So I don't know why he married me, seeing as I'm a Methodist, unless he thought I had more money than I do. Told me he was a widower, told me all about how his first wife died of cancer—" She blew her nose again, dropped the tissue into the trash can, grabbed another, and wiped her eyes. "It wasn't until after we were married that I found out he'd had three wives before me. But none of 'em were dead. He'd been divorced three times. He's like a cuckoo, going around leaving his young in everybody else's nest— expecting me to pay his child support, because *he* didn't have any *money,* never mind that he had the money to travel in style.

"I don't know why he married me. *I* couldn't have any more babies for him and he ought to have known that, but he used to get so mad at me for it, like it was my fault I was fifty-two—I looked younger when I married him. I did. You can't tell it now, though. He's enough to give gray hair and wrinkles to a saint. One year. One year I stuck it out, but it was just awful practically the whole time, and then he had the nerve to bring one of his girlfriends *home.* I was out to the Elks playing bingo and Marian, that's my neighbor and she always goes with me, she got sick and I had to take her home so I came home early and there he was with that awful woman in my very *bed,* the old goat, and he's already had one heart attack that I know of and you'd think he'd have better sense! And he had the nerve to tell me it was okay because I wasn't acting like a wife to him anymore and anyway they weren't *doing anything.* I could see what they weren't doing, and I could see what they were doing, and if that's not anything then I'm a monkey's uncle.

"Well, of course I threw him out, stood over him and made him pack up all his stuff that very minute and then I slept in the guest room until I got that bed replaced. I certainly wasn't going to sleep in it after—oh, you don't want to know that! And we aren't even divorced yet and he's already gotten and broken up with two fiancées. And he's got this knack—he can always make anybody feel *sorry* for him. And he really had been sick before he married me, but he was obnoxious even when he wasn't sick."

Words were pouring out now. This might be the first time she

. . . . .

33

had really let herself go, and Matilda and I listened patiently as she talked and cried. Matilda occasionally, silently, put another tissue into her hand, and I didn't move from my position by the door.

"After I threw him out he kept coming over here, trying to make me sorry for him, and he asked me to let him keep using my answering machine until he got a phone of his own, because he was really short of money, so I let him because, you know, it's one of that kind you can get the messages remote, but then he brought a girlfriend over here *again* and had the nerve to say it shouldn't matter to me if we were getting divorced and anyway they weren't *doing anything* and I thought, Here we go again. Well, really! Man's an idiot! And then he got sick again and had the nerve to tell me I ought to let him come back here to recover because I *am* still his *wife*. Well, I can't help it if the divorce courts are slow, but I do *not* consider myself his wife. I told him go recover at one of his girl-friends' places. So I haven't seen him in a month and I hope I never see him again." She blew her nose, wiped her eyes, and looked up at Matilda. "How much does he owe you?" she asked.

"Three thousand dollars already," Matilda answered, "and more to come."

"Oh, dearie, I'm sorry, I really am, but you're never going to see that money. He *never* pays bills. That was one of the things I found out after I married him. He never pays bills. Even with my money, if I give him the money to pay bills, even if it's my money and my bills he'll take it and blow it on something else, and I'm sorry, but I really *can't* be responsible for bills he runs up now."

"Of course you can't," Matilda agreed quietly. "It's his responsibility."

"Responsibility!" Mrs. Gaines gave a short bark of laughter. "Dearie, he doesn't know what responsibility is. So even if you do find him—and he travels a lot, you know. He gives seminars about genealogy, and sometimes he does genealogy work for people, you know, finding out who they're descended from and all that. I think that's silly, don't you? I mean, who *cares* who you're descended from? It doesn't have anything to do with *you*. It matters more what the people descended from *you* do, doesn't it, because that's something you might have a little control over.

"But there, I know lots of people disagree with me about genealogy. Look, I'll tell you what I'll do. I'll give you, let's see, I have the phone numbers of both his fiancées, well, all three actually, the two he's already dumped—or maybe they got smart and dumped him—and the one he's engaged to right now, and one of his ex-wives, the only one I get along with. Will that help?"

"It might," Matilda said. Her voice wasn't quite shaking, but I knew what the loss of six thousand dollars—the three she should have earned for the two months she'd already put in on the book plus the other three thousand dollars he was ultimately supposed to pay her—would mean to her. I knew, and I wasn't sure Dora Gaines ever would.

But I got paper towels and Simple Green solution and went and cleaned fingerprint powder off a windowsill and the floor beneath it, and off the white paint on a ravaged bookcase, which didn't in my mind add up to fingerprint powder everywhere, while Matilda put books back on shelves and Mrs. Gaines copied out names and addresses.

One part of my mind, even then, wondered about a burglar who'd gone after nothing but books and paper. But there weren't, yet, any connections to be made.

Within about half an hour Matilda and I were back in my car.

"What now?" she asked me. "I know you've got other things to do, but if I *do* locate him I might need to be able to go where he is, and—"

"I'd rather spend the day with you than go play with a computer," I said candidly.

"There speaks the voice of truth."

"She's probably right that the money is gone," I added.

"I'm not so sure about that," Matilda said. "See, I've got a lot of his books and papers, stuff he gave me for research. And I'm going

. . . . .

35

to hold every one of them hostage until he pays me."

I couldn't help laughing at that.

"I can do that, can't I?" Matilda asked. "I mean legally?"

"I'm no lawyer. But it sounds to me like you can—I don't see much difference between that and a mechanic's lien."

"That's what I thought." she settled herself composedly on the seat with her hands behind her neck. Then, thinking about it, she fastened her seat belt before resuming her deliberately nonchalant pose. "*Is* he a Mormon?" she asked then.

"How should I know? I don't know all the Mormons in Fort Worth. I don't even know all the ones in my ward, and there's two full stakes in town."

"So what's a ward and what's a stake?"

"A ward is a congregation, only it's defined by geography—if you live inside the boundaries of one ward that's the ward you belong to. A stake is a larger geographical division, and it might contain anywhere from three to seven wards. Usually three or sometimes four wards will meet at different times in the same stake center."

"And that's the church building."

"Uh-huh."

"So that's why you go to church at such weird times sometimes."

"Yep."

"Well, is there ever a time when all the stakes meet together?"

"There's stake conference, when all the wards in one stake—"

"Did you ever see him in—"

"Matilda, it's a crowd like for a football game. I couldn't possibly notice somebody I don't know there. I have enough trouble noticing people I *do* know. And regional conference, forget it, that's thousands of people."

"Could you find out?"

"I suppose I could, but why?"

She shrugged. "I don't know. Maybe it would help find him."

"He hasn't legally been reported missing yet," I pointed out.

"Oh, yeah, that's right."

I took her to the grocery store, where of course I didn't dare offer to supplement the fifteen dollars she had to buy groceries, although I did successfully insist on buying a couple of boxes of my own herbal tea to keep at her place, and then we went back to her apartment and I sat there while she started telephoning, using the speaker phone she'd gotten several months ago so she'd have both hands free to turn over papers while she was talking with writing clients.

I don't know when it was that I started wondering. I know I sat and watched four telephone calls, three of which reached nobody and the fourth of which reached Jennifer Webster, an ex-wife who was about as excited and concerned over the disappearance of Marvin Tutwiler as Dora Gaines was. "She's the only one of my wives-in-law that makes good sense," Ms. Webster emphasized.

"Wives-in-law?" Matilda repeated, sounding slightly dazed.

"Well, I've got to call them something. I mean, Julene and Nell and Amy and me, our kids are all half-siblings, and we figure we ought to keep them in touch at least enough so they know each other, so they don't, you know, grow up and accidentally fall in love or something because they don't know who each other is. Are. Whatever."

"I see," Matilda said. "Well, I guess that makes sense. But I thought he just had three ex-wives and the one he's married to now."

"Who told you *that*? Never mind, it was probably somebody he told it to. He always was a liar. He's had—" She chuckled suddenly. "Like that woman at the well, in the Bible, only the other way around. He's had seven wives and the woman he's with now isn't his. Only really I think it's just five."

"Words fail me," Matilda said. "Well, anyhow, if you see him or hear from him—"

"I won't," Ms. Webster interrupted.

. . . . .

"Well, but if you do, you know, tell him I'm holding his books hostage until he pays me."

Ms. Webster's laughter, even over the telephone, chimed with merriment, and she said, "Lots of luck. But I'll tell him if I see him."

I must have been wondering by then, because I remember I leaned forward and said quickly, "Don't hang up. I'm Deb Ralston, I'm a police officer."

"What's the police interest?" Mrs. Webster asked. "I mean, he's an awful liar, but I don't think he actually breaks the law."

"I don't know that there is any police interest; I'm just a friend of Ms. Greenwood. But there might be, so can you give me Amy and Julene and Nell's full names and phone numbers?"

"Yeah, I guess," Ms. Webster said. "But they won't hear from him if I don't."

Now we had all the women we *knew* he was associated with: four ex-wives, one current-but-soon-to-be-ex-wife, two ex-fiancées, and one current fiancée. On the previous women's answering machines, Matilda had left the same message: "If you see him, tell him I'm not writing another word until I'm paid, and I'm going to hold every book and sheet of paper he gave me hostage until he pays me every last cent of what we agreed on."

The answering machines, of course, said nothing.

She went on calling. Two ex-wives were not home and had no answering machines. The remaining ex-wife, one Amy Dorne, laughed and said, "Lots of luck. If you can get him to pay you, you're the first one to do it—but I don't think anybody's ever held his books hostage before. That might do it, if he's got the money. He does care about his books. That's about all he does care about, if you ask me."

"Do you think he does?" Matilda asked. "Have the money, I mean?"

"Sometimes. I mean, he can leech off me and every other woman he meets, and he can leave the kids to starve in the streets for all he cares, but he can't leech off gasoline stations and motels and restaurants. And he does travel a lot, and he likes to go first class."

The last call—Matilda and I had agreed deliberately to leave it for last—was to Tutwiler's present fiancée, Janet Malone.

Unlike the other women, she was nervous. In fact, she was downright scared. Marvin was supposed to take her out to a late dinner Thursday night. He hadn't. He hadn't shown up, and he hadn't called, and she hadn't heard from him since, and she was scared he'd had another heart attack. He'd had that terrible one about three years ago, way before they met, and then he'd had another one right after they met, not that *that woman he was married to* cared—she'd just thrown him out on the street like a dog, sick as he was, but she'd thought he was doing better now, but she went to his apartment and he wasn't there and his car was gone. She'd tried to report him missing, but the person at the police department had refused to take the report because she wasn't a relative and didn't live with him. And to think he might be lying dead in a ditch somewhere and nobody even *looking* for him. . . .

She gabbled about as much as Dora Gaines did. Apparently Marvin had some sort of weakness, probably lately developed, for gabblers.

When Matilda finished that call and got off the phone, I asked, "What did he look like?"

"What do you mean, 'did'?" Matilda demanded. "Do you agree with her that he might have had another heart attack, maybe died from it this time? Actually, I guess he could have." Without waiting for an answer, she went on, "Oh, he's about five-ten, kinda chubby—call him two hundred pounds, I guess. Blue eyes. He looks older than he claims to be—white hair, ruddy face."

"Do you know anything about these heart attacks we kept hearing about?" I asked.

"Oh, yes, that's part of why I did agree to wait to get paid and waited so long before I started getting nasty. He'd just gotten over one when he came to see me the first time, and then while I was working he had to go into the hospital for some sort of procedure and I think he had another heart attack in the hospital."

Sure sounds like Uncle George to me, I thought, *except I can't imagine how he'd have gotten to the test field, much less gotten to the field already embalmed.* "Did you notice whether he bites his fingernails?"

"Oh, gosh, no, Deb, he looks to me like he gets a regular manicure—everything but glue-on nails and red nail polish. Why? Do you think you know where he is?"

"There's a possibility I might," I said. "And if he is . . ." I began to explain, and Matilda looked suitably appalled.

I didn't have any of the crime-scene pictures with me. Why should I? This was my day off. I wasn't planning to work on identifying the corpse today.

I called Dora Gaines, first, and got confirmation of two things: Tutwiler had false teeth, and, so far as she knew, Tutwiler didn't have a passport and hadn't been in the military. I asked, then, about heart surgery.

He'd had triple bypass surgery.

Bingo, I was beginning to feel. Got him—except for that embalming. But I could figure that out later. (Have I mentioned that there are times when I tend to be unduly optimistic?)

She didn't have any pictures of him. She'd burned every one of them, in a ceremonial bonfire in her backyard. "Thanks," I said. "I'll see if somebody else has some."

"Try the fiancée again," Matilda suggested after I hung up.

"Give me her phone number," I said.

Matilda slid the index card and the phone over to me, and I dialed. "Janet Malone?" I asked a moment later. "I'm Detective Deb Ralston. I'm a friend of Matilda Greenwood, and she just told me about your fiancé going missing. Do you mind if I ask you a few questions?"

"No, go ahead. Do you think something's happened to him?" She sounded young, frightened, and a little bit silly.

· · · · ·

"I hope not," I said as soothingly as I could manage, "but I think it might be useful for me just to take the report for now. I'm sorry the person you talked to wouldn't do it. When was last time you saw him?"

"Wednesday—Wednesday afternoon, but he called me Thursday and said he was going to get some money and he'd take me out to a real night on the town—you know, mostly we've been having video dates, he'll get a video and bring it over and I'll make dinner and we'll watch the video. It's not like I couldn't afford to take us out, but you know, he's all man, wants to pay his own way or not go at all. His first wife, up to the moment she died, she never had to work a day in her life. But then his second wife, she just didn't care about being treated like a princess and that's why she divorced him. And his third wife, well, I told you about her."

That was not exactly what I had heard about him—especially from his very-much-alive first wife—but I didn't comment. Anyway, he must have put up some sort of façade before getting married, or he wouldn't have managed to hook so many otherwise fairly sensible women. "So Thursday he was clearly expecting money?"

"Oh, yes, a lot of it, and he was real excited—You don't think he'd just get the money and go off and leave me, do you? I mean he hadn't had much money lately, but he works real hard, but he has to pay all this alimony—"

"Are you sure it isn't child support?" I asked, as tactfully as I could. To the best of my knowledge, it's only in rather unusual situations that Texas provides for alimony, if it does at all. And whatever it was, the consensus was that he wasn't paying it.

"Well, maybe that's what it was," she said. "I don't know, he's got I guess six or eight kids, and he does have to pay a lot of child support."

But he doesn't do it, I thought. I'd heard the angry words from one ex-wife Matilda had talked to: Marvin was approximately four years behind in child support, which he was always going to catch

· · · · ·

up on real soon. Not that that shortage kept him from making numerous expensive trips all over the country, even when he was between wives and didn't have anybody else's income to live on.

Never mind the rest of the conversation. Sufficeth to say that Janet Malone had money. Not to compare with my son-in-law, of course, few people do, but enough that she didn't have to work and Marvin wouldn't have had to work either, if he'd married her. Marvin had caught himself a live one this time, and unless he'd come up with *mucho dinero* himself he wasn't going to bail out on her. Especially considering that he was aging and his health was demonstrably bad.

Ergo, he really was missing.

Ergo, he might be the body Olead had found Saturday.

Except that if he'd had another heart attack, which seemed perfectly possible given the situation, what was the body doing in the experiment—uninvited? And embalmed, which fact frankly was driving me crazy. In fact, the last case I could remember being this crazy-making was the time the owner of a barbecue kitchen had dashed outside one evening, thirty-eight in hand, yelling at somebody, and been found ten minutes and three audible shots later under a tree dead, shot through the heart, with two rounds gone from his pistol, without the trace of a hole in his undershirt, shirt, or bib apron. We never did clear that one, but I had long since reached the point where I didn't even care who did it. I just wanted the perp to write me a letter, as anonymous as he wanted it to be, and tell me how in the heck he did it.

That was how I felt about this case. Identifying Uncle George— whether or not Uncle George turned out to be Marvin Tutwiler— wouldn't answer most of the questions, but at least it would provide a starting point.

I called Captain Millner, who assured me our corpse was still unidentified and invited me to bring my possible witnesses to see whether they could make identifications.

At this point I was not ready to bring in Amy Dorne, Jennifer

Webster, or even Dora Gaines, much less Janet Malone. Instead I went over to Malone's house and collected a couple of pictures of Marvin Tutwiler.

From the pictures, I could not say the corpse was Marvin Tutwiler. I also could not say the corpse was not Marvin Tutwiler. And I still wasn't prepared to ask any of the women who'd been involved with Tutwiler to look at the corpse.

Back in the car, I said, "I've got to find out for sure. Matilda, would you mind—?"

"Of course I mind," she retorted. "But you might as well take me anyway. Somebody's got to be the first to look at him who might have known him, and you certainly can't take that nitwit. But if you have some pictures of the corpse, is it okay for me to look at them first? If I can say no from them, then that's as far as it needs to go. I know if I'm not sure, or if I think it is, then I still have to look at the real body, but . . ."

Not surprisingly, Matilda looked at the first photograph, shoved it away from her, and shook her head, looking about as pale as a full-blooded Comanche can look. "No, I don't know. It might be him, but Deb, I never saw anybody without his nose. I don't know. I really and truly don't know."

"Do you think if you saw the body itself . . ."

She swallowed hard. "I'd really rather not. But if you think I need to—Yeah, maybe. I don't know. Okay, I guess so. Better me than Janet Malone, anyway."

The corpse, only a few degrees above freezing where it was held in the morgue, smelled rotten despite the chemical tang of the embalming fluid (which at most is a temporary measure), and the morgue, as it always does, smelled like rancid raw meat. Not that the viewing did any good.

"Deb, I still don't know," Matilda said. "It could be him. It's the right size and all that. But—I just don't know."

I can't say I was surprised.

We went back to the police station, where I made a fast oral report to a tape recorder, told another detective what was going on, and departed quickly, it still being theoretically my day off (though I had racked up another three hours of comp time I would probably be able to take only in the millenium) and then took Matilda back home.

By then it was four o'clock and it would have been time for me to go home even if I had officially been working, but I had the bit in my teeth. I wanted to find out who the heck this corpse was. I drove back to the police station.

I should have gotten those names and phone numbers from Matilda before I left her.

Well, I didn't. So I called her from the office and got names and phone numbers, and called everybody on that list, and got more names and phone numbers from each of them, along with all the information they could or would give me. A few, especially Janet Malone (despite my having talked with her earlier), were somewhat alarmed at now-official telephone calls from a police officer. Most weren't.

By five-thirty, I was about ready to start throwing things from sheer frustration.

Marvin Tutwiler had no fingerprints on record.

Marvin Tutwiler had false teeth, which could easily have been identified by his dentist, but our corpse's false teeth were missing.

There were no jaw X rays available, because he'd started going to his present dentist after he already had false teeth, and his previous dentist had died and his records had presumably been dispersed or destroyed.

Marvin Tutwiler had never, so far as anybody was able to tell me, had a broken bone, so there would have been no long-bone X rays.

Marvin Tutwiler had never been arrested, so there were no mug shots.

I called Irene, who, like me, should have gone home already but hadn't, and then I called Dora Gaines, and then I called a judge and told him to expect me, and then I started writing a search warrant.

*   *   *

·   ·   ·   ·   ·

It should have been very simple, one of the normal things we do when faced with an unidentified body we think we can tie a name to. Go to the person's dwelling, locate a few things normally handled only by the person the body might be, search for fingerprints, compare the fingerprints to those of the body. The FBI disaster squad does it routinely after airplane crashes; one woman they were able to identify only from her fingerprint on a glass punchbowl she'd put away two Christmases before the crash.

Once I got the search warrant signed, Irene and I went over to the boardinghouse where Marvin Tutwiler had lived. It was not beautiful. It was not elegant, though the house, forty years ago, might have been. It was utilitarian. The landlady, one Mrs. Keating, reluctantly agreed to let us into his room only after we presented the search warrant, our identification, and a lengthy explanation of what we were doing there.

But she hadn't seen him since Thursday either, when he had driven off in the morning as usual. She had begun wondering whether he had skipped out on the two months' rent he owed her. "Not that there's any reason why he should," she emphasized over her shoulder, as we followed her up the stairs, "and when he's lived here before there've been times he's got way behind and caught up, but, well, you never know, especially with these traveling gentlemen. And he *does* usually tell me when he's going to be gone." She paused at the door of a corner room and tried to insert the key in its lock. "Well—that's odd."

"What is?" I asked.

"This door's not even locked."

"Does Mr. Tutwiler usually leave it locked?"

"Oh, yes, very particular he is with all those papers of his, like they were some sort of—oh my goodness!"

She had flung the door open. She stepped back, hand pressed to her chest, and I moved forward with Irene right beside me.

The room had been tossed, about as thoroughly as I've ever seen a room tossed.

.   .   .   .   .

Three
· · · · ·

"WELL, WELL, WELL," Irene said softly.

But for once, I saw far more at a crime scene than she did—more not in terms of objects present or absent, but in terms of overall implications. She had no reason, yet, to connect the burglary of Dora Gaines's house with the tossing of Marvin Tutwiler's room, or to connect either of those with the unknown corpse we were all, by now, calling Uncle George. I did.

"But when—" Mrs. Keating got out. She stammered a little, almost inarticulately, before adding, "And why?"

"That's what we're going to have to find out," I said briskly. I didn't have to say anything else to Irene; she was already headed for the front door to bring in the complete crime-scene kit to supplement the small fingerprint kit she'd had in her hand when she entered with me. Beside me, as we waited, Mrs. Keating was making small sounds of horror and disgust.

While Irene was gone, I asked Mrs. Keating how many boarders she had.

"Nine," she told me, her eyes still fixed on the room. "Nine altogether. Only four here all the time. The other five are railroad men; they keep rooms for when they've got short layovers. Long layovers of course they deadhead home and back. My husband, he was a railroad man. It's not the work that kills railroad men, at least not most of the time, it's all them damn layovers."

"What's a layover?" I asked.

Her explanation was rather vague, but it added up to this: A train leaves a junction point with a full crew, most of whom live in the town where that junction point is located. That crew takes the train a certain distance, varied of course according to the line and the route, and then another crew takes over. The first crew then has a "layover" until another train arrives, heading the other way, which that crew is scheduled to take back to the junction point. The layover may be very short, only two or three hours, in which case the railroader may not even leave the station except to eat. The layover may be longer, eighteen to thirty hours, in which case the railroader is expected to find his own place to eat and sleep during the layover. And the layover might be longer yet, two or three days, in which case the railroader may ride the next freight train to his home, "deadheading" rather than working as a crew member, and if he does, then he will later deadhead on another freight train back to the junction point, where he will once again serve as crew-man.

This whole thing is complicated by the fact that freight-train schedules, even today, may be no more than approximate, with hours of leeway on various days. The "caller" will notify the rail-roader when to be at the station, but the railroader may have as little as half an hour's notice. This means that unless he keeps his own car at the distant station, which most don't, he's got to board within walking distance of the station.

This fact accounts, at least in part, for the multitude of small hotels, cafés, and boardinghouses that grew up near all the old train stations. Nowadays, with faster trains and fewer crews, the crews go farther and, often, wind up with longer layovers and fewer junction points. So the system of cheap hotels, cafés, and boardinghouses perforce continues.

Many of those small, often unlicensed, boardinghouses are run— as this one was—by widows of railroad men who had built or bought houses twenty, thirty, fifty years ago near junction points. Old houses built for large families are perfectly suited for boarding-

* * * * *

houses. Advertising, of course, isn't necessary. Word gets around.

I didn't ask whether this was a licensed boardinghouse. If the neighbors don't complain, and in railroad neighborhoods the neighbors usually don't complain, normally nobody cares. I certainly didn't care. It was her house. But there were other questions I had to ask.

"Since last Thursday, how many times have there been when the house was entirely empty?" I asked. "And can you give me any kind of approximate idea when those times were?"

"None," she said flatly. "The house is never empty; I'm afraid of burglars, and I don't go out without one or two of the railroad men are here. But"—her eyes turned back to the room—"I guess they sleep pretty heavy."

By this time Irene was back, with briefcase-size kits in both hands and slung over her shoulders, and without her saying anything I moved out of her way and gently moved Mrs. Keating with me. Irene set the kits down just about where we had been standing and opened the first kit, a camera bag.

Normally, the first thing that happens at a crime scene is a complete walk-through. When I was in Ident I usually did that walk-through the same way Irene does it now, with my hands clasped behind my back so that if I started, through excitement or impulse, to touch something I shouldn't touch, I'd have time in the second or two it would take me to unclasp my hands to remember not to handle whatever it was.

It was impossible to do a walk-through of this scene. I had seen a room this thoroughly disorganized only once before, the day I met Olead Baker, who is now my son-in-law. The man who had framed him for the murder of his mother, stepfather, and half-sister had spent most of the night piling furniture in all the rooms, in such incredible jumbles that the rooms looked like a giant's game of pick-up sticks.

The second step is to stand in the doorway and photograph the room, panning slowly clockwise until the entire room has been

. . . . .

covered, and then to walk directly across the room and photograph back toward the door from which the other photos had been taken. The first part of this plan was doable. The second was not, because there was not enough cleared space in the floor to walk through.

The third step is to take triangulated measurements and close-up photos of anything of major interest; then evidence collection and fingerprinting begin.

This time the third step and the fourth and fifth (which often blur together anyway) would all blur together. And Irene and I were in for a very long night. Mrs. Keating, I supposed, was in for an even longer one, if she intended to clean all this up tonight. In view of her age, I hoped she'd have better sense.

As Irene began to take pictures, I asked Mrs. Keating to let me use her phone. She showed me an extension in the upstairs hall, just about ten feet from where I stood, and I called home. Cameron answered; at four, he's just now getting the hang of using the telephone, and he's very proud of himself for it. "Is Daddy there?" I asked.

"Yeah, but he's watching telebision."

"Well, tell him I need to talk to him."

Cameron was not ready to get off the phone yet. "Are you coming home pretty soon?" His voice was hopeful, and I felt like a rat cubed.

"Fairly soon, but probably not till after you're in bed. I'm sorry," I added hastily, over his protesting *Aw, Mom!* "Get Daddy for me," I said again.

I told Harry where I was. I told him what I was doing. I did not expect him to be pleased. That was just as well, because he was not pleased. "Lori went over to Becky's," he told me glumly, obliquely pointing out that he and Cameron would be all alone by themselves and probably would starve to death during the two or three more hours before Lori or I got home.

Lori, who will probably be our daughter-in-law one day, has lived with us ever since we discovered that the aunt she'd been

. . . . .

49

staying with since her mother's suicide blamed her—constantly, loudly—for that awful death. Having assumed the rule of daughter in the house, she normally cooks when I am not there or am otherwise indisposed.

"How's Becky doing?" I asked, ignoring Harry's implication. Of course Harry can cook. He just prefers not to, unless he can barbecue outside with dramatic flourishes. And the refrigerator, freezer, and cupboards were quite full. Becky is expecting baby number four—she had her first three between her older sister Vicky's first and second—and she usually has a house full of disturbed teenagers for whom she and Olead act as "safe house" guardians.

"She's fine, but Lori needed some help with her algebra and I couldn't do it the way the school does."

Lori sustained some brain damage in the automobile accident that kept her comatose for months; she has never been particularly gifted in math, but what little bump of math talent she did have seems to have been knocked out of her. Harry, unlike me, is good in math, but the rules for how things are done change periodically, not much, but just enough that parents' math skills rarely help their teenagers. Becky is close enough to Lori's age that she might be able to help.

"I guess Cameron and I will send out for pizzas," Harry added gloomily. "We would go out and get hamburgers, but Lori has the truck." This, of course, was the new truck, bought to replace the old truck, which had blown up in an explosion at a restaurant not long ago. As this was Harry's first *really* new truck, he was as nervous over it as a hen with one chick, but he was valiantly letting Lori use it just as he had let Hal, and then Lori, use the old one.

Unlike the earlier implication, these supper plans were probably not calculated to make me feel guilty—Harry and Cameron like pizza as much as they do hamburgers—but they succeeded in doing so anyway. "I'm sorry," I said, "but this looks like it's turning into something, and I don't know when I'll be home."

"I gathered that. You're still on that found body?"

. . . . .

"Sort of." I didn't want to try to explain things at great length right now.

"You were supposed to be off today."

"I know," I said. "But you know how it goes."

"Yeah. I know how it goes, all too well. Are you alone?"

"No, I have Irene with me."

"Good, she won't let you get in too much trouble."

"There's no trouble to get into, Harry, really. We're just processing a crime scene. I'll come home soon as I can."

"Stop and get something to eat on the way home, Deb. There's no sense in you having to eat cold pizza or come home and cook after a long day."

Gee, he *was* in a good mood; he didn't even reproach me—out loud—for getting involved in police work on my day off.

"Aunt Darla called," he added. "Three times."

"Oh dear," I said involuntarily. I had been hoping she would forget, but I should have known better.

Aunt Darla, my mother's sister, has decided I should join her Daughters of the American Flag chapter. That's sort of a clone of the DAR, founded about fifteen years ago by some women who got mad at the DAR for some reason never adequately explained to me (or at least if it was explained I didn't listen). In blithe disregard of copyright laws, they use all the same forms that the DAR uses, photocopied from originals with *Daughters of the American Revolution* whited out and *Daughters of the American Flag* inked in.

I do not have the time, or the interest, to take part in these things. But my mother begged me to join, just to please Aunt Darla, who has had a difficult life. I do not consider pleasing Aunt Darla, who brought much of her difficult life on herself (mainly by making herself so disagreeable to her offspring, my cousins, that they have moved several thousand miles away from her), to be a high priority, but I had about decided I would join anyway just to get Mom off my back, and then conveniently be unable to go to

. . . . .

many meetings. (That would not be difficult; they meet during the day, when I'm normally at work.)

I had requested a vacation day Wednesday so that I could go to a DAF meeting, to be properly introduced to the DAF, formally invited to join, and given an application form. When I made the request, I hoped like mad that Captain Millner would find some reason why I couldn't possibly take Wednesday off, as that would delay the whole thing for at least another month, but unfortunately he had granted me the day. Now all I could hope was that I got called in at the last minute.

"What did you tell her?" I asked.

"I told her you were working late," he said, "and would call her back later. But you know her."

I know her. She doesn't believe a message will *really* get delivered, or that anybody will *really* call back. (This second belief is not altogether unreasonable; people often do not call her back, for very good reasons.) As it is impossible to have a telephone conversation of less than half an hour with her, I certainly was not going to call her now, especially since Irene, as impatient as Aunt Darla, was down the hall yelling, "Deb, are you going to come help me, or do I need to call for backup?"

"I've got to go, Harry," I said hastily. "Just—I'm sorry she's pestering you. If she calls again, tell her I've taken the day off Wednesday and I'll be there unless I wind up having to work anyway. All *right,* Irene, I'm coming!"

I dashed back down the hall, to find Irene fingerprinting the legs of a very old, and very battered, oaken chair that was lying on its side. After helping her for about fifteen minutes, I left her for the moment and went to talk to residents of the boardinghouse.

We already knew that Mrs. Keating had seen and heard nothing. I expected everybody else to have seen and heard nothing.

Mrs. Keating told me that all four of the permanent residents, as well as three of the temporary ones, were presently in the house, and I decided that the easy way to do this was to meet with them all

· · · · ·

together. Normally police don't do that, but I had no reason whatever to suppose any of them were involved in the crime or that any
two or more of them had any need to get together and conflate
testimony.

Mrs. Keating parked me in a large and gloomy Victorian parlor,
with a shawl (black with large pink roses and black fringe) draped
over an extremely old upright mirror spinet, and offered me my
choice of fourteen assorted chairs ranging from an old—very old—
dark blue Queen Anne chair to a couple of yellow Formica kitchen
chairs that seemed to match Matilda's table to a trio of stained
orange-linen-and-unwaxed-walnut Danish modern contraptions,
a green-print chintz couch, and a faded red-plush-and-unwaxed-
mahogany loveseat. All of this furniture was strewn about the room
rather haphazardly, along with an assortment of would-be and real
maple, walnut, and mahogany end tables and coffee tables beset
with old lamps, crocheted doilies, and oddments of the sort found
in roadside souvenir shops.

The people, I could not help observing, seemed to clash with
one another—at least in appearance—about as much as the seating
arrangements did.

I got names: Victoria Hardage, seventy-three, retired high-
school mathematics teacher, very thin, gray-haired, in a gray dress
with a white lace collar, sitting bolt upright in a straight chair despite the cane in her left hand; Glen Scarlatti, forty-one, nightclub
magician, in tan slacks, an imitation alligator shirt, and tan Hush
Puppies, chubby, balding brown hair, sprawled in a club chair; Lala
Singh, twenty, college student, in a sari and sandals with her dark
hair up in a bun and four narrow bangle bracelets on each wrist; and
Tony Parrott, who refused to tell his age (but he looked about
forty), disabled, large and chubby, with tousled brown hair and
pallid skin, with a thick tongue protruding slightly from his mouth.
Only two of the five railroad men had come to the parlor; two
were working or at their real homes, and one would not get out of
bed. The two who came were Ed Lowell, thirty-six, brakeman,

. . . . .

and Arnold Jones, forty-nine, conductor. Both of them were wearing Levi's, blue chambray shirts, railroad boots, and expensive-looking watches.

Feeling like an idiot (although I had arranged this myself in the name of logic, I really hate the kind of situation where all the potential witnesses are gathered together and I'm sitting in front of them as if I were pretending to be Hercule Poirot, especially in a setting like this in which Poirot would certainly be more comfortable than I) I made explanations and started asking questions. At this time I didn't mention any possibility of Tutwiler's death; I simply asked about the trashing of his room.

"I heard nothing," Mrs. Hardage said precisely, "but I would not be surprised at anything. Mr. Tutwiler is a *most* unpleasant person, with a superficial charm that might fool the unwitting."

"But you haven't seen any strangers here?" I probed.

"None," she said, "unless—" She seemed to hesitate.

"Unless what?"

Instead of answering me, she turned to Mrs. Keating. "*Did* you ask a gentleman to come and work on the furnace last Friday about three P.M., when you were gone shopping?"

Mrs. Keating seemed to swell; her shoulders rose and her lips pursed. "I most certainly did *not*. The furnace doesn't need any work, and if it did my son would come and do it."

"Well, there was sure as hell a repairman here," Scarlatti said, "and he made the most incredible racket in the basement. I was trying to sleep, I was doing a show that night, and he made enough noise to wake the dead. Even Tony heard him, didn't you, Tony?"

"Heard wha-a-t?" He spoke very slowly, and looked as if his tongue was too big for his mouth.

"Last Friday. The noise in the basement."

"Was it Friday?"

By now I had deduced that Tony Parrott was somewhat retarded, but I didn't want to interrupt my witnesses when they were in full gallop.

. . . . .

"Yeah, sure, you remember, you were scared—"

"*Ghosts,*" Parrott said. "Inna basement. Ghosts—ghosts inna basement. Make a lot of noise. Bang, bang, bang!" He began to illustrate by slamming huge fists down on an empty metal chair, and Mrs. Hardage quickly corralled him.

"There are no ghosts," she said. "If someone was in the basement, it was a person being naughty." She glanced at me. "But it *was* quite loud, and I suggest that you now have your time of occurrence."

"I expect I do," I said. "Is anything stored in the basement?"

Obviously there were things stored in the basement; Mrs. Keating fairly leaped from her chair and dashed toward a hall door, with me in full gallop behind her and Mrs. Hardage, spry beyond her years and despite her cane, right behind me, and Tony Parrott, Glen Scarlatti, and Lala Singh trailing behind us. The railroad men didn't follow, but there was no reason they should have anything stored in this house.

The basement, a large room only partially below ground, was full of assorted trunks and boxes. Some of them—labeled HARDAGE, SCARLATTI, PARROTT, SINGH—were pristine except for thick layers of dust. But the contents of others, especially books and papers, were scattered all over the floor.

But strewing books and papers wouldn't cause the noise that had been reported to me. I—or somebody else, like maybe the crime-scene crew—would have to look farther for a reason for that.

Asking Mrs. Hardage, who seemed the calmest of the group, to get everybody else back upstairs and into the parlor, I checked quickly as much as I could without disturbing evidence.

The boxes that had been opened were unlabeled or were labeled TUTWILER. And I still couldn't see anything that would have caused a noise.

Whether or not Uncle George was Marvin Tutwiler—and by now I felt pretty sure he was—I had no lingering doubt as to whether Marvin Tutwiler was dead. And whoever killed him very

. . . . .

much wanted something he had and was looking everywhere the object—probably one or more books or papers, assuming, probably correctly, that this burglar was the same as Dora Gaines's burglar—might conceivably be found.

Had someone also considered hiding the body in this basement before deciding to transport it to the spot where it was found?

I went back upstairs, told Irene (who swore), and then returned to the parlor to get a description first of the "furnace repairman" and then of the noise.

Only Victoria Hardage admitted to actually seeing the man, but she undoubtedly had the best memory of the entire group anyway. "He was about six feet four inches tall," she said precisely, "and I would guess that he weighed about two hundred and thirty pounds. He had brown hair and blue eyes, and his skin was rather pale, as if he did not get outdoors often. From his vocal—ah—deficiencies and his facial expression, I believe that he was probably mentally deficient by twenty to thirty percent." Her eyes asked me to understand; her eyes told me there were some words she felt unhappy using in front of Tony Parrott. But that was all right; she had adequately conveyed to me that she believed his IQ was somewhere between seventy and eighty: trainable but probably not educable.

Which immediately posed a problem. "In that case," I said, "how could he have known what books or papers to look for?"

"Oh dear," she said. "I didn't think of that . . . but I'm not wrong. Truly I'm not. I began as a mathematics teacher but I taught special education for twelve years. I *know* these things."

"Was someone else with him?"

"Someone else must have been," she said, "as he arrived by automobile and I do not believe he would be able to drive. But"—she sounded as if she were confessing a terrible sin—"I really did not notice his companion at all. Not even to notice whether the companion was male or female."

"How about the car?" I asked.

She shook her head. "I'm afraid I am not very knowledgeable about automobiles. It was gray, and it looked quite new to me, but of course it might really have only been well cared for. Mr. Scarlatti, did you see it?"

Never mind the rest. Mr. Scarlatti hadn't seen the car or either person; he had alternated between pulling a pillow over his head and trying to sleep, and trying to comfort Tony Parrott, who was becoming hysterical thanks to the noise. Ms. Singh had been in class, at Texas Christian University. Neither Mr. Lowell nor Mr. Jones had been present at all.

I asked, then, about the nature of the noise, and after some hesitation and consulting with one another, they all seemed to agree that the noise had sounded like hammer strokes made near loose metal.

I thanked them all, asked Mrs. Keating to be sure nobody touched anything in the basement until we had finished with the crime scene, which might not be until tomorrow, and went back into the basement.

The side walls of the basement were partly dirt and partly brick, and the floor was hard-packed dirt. When looking for metal, loose or otherwise, the only thing I found was the furnace and the metal flues leading to various rooms and to one wall, where it apparently went up to heat the second floor also.

On the ground under the point where the flue began to ascend the wall, I found a little dirt that seemed to have been loosened by the blade and point of a pickax; that supposition was strengthened by the fact that a pickax, its point fouled with clinging crumbs of dirt, lay in the middle of it.

Unfortunately the undressed wooden handle was worn smooth and dirty from age and use; there would be no chance whatever of getting fingerprints off it.

But the use of that pickax this close to the flue could certainly have caused the noise I had been told about.

I went to the basement stairs and called up to Mrs. Keating, who

. . . . .

hurried back down to me. "Is this yours?" I asked her.

She peered at the pickax. "I think so," she said. "At least my husband had one. But I've never used it, and he's been gone fourteen years now."

"Where would it have been kept?"

"Here." She led me to a closed door and opened it for me. I could see nothing at all but darkness until she pulled the string of an old light fixture, and the blaze of an unshaded hundred-watt bulb illumined a room of shelves containing an assortment of tools and fruit jars, some of them full and some empty and cobwebby inside.

I thanked her, asked her again to leave things alone, and went back upstairs to help Irene. But I was thinking as fast as I could. A hypothesis, too vague yet to be called a theory, was beginning to build in my mind.

Whoever killed Marvin Tutwiler—because I was sure, now, that Uncle George had to be Marvin Tutwiler—had killed him Thursday night, except—wait a minute—nobody killed Marvin Tutwiler. That, we *knew*. He had died of a heart attack. At least if Marvin Tutwiler was Uncle George he had died of a heart attack.

So somebody had made him so angry he died of a heart attack, and whoever it was panicked because Marvin had something the perp needed desperately, and now he couldn't tell the perp where it was. The perp was familiar enough with this house to know where tools were kept, and had tried first to bury Marvin in the dirt floor until he realized the dirt was too hard packed to make that possible, was familiar enough with the experiment not only to know about it but to be able to get the body inside, which implied access to a key. And he—assuming it was a "he"—had burglarized the house of Dora Gaines, who had been Mrs. Tutwiler, and had tossed Marvin Tutwiler's room in his attempt to get whatever it was. . . .

Was severely mentally retarded but had enough intelligence to recognize whatever he was looking for when he saw it?

And had tried to bury Marvin Tutwiler in this basement—*after* he'd been embalmed?

. . . . .

58

Not a bit of this made even a shred of sense.

I'd think about it later. Right now I'd concentrate on the task before me, which was Marvin Tutwiler's bedroom.

Crime-scene work is nitpicky; I've known it to take three days to work, adequately, a crime scene that was *inside* a sedan. This room wasn't that bad, but still it was after ten before we got through. By this time the room was back in semi-order, as Mrs. Keating had followed determinedly after us with pails of soapy water and dirty rags to wash off the fingerprint powder as soon as Irene had either lifted prints or declared them nonusable, and Irene and I had hoisted furniture back into place for her because it was obvious that if we didn't she would, and she looked to be about eighty-five years old.

"Now I need one more thing," Irene said. "Mrs. Keating, I need to get some elimination prints from you."

Mrs. Keating bridled, as many people do when faced with this request, and as she always does, Irene proceeded to explain. "The thing is, we know you had a legal right to be in there. But you may well have left fingerprints. We need to be able to see which finger-prints are yours, so that we can eliminate them immediately instead of wasting a lot of time trying to find them in a criminal fingerprint file."

It took a little more explanation, and a little more cajoling, but finally Mrs. Keating consented to be fingerprinted in her kitchen, where she could immediately wash her hands with soap and water.

Only then did Irene go down the stairs to look at the basement. She swore a few more times, took some pictures, told Mrs. Keating we were through with the bedroom but not the basement, and asked Mrs. Keating to lock the basement door so that her people could work this scene tomorrow. Then she X'd strips of yellow CRIME SCENE! DO NOT DISTURB! tape over the locked door and told me we were leaving.

Outside, Irene said that so far she had prints of four people: One of them was very large, one of them was about the same size as

* * * * *

Uncle George (or, at least, had hands about the same size as Uncle George's), and two of them were rather small. Presumably one small set, from very wrinkled hands, would turn out to be Mrs. Keating's. That would leave three sets of unidentified prints, one that might be Uncle George and two that almost certainly weren't.

Then we caravaned back to the police station—I had taken my car to the Keating house, expecting to be able to leave as soon as Irene collected prints we could assume were made by Marvin Tutwiler, as we certainly had no reason to expect a burglary—and Irene sat down with the fingerprint lifts and began to compare them first to Mrs. Keating's prints, from which she was able to eliminate a good many lifts, and then to Uncle George's prints. To my amazement, since I last inquired into the matter, she had actually managed, doubtless with help from somebody in the medical examiner's office, to get a full set of prints from Uncle George.

After a while she sighed and then, laboriously, started through the collected latent prints again, still comparing them to Uncle George's prints.

Finally she sat back, looked at me, and shook her head.

"You've got to be kidding," I said.

"I wish I was. But Uncle George never touched a thing in that room. And he had good, strong ridge detail, Deb."

"I thought you said it was fragile."

She sighed. "I said his skin was fragile. It was. He'd been sick, and the body was beginning to decay. But his hands originally had good strong ridge detail. He'd have left good prints. So he didn't live there. That's all there is to it. We've got the front end of one case and the hind end of another, and any way you want to cut it, the front end of a camel and the rear end of a horse do not add up to a moose."

Ergo, Uncle George was not Marvin Tutwiler. Uncle George was still unidentified, and Marvin Tutwiler was still missing. So why the *hell* had somebody tossed Dora Gaines's house and Marvin Tutwiler's room and his possessions and possible possessions stored in Mrs. Keating's basement as well as—apparently—starting to dig a grave there?

I hadn't the slightest idea, and obviously Irene didn't either.

"Rats," I said. "I'm going home."

"I will in a minute," Irene said.

As I headed out the door, I heard her instructing the night Ident crew to run as many of the lifts as they had time to on AFIS during the night and leave her the results, so she could work on the rest in the morning.

Harry was right. I was feeling half-starved, and I definitely did not want either to go home and cook or to sup on cold pizza. I stopped at a coffee shop for grilled halibut and a baked potato, and then went on home.

The truck was in the driveway, so Lori—with or without completing her algebra—was back home. Pat, our half pit bull, welcomed me eagerly but drowsily and then curled back up in a ball with Ivory, the cocker spaniel, who hadn't wakened at all and who in fact was snoring rather loudly. When I entered I found that only Harry was still up. At eleven-forty, that wasn't surprising. What was surprising was that instead of being glued to his computer, taking part in dozens of bulletin-board discussions, he was lying on the couch, watching television. I've begun to see a few small signs that his love affair with computers is winding down. I would be pleased by that if I weren't afraid of what he would get into next: Our house is littered with ham radios, CB radios, and electric trains, and he *still* hasn't sold the single-engine plane he flies no more than about once a year now but still pays insurance and hangar rent on twelve months out of the year.

On my arrival, he cheerfully turned off the television and accompanied me to bed, except that I detoured through the bathroom, where I spent somewhat more time than I had planned on because I went to sleep in the bathtub, leaning back on the ducky little bathtub pillow Cameron (with help from one or more of his sisters) gave me last Mother's Day, until Harry woke me, sometime after midnight, and suggested I remove myself from the now-tepid water before I totally shriveled into a prune.

Of course I still woke up at six-thirty, in plenty of time to make breakfast for the multitudes.

I was still so sleepy I was half nauseated, but I knew perfectly well from past experience I'd be fine by about nine-thirty, which meant that I couldn't—reasonably—call in and announce myself sick. But I really didn't have anything official going on yet, because the Uncle-George-and-Marvin-Tutwiler case hadn't been officially assigned to me yet and might not be. What the heck, might as well go for broke, I thought, and picked up the phone to call Captain Millner.

Miracles never cease: He actually allowed me to take a day of comp time! This allowed me to finish my waking quite leisurely, wandering around the house in my nightgown (like almost all my nightgowns, it was a practical cotton muumuu I was still sewing from a pattern I'd been using for twenty-five years and saw no need to change).

Lori was gone to Seminary in the truck, and I got Cameron bathed and dressed in the front bathroom while Harry was showering and shaving. That used not to be possible, until Harry got ambitious a few months ago and decided to install a second hot-water heater so that we'd have one of our very own and be able to take hot showers (or, in my case, hot soaks) no matter what the front bathroom, dishwasher, or clothes washer happened to be doing.

It would have been nice if he'd thought of that when we had three offspring at home, or when we had two or three and one of them was Hal. Cameron doesn't use much hot water yet. Of course Lori, like most teenage girls, washes her hair every day—what ever became of the shampoo-on-Saturday routine?—but I don't know how much longer we'll have Lori with us.

Anyway, it was nice to have the extra hot water. By the time Lori got home from Seminary I had pancakes made and sitting in the microwave, in stacks with their layers separated by paper towels, waiting for everybody to be ready to sit down at once for breakfast.

An added miracle: Everybody actually ate. At one time. With nobody having to leap from the table and dash away, either to catch a school bus on time or to get to work on time. "Cameron," I said, "do you want to go to school this morning, or stay home and help Mom?"

It didn't take him long to make up his mind. "School," he said instantly.

I should have expected that answer. Youngsters in play school tend to be quite eager. I hoped he would retain that eagerness as he got older.

Harry took Cameron to school and himself to work, Lori left on the school bus, and I called Ident to see whether Irene was there or had gone back to Mrs. Keating's boardinghouse, and whether she had any names tied to prints yet. She'd sent Bob, her second-in-command, out to do the basement, and as to names, "No, I don't," she almost snarled. "You know I'll tell you when I do."

"I know," I said humbly, "but I'm taking a comp day today, so I'll be at home. Listen, do you remember that burglary at Dora Gaines's house Monday?" I knew she would. Irene's memory is phenomenal; despite all the crime in a city the size of Fort Worth, if Ident was called to a case she'd remember it, at least for the few weeks or months it was being actively investigated.

"Yeah, what about it?"

"Did you go to it?"

"No, Sarah did."

Sarah Collins, one baby later, wasn't quite as drop-dead gorgeous as she had been the first time I saw her, mainly because she had added—and kept—about forty extra pounds, but her appearance was still striking. The best I could figure out from things that she had said to me, she was a mixture of Black, White, Hispanic, Chinese, and Native American, and if that so-called mongrel race the racist hystericals keep talking about is going to turn out looking anything like her, I hope it arrives real soon. Her brain was as sharp as her looks, so she was turning out to be a top-notch Ident officer.

"Did she get any good prints?"

"Yeah," Irene said, "why?"

"Check them, would you, and see whether any of them match prints you got last night."

"I assume you have a good reason for that request."

"I do."

"Okay, give me your home number."

She called me back only ten minutes later, while I was still stacking dishes in the dishwasher, and said, "Your crystal ball was right on target."

"Oh?"

"Two of them. The big one and the small one." Male and female, I guessed but did not say to Irene because there is no real way of telling sex from fingerprints, and on anything to do with fingerprints, Irene refuses to speculate.

By now I'd really rather have gone on to work, because there was something complicated going on and I wanted my hands on it. But I get to take comp days so seldom I was determined to take this one whether I wanted it or not, so I was glad when the mail came, bringing a letter from my son Hal, who is now serving his two-year Mormon mission in Nevada and who, by mission rules, is allowed only one phone call home a year, on Christmas day.

I had just finished reading the letter when Matilda called and said, "Deb, I've been burglarized."

Four

. . . . .

NOW, I TRUST I need not say that, laying aside my natural sympathy for a distressed friend, I found this an extremely interesting development. Because anybody with even a casual knowledge of Marvin Tutwiler and a halfway decent knowledge of how to locate information might be able to locate Mrs. Keating's boardinghouse, might be able to locate Mrs. Gaines, who had been Mrs. Tutwiler. But how many people would be able to trace Marvin Tutwiler— or, rather, Marvin Tutwiler's papers—to the home of a so-called psychic who was doing his ghostwriting?

Well, maybe that thought wasn't quite fair. Matilda had taken out an ad in the Yellow Pages under "Writers": MATILDA GREEN-WOOD, M.A., ALL KINDS OF COMMISSIONED WRITING, with her phone number but not her address. There weren't very many other writers in the Yellow Pages. So if the perp knew Tutwiler was having some writing done he might be able to find out, or figure out, who was doing the writing.

Of course I was reasoning well ahead of data; this is one of my besetting sins, and I reminded myself of that fact. If we could just be sure that Tutwiler was dead, if Uncle George had just turned out to be Tutwiler. . . .

I started imagining all kinds of scenarios in which Tutwiler for some reason had very dry skin and therefore didn't leave fingerprints, even in his own room. But in that case who *did* leave the fingerprints that we'd assumed must be those of Tutwiler in that room?

. . . . .

"Deb?" Matilda said. "Are you still there?"

"Yes, I was thinking. Have you called the police yet?"

"Only you."

"You're really going to have to make an official report."

"But Deb, I don't think they actually *took* anything."

"That's immaterial. We—police—need to know the burglary pattern in any area, to stand any chance of clearing any of the burglaries. And that means calling the police department and making an official report."

"You know why I don't like to do that," Matilda said. "I mean, so many people think I'm some sort of con artist—"

"Gee, Matilda, I just can't for the life of me figure out why anybody would think you're a con artist."

Matilda had the grace to laugh at that. Her spiritualist "church," with its red wooden billboard shaped like a hand held up, palm facing out, had been planned carefully to fit a stereotype. She knew exactly what she looked like. She had set herself up to look that way.

"Oh, I know," she said. "But—all right, if I have to call them I will, but you said yesterday you might be off today, and—I know it's presumptuous, and you're probably busy, but if you would just come over and look at it first, then you'd know if it was worth reporting officially. I mean, why set myself up for a hassle if I don't have to?"

"It's not in the least presumptuous," I said, "and I'll be over in about fifteen minutes. In the meantime, don't touch anything it looks like they might have handled."

"I knew that much," she said. "But just about all of it is stuff I've already handled plenty of times before. See you."

She hung up, and I went to pull off my nightgown and make a quick dash under the shower before throwing on my clothes.

It was about ten-thirty when I parked in the dirt lot near the rickety building right beside Matilda's light blue twenty-odd-year-old Ford Fairlane, which looked like a refugee from a demolition derby but presumably was fixed again, at least temporarily. Matilda, in the same batik skirt she'd worn yesterday but a different blouse—this one deep brown, long sleeved, with a scoop neck—was sitting on the bottom-stair tread waiting for me, and she rose gracefully, dusted her behind with her hands, and walked toward me. "I thought I'd be better off waiting outside," she told me. "That way I wouldn't be so tempted to start straightening things." She glanced at the sky. "I was pretty sure it wouldn't start raining quite yet."

"Though I don't know how much longer it will hold off," I agreed. Black clouds had begun massing in the north about half an hour earlier, and I was wearing the poplin jacket I usually substitute for a raincoat, because I'd rather get wet than have half a mile of extra fabric billowing around my legs.

She preceded me up the stairs and unlocked the door. "Thank goodness they didn't take the stereo," she said. "I don't know what I'd do without it." She turned it on and put an old 33⅓ record on the turntable, turning to me as a sweet alto singing "Heading home, heading home, my home is over Jordan" began to fill the small room.

"I like that one," I said.

"Yeah, it's one of my favorites. If people could learn to think of dying as heading home, they wouldn't be so scared of it. They didn't do anything in the kitchen, either," she added over her shoulder, in an abrupt change of topic, "so I'll make us some tea."

"What kind?" I asked, as I always did, and she told me she was trying a new one this time and she wouldn't tell me its name until I told her whether I liked it.

"I went out first thing this morning to get my car," she said, rinsing out the kettle and filling it with fresh water before striking a match to light the front right burner of the small, old, gas cook-stove. "You know that garage I usually use; it's so close I just walked over there right after breakfast. I don't know how long I was gone, probably about an hour, and when I got back I found this." She gestured toward the mess that had yesterday been an assortment of halfway tidy stacks of paper.

"Have you checked your bedroom?"

"Yeah, they pulled out everything in the bookshelves in there, but nothing else was touched."

Clasping my hands behind my back, I approached the living-room corner Matilda used as an office and examined, as closely as I could without touching, the wild disorder. There were unopened but ratty-looking stationery boxes labeled MACROBIOTIC MS., DOO-LEY FAM. HIST. MS., CAN'T WIN FOR LOSING NOTES, HIST. OF COMAN-CHES IN TEXAS, and so forth. As in the boardinghouse basement, the boxes that had been opened, and the papers that had been scattered, were either unlabeled or were labeled TUTWILER. And all the gene-alogy books were pulled out, although none of the other books in the front room were.

We had a connection.

At least we had a connection between Tutwiler and this bur-glary, and almost certainly a connection linking this burglary, the one at the boardinghouse, and the one at Mrs. Gaines's house. What else all of this connected with I wasn't totally sure yet.

"We've got to have somebody come out," I said. "Let me make a phone call, and then I'll explain." With the very familiar feeling that once again the universe had set my agenda without the least consultation with me as to what *I* wanted my agenda to be, I went to the kitchen phone rather than the speaker phone near the work area and called Ident. With Sarah en route, I called Captain Mill-ner. This time I gave him a full report.

"That's the damnedest thing I ever heard of," he informed me.

"No shit, Sherlock," I agreed. "But—what does it look like to you? I mean, we have a body we can't identify and we have a missing person and somebody's searching all his possessions, but the missing person is not the body although they're about the same size and age and have—had—the same health problems, but I'm sure the two cases are connected—"

"Why are you sure of that?" he interrupted.

"Well, because——" I came to a dead halt, thinking. "I don't know," I said finally. "I guess there's not any reason why they have to be, but——"

"But there's also not any reason why they can't be," he said. "I see your reasoning. And I agree that there's at least a chance, maybe a good chance, that they're connected. You've been assuming from the start they were connected because you thought the body was Tutwiler's, and now you know it isn't."

"No I don't, not for sure," I interposed.

"Ri-i-i-ght, Deb," he said. "Then let's put it this way: If I were on a jury I'd vote this body not guilty of being Tutwiler. How's that?"

"Okay," I said meekly.

"Your hunches tend to be good," he went on, "but a hunch, or a chance, isn't a fact. So far all the *facts* we have consist of one missing person and one found body, and by the way Missing Persons is working on both of those now, and two—now three—burglaries. Have you called Ident?"

Assured on that point, he said, "Keep me posted. I still don't know whether we have a case at all. It's obvious *Burglary* has a case, and *Missing Persons* has a case, but——"

"But," I agreed. "Yeah—until we know a little more, there's no real reason to assume Major Case has a case. Well, whether I'm on it or not, Matilda's my friend and I'm off today, so I'm out here."

"Okay," Millner said. He told me again to keep him posted, and then he hung up.

"One thing happened yesterday afternoon that you might ought to know about," Matilda told me as she poured boiling water into a two-quart Pyrex measuring cup that contained a reusable muslin tea bag filled with a green leafy substance, which, if anybody other than Matilda were using it, I'd be tempted to run drug-kit tests on. "Dora Gaines called me. She said one of Marvin's genealogy research clients called her—said she'd been calling her all weekend and couldn't get an answer—well, you know she, Dora that is, told us she'd left her answering machine turned off—and she, the client I mean, wanted her genealogy no matter how incomplete it was. She wanted everything Marvin had done about her ancestral line, and Dora told her she didn't know where it was but she'd ask me if I knew."

"Who was the client?"

"Dora didn't tell me. She just asked for all Marvin's papers, in case she got more phone calls like that, and I said until I knew for sure Marvin was dead I was holding his papers hostage. Deb, are you sure I can do that?"

"No," I said, "but I'm not sure you can't, and I really think you probably can. Well, I'll just call Dora right now."

I did so. Dora—who, I gathered, was retired, or at least didn't work outside her home during the day—answered the phone. "I don't know who it was either," she told me after I explained why I was calling. "Whoever it was, she left a couple of calls on my answering machine Thursday, before I turned it off before I went out of town Friday, but I couldn't call back because she never did leave her name or anything."

"And of course you don't have Caller ID?"

"No, what would I need it for?"

"No reason," I said. "For that matter I don't have it either, though I guess I'll have to get it eventually."

"Anyway," Dora added, "when she called me last night I asked, but she didn't tell me—she said if I didn't have the papers then it didn't matter, did it?"

"Well, it would have helped if you'd been able to get her name, but if you couldn't, you couldn't. Let me be sure I understand you: You told her you didn't have his papers and that Matilda did, right?"

"Right."

"Tell me one more thing: When you mentioned Matilda, did you actually give her name?"

"Yes, wasn't that all right?" Dora Gaines sounded mildly alarmed now.

"She didn't tell you not to. Thanks for the clarification, though. Thank you," I said, and hung up. "Well, that answers that. He—she—they—didn't have to track you down. Dora Gaines told them where to find you. Matilda, do you think you can find that list we had of—never mind," I said hastily as she started to head for the work area.

"Oh, yeah, don't touch," she reminded herself, and sat down again on a high stool by the kitchen counter.

Sitting on the high stool facing her, I called Dora Gaines again and asked again for the same phone numbers she'd already given us. Her interest, when I explained why we needed them again, was strong but had to go unsatisfied except for a very brief explanation, during which she gabbled repeated apologies: She wouldn't have told them where to find Matilda if she'd had any idea this would happen; she was so sorry Matilda had had this inconvenience on top of going unpaid. I managed to get off the phone rather later than I had expected to, but without any display of bad manners.

After ten more telephone calls, by which time Sarah had arrived and begun processing the crime scene, I had discovered that some, but not all, of Marvin's assortment of former, present, would-be, and presumed future wives had received telephone calls from a woman—she sounded kind of middle-aged, one ex-wife said—asking for Marvin's papers. At least two women said she sounded pretty frantic.

Well, what did that add to our knowledge? We already knew that somebody, probably several somebodies, probably one of them female, wanted something from Marvin's papers very badly, probably her own genealogy—but I couldn't imagine anybody's genealogy being worth murder, or even burglary. And I couldn't imagine Dora Gaines, or anybody else, giving out that list to an inadequately identified caller over the telephone. Nevertheless . . .

I called Dora Gaines again, and asked.

. . . . .

"Oh, yes, she asked if I knew anybody else whom Marvin might have stored papers with, and you know him, he was just like a cuckoo, leaving everything in everybody else's nest—"

I thanked her, wished silently for an epidemic of a virus that would spread common sense, and managed to get off the phone.

"Let me guess," Matilda said. "She did."

"She did."

After shaking her head, Matilda began tidying her kitchen, and I went back to thinking about the case. From fingerprints, we thought at least one of the somebodies might be a woman; from eyewitnesses we knew at least one of the somebodies was male and probably retarded. We now knew that a woman was involved at least to the extent of making telephone calls.

I gave up on thinking just as I had given up on calling, and just sat and watched Sarah for a while. She's nothing like as judgmental as Irene is, although she's just as careful at crime scenes, and as she worked she asked Matilda all kinds of interested questions about her channeling—which I consider to be Matilda's subconscious mind fooling an otherwise intelligent woman—as well as about her spiritualist church and her ghostwriting.

"Might as well check on this," she said, and picked up—with tweezers of course—several papers that Matilda had identified as being in Marvin Tutwiler's handwriting. "Everybody hold your nose," she added, picking up an aerosol can in her right hand. After that warning she walked out on the stair landing to spray the papers, and even so the metallic smell of ninhydrin—triketohydrindine hydrate, also called 1,2,3-indantrione monohydrate, dissolved in acetone (I mention this just in case you're a chemist)—filled the air. She took out each paper, sprayed it, and brought it back in, one at a time, and hung each one on the small wire clothesline Matilda had strung across the back of her kitchen, fastening it with the plastic-coated metal clips Matilda keeps there. "I wouldn't do this if you had a fabric line or wooden clothespins," she commented, "because this stuff might stain them and then rub off on your clothes. Do you have a small hair-dryer I could use?"

. . . . .

72

"Yeah, sure," said Matilda, who had been watching bemusedly. She went down the hall, returning with a blue hair-dryer.

Sarah blew a gust of hot air over the row of papers, and the three of us watched as the whiteness slowly began to bloom with purple fingerprints. "Ninhydrin was known as a specific reagent for protein for fifty years before anybody thought of using it to check for fingerprints," she commented. "Makes you wonder, doesn't it?" Then she got out of her briefcase a set of photographs of fingerprints and a lighted magnifier and began to compare, with the papers still hanging in front of her.

"Deb," she said a few minutes later, over her shoulder, "the bigger prints on these papers match the prints Irene got from the most personal stuff in Tutwiler's bedroom. So a dime'll get you a dollar they're Tutwiler's fingerprints."

"But not Uncle George's," I said morosely.

"Definitely not Uncle George's. There's another set of large-size prints that match the other large one from the Keating burglary, And there are a couple of sets of smaller prints here; most likely they're Matilda's and your other burglar's, but I didn't bring the other burglar's prints with me. I'll go ahead and package these now, and then, Matilda, I'll need to get elimination prints from you."

And that was the point the investigation had reached—with Matilda being fingerprinted in her kitchen—when Captain Millner called me back. "De-e-e-eb," he said, "come to Papa. Major Case has a case."

That "come to Papa" phrase is not my most favorite of all the things he ever says, as it usually presages something nasty, complicated, time-consuming, or—usually—all three. In this case it rapidly became even more disagreeable, as he added, "On second thought, just go home and pack for an overnight stay. I'll meet you there and tell you what's going on while I drive you to the airport."

". . . died in Fort Worth," Captain Millner was saying, his eyes fixed on the highway, "at some sort of meeting; it was his third heart attack. He'd already had triple bypass and that had filled back

. . . . .

73

up, and then they'd done another angiogram and tried to use the tubes from the angiogram to blow the heart vessels open again and that didn't work, and he was supposed to take it real easy. But he insisted he *had* to go to this meeting in Fort Worth despite all medical advice, and the results were just what the doctor had predicted, and of course the family ordered the body shipped home to San Francisco."

"Uh-huh." I was still trying to collect my scattered thoughts, after calling Harry (who was not pleased by the news); stopping by the bank to get some cash; driving home in a chilly, nasty rain; changing clothes; unloading my pistol and putting it and its ammo in separate corners of my gym bag; and hastily shoving enough clothes for an overnight stay into said gym bag and then locking it by putting a bicycle lock through the holes in the tabs of three zippers, because even a federal agent, much less a city cop going out of her jurisdiction, can't carry a loaded gun onto an airplane. In spite of all this I'd still managed to get outside in time to catch Captain Millner *before* he tried to enter a front yard that the dogs, or at least one dog, think belongs to them. Pat seems to have decided that since Ivory is so indiscriminately friendly it's his job to protect Ivory as well as the family, and he's become correspondingly more obnoxious.

"And what got to San Francisco wasn't Uncle George," Captain Millner continued.

"Uncle George?" I asked involuntarily.

"Yeah, kind of a funny coincidence, wasn't it?" he said. "I mean, we'd been calling the body Uncle George and sure enough it *is* Uncle George. George Milton. Had been married but wife dead about ten years. No children, but a lot of nieces and nephews, all of them very fond of him. So you can imagine the reaction when the guy at Driscoll's—"

"Driscoll's?" I interrupted.

"Funeral home. I correct myself. Mortuary chapel in San Francisco. Advertises that it takes care of shipping bodies anywhere.

*   *   *   *   *

74

Seems no bodies are buried inside the city limits of San Francisco anymore, so people have a choice of using a cemetery somewhere out in one of the nearby counties, using a cemetery somewhere else in the country, or cremating. Hence, a lot of bodies are shipped out of San Francisco. Obviously Driscoll's also receives shipments. Anyhow, the guy at Driscoll's opened the shipping coffin to get the body all pretty for the funeral—and it wasn't Uncle George."

"Oh?"

"It was somebody else entirely. He bore some resemblance to Uncle George, enough that the funeral home might not have thought much at first, except that the body hadn't been embalmed. And it's absolutely illegal to ship bodies across state lines without embalming them."

"And it was in shipment how long?" I asked dourly.

"Well, it left Fort Worth on a Saturday morning train," Millner said cheerfully. "And it's now Tuesday—you can figure it out yourself."

"I'm afraid I can."

"Well, it's not *that* bad," Millner said. "I mean, it *is* November and the boxcar wasn't heated. So anyhow, the guy at Driscoll's called Mullins Brothers, who'd prepared the shipment here, and Mullins Brothers checked their records and said absolutely, positively, Uncle George had been embalmed. And then Driscoll's checked again and that time they noticed their corpse was still in street clothes, pretty dirty, and that's when they called the San Francisco Police Department. So a uniform officer went out there first and nosed around a little and thought it looked real funny, and then she called Homicide, and a Homicide inspector went out there and he noticed the corpse had what looked to him like a depressed skull fracture, so then he called the coroner."

"So you were actually called by—"

"One Inspector Brooks. Who says he has no doubt the body that got to San Francisco had been murdered. And says the deputy coroner who went out there agrees with him."

"But—" I began.

"But what?" Stopped briefly before entering the flow of traffic where one freeway merged into another, he glanced at me.

"But what makes you so sure their Uncle George is our Uncle George? Because don't forget, I recognized him. Our Uncle George, that is. Not that I knew his name, I mean, but he was somebody I'd seen before. So if he's from San Francisco—"

"He was here to meet with some people from the Fort Worth Elks lodges."

"Oh," I said, and memory began to stir in me. Friday night two and a half weeks ago. Despite my dislike for smoke-filled rooms, I care enough about Harry's interests that I accompany him to parties at his lodge. That Friday night I had wandered around in an evening gown with a glass of club soda and, from 8 P.M. until 1 A.M., dutifully smiled at and shaken hands with numerous people, some of whom I knew and liked but many of whom I did not know, had never seen before, and expected never to meet again. And—yes, that's right—the man who later became the corpse we'd called Uncle George had been there. And I'd met him once or twice before, in past years. "I should have shown the pictures to Harry," I muttered, and then turned my mind once again more directly onto business. "So Uncle George, or rather, Uncle George's body, was supposed to be shipped to San Francisco, and instead he wound up in our experiment, and somebody else wound up in Uncle George's coffin."

"Marvin Tutwiler wound up in Uncle George's coffin," Captain Millner said.

"Probably. You don't know for sure, yet, though, do you?"

"No. If I did I wouldn't have to send you to San Francisco."

"You could just fax fingerprints."

"Your ticket is already bought. Stop grumbling. You've never been to San Francisco before, have you?" Captain Miller was heading, now, down one of the roads inside DFW International Airport.

. . . . .

"No, but I was planning to go with Harry, sometime on vacation."

"So? You're getting an advance trip."

"Oh, right," I muttered. "So I can go look at corpses there too. All right, never mind. Is somebody meeting me at the airport, or do I need to rent a car?"

"Somebody's meeting you. Inspector Brooks. And you and he together will work out the agenda from there out. At least you won't have to watch the autopsy; they've already done that. The report'll probably be ready time you get there, except for toxicology and so forth. Of course."

"Of course," I agreed. Toxicology reports can take several weeks. Not that you need to look very far for probable cause of death if you've got a depressed skull fracture, but you still do a toxicological workup too, just in case. "But I still don't know what you want me to *do* there."

"You get to read all their case reports on Uncle George. You get to ask questions about Uncle George, if any seem indicated. You get to bring the corpse back here."

"I can hardly wait," I said, rather embarrassed to find my spirits were rising a bit, not at the prospect of bringing back a corpse or talking to Uncle George's nieces and nephews—the reason for which I still could not understand, in view of the fact that there was no doubt that Uncle George had died a natural death—but at the prospect of getting a look at San Francisco.

Then I realized that the main reason my spirits were rising was the fact that now I didn't have to go to Aunt Darla's DAF meeting Wednesday.

Captain Millner blithely parked in a fire lane, handed me a city credit card, told me where my ticket was waiting, told me to call when I knew when I was coming home and he'd see to it somebody picked me up, and drove off, leaving me standing on the curb.

*   *   *

.   .   .   .   .

Of course police on official business don't fly first class. This means that I got two half-cans of Diet Sprite and a couple of bags of peanuts in flight. Although I had had a decent breakfast, it was now well past lunchtime and I was feeling half-starved by the time I got off the plane to see a well-dressed Black man looking directly over my head while holding a sign that said DETECTIVE RALSTON. I approached him.

"Hi, I'm Deb Ralston. I guess you're Inspector Brooks."

He looked rather startled. I suppose Captain Millner once again had forgotten to mention that Detective Ralston is female. But for the most part San Francisco operates in the twentieth century, and there was no problem. Brooks—who immediately asked me to call him Ray—said, "Did the airline feed you?"

"It did not," I said, "and if you expect me to look at a corpse in an imperfect state of repair, I recommend you feed me first. My stomach acts peculiar when it's empty."

"I'll take you somewhere decent for supper," he promised, "but how about a burger for now? Or would you rather have nachos?"

After collecting my luggage, I stopped in the rest room to re-arm myself, in view of the fact that I was on official business. Then we left the terminal into—guess what?—a chilly, nasty, rain that felt somehow heavier than the one I had left behind in Fort Worth. I was glad I'd brought my poplin jacket, which has a red flannel lining and about twenty pockets so that I can put my hands in my pockets without dislodging all my other pocket contents.

We settled on hamburgers for lunch. Brooks—Ray, I suppose I should say—drove through the airport area into the closest town (which was wall-to-wall motels and restaurants) and stopped at a McDonald's, after which it took about twenty minutes, mainly on the freeway, for him to drive downtown to the Hall of Justice on Bryant Street. The building, often prominently displayed in Dirty Harry movies, was about seven or eight stories high and looked sort of like a large white cube. In front of it was a grotesque arrangement of what looked like black metal drainpipes making dozens of unrelated right angles; occasionally two or three of the pipes were attached with black-enameled half-circles. "What's that?" I asked.

"The city thinks it's a statue," he said, and grinned. "I think it stands for the screwballs who make the laws and expect us poor sods to remember them all."

I could identify with that feeling.

We went first to his office, where he sat down, grabbed an unoccupied chair from another desk for me, and said, "Okay, what goodies did you bring us?"

I started unloading my own briefcase—the nice briefcase-purse-pistol bag I'd bought last year, although I normally carry my pistol in a shoulder holster when I'm on duty—and laid on the desk photographs of as many of the fingerprints presumably belonging to Marvin Tutwiler as Irene had been able to supply me, along with photographs—both original and computer-enhanced to replace the nose—and fingerprints of our Uncle George.

Ray brought out photographs of George Milton, and we put his photographs and mine side by side. He looked at me, I looked at him, and we both nodded. "All right," he said, scooping up his photos and mine as if he were collecting a winning poker hand, "let's head for Ident."

We headed for Ident, where I managed with some difficulty not to drool on all the equipment they have and we lack, and an Ident tech named Henry Song brought out fingerprints he had collected at George Milton's house after learning of the confusion of corpses. He threw enlargements of George Milton's right forefinger and our Uncle George's right forefinger up on a comparator, and we all looked at them. Song started grinning first, within about forty-five seconds, but Ray and I—neither of us fingerprint experts, but both of us moderately familiar with fingerprints—were beginning similar grins by the time Song's grin was complete.

"One down, one to go," Ray said.

I handed him my photographs of the right index fingerprint we assumed was probably Marvin Tutwiler's, and he put it into the left side of the comparator, with the right index fingerprint of the un-known corpse who'd arrived in George Milton's coffin on the right side.

Song grinned again. "Bingo," he said softly.

And that was that. Uncle George was George Milton, and Mar-vin Tutwiler had arrived in San Francisco in George Milton's cof-fin, and if Marvin Tutwiler was in as bad a condition as it had sounded over the phone, then somebody in Fort Worth, whether it was Homicide or Major Case, had a case.

"Let's you and me go visit Mr. Tutwiler," Ray said.

Mr. Tutwiler, as presented to me by deputy coroner Richard Stein, M.D., was not a prepossessing sight. He had been about the same height and weight as Uncle George, and his coloring probably had been the same. He had a similar scar down the middle of his chest, although it was hard to spot now because one of the incisions from the autopsy had been made right beside it, and he had about the same amount of hair. Unlike Uncle George, his nose and eyes had not been nibbled on by rodents. But also unlike Uncle George, he hadn't been embalmed, and he'd spent part of Saturday, all day Sunday, and part of Monday in a sealed box on a train.

His features were swollen with body fluids and streaked with the purple, black, and green of decomposition.

I was glad we had been able to identify him by fingerprints, because I doubted anybody would ever be able to identify him visually now.

"Pending toxicology reports, which I really don't expect to get anything from, here's your cause of death," Stein said, casually—though with properly gloved hands—lifting off the back of the skull. "It's easier to see from the inside." He gestured.

Yes, it was pretty easy to see from the inside. It was also easy to see from the outside, for anybody who was looking for it. I would say that Mr. Tutwiler had been struck on the head with, or had fallen and struck his head on, something with a decided corner on it. The right side of his temple was caved in to an appalling degree.

"Looks like somebody slammed his head against the corner of something," Stein added. "I really don't see how anybody could have hit him with anything and gotten that result."

Stein showed me the brain, now floating in a neat jar of formaldehyde. "You can see the damage here," he said. "No, not there, look here, right where the frontal lobe, parietal lobe, and temporal lobe all join together, see that? Totally smashed in. Well, the poor devil couldn't have lived long—I don't know, maybe half an hour or so at the outside. It probably wasn't instantly fatal, but it might as well have been. Maybe if somebody had gotten him right to the hospital his body might have gone on living for a while, but not him, if you get what I mean. I mean, that's pure jackassery, to keep somebody alive on machines after something like that, unless it's just long enough to harvest transplants and then unplug, and this poor fellow, nobody would have wanted his heart or liver or eyes."

He continued to speak as he worked. "He ate too much"—emphatic slam of brain jar onto counter—"smoked too much"—he turned toward the slab on which the body lay—"drank too much"—he crashed the slab back into the cooler—"didn't get any exercise"—he slammed the cooler door shut—"probably had been impotent for years"—he shucked off the plastic gloves and dropped them into the trash can—"and with those cataracts, he damn sure shouldn't have been driving." He turned on a water faucet and began briskly to wash his hands.

"So you know who he is," he said, turning to me as he dried his hands.

"Yeah," I said. "Marvin Tutwiler. From Fort Worth, Texas. And for somebody who was impotent, he sure did have a lot of female company."

"Oh, that's real common," Stein said. "Guy can't get it up for one woman, he decides it's her fault so he goes looking for another woman." He tossed the towel into a dirty linen bin and grabbed a pen. "Marvin—Tutwiler," he muttered, writing on the numbered form that matched the number on the corpse's toe and the number above the cooler vault the corpse was in. "How do you spell that? You got a date of birth?"

Of course I had brought all that stuff with me. I provided date of birth, name of next of kin (Dora Gaines, whose divorce had not yet come through, and she was not going to be happy about being expected to pay for Marvin's funeral), address, and so forth.

"Where do you want it shipped?" Stein demanded. "We'll have to prepare the body here, of course; can't send it back across state lines unembalmed, even if it did arrive that way."

Eventually we agreed that Marvin Tutwiler would be shipped to the Tarrant County Medical Examiner's Office by air freight, that I did not necessarily have to be on the same flight, that on arriving home I would see to the air-freighting of Uncle George, and that I would take with me to Fort Worth the preliminary autopsy report, which Stein's secretary was typing at this moment and would have ready in half an hour. Stein would have toxicology and other reports still pending sent in duplicate both to me and to the Tarrant County Medical Examiner's Office.

It was, by now, four-thirty in San Francisco, which made it six-thirty at home. I figured I'd better give Matilda the bad news, which I expected she was about resigned to anyway, that Marvin Tutwiler was no longer around to pay her for the writing he'd ordered.

I borrowed a phone in the coroner's office and used my police-department telephone charge-card for this one. The phone rang and rang, with no answer. That was odd, but come to think of it, Tuesday is the night Matilda has one of her "public sessions" of channeling, and she tends to take the phone off the hook to rest up for it.

I called home, and Harry answered instantly. I thought that a little odd, until he said, "I just got off the phone with Matilda and I was about to call Millner."

"Oh?" I said.

· · · · ·

"Yeah. Deb, there's something bad wrong. First she asked for you, and then pretended she was talking to you—it was like somebody was listening to her end. She told me—you—to get that genealogy stuff she asked you to store for her and take it by her office. I said, 'I don't think Deb's storing any genealogy stuff for you,' and she said, 'Oh, that's right, you did put it in the safe deposit box, didn't you? Well, get it tomorrow, please. I won't be there, so just put it in my outdoor mailbox.' And then she said, 'But don't miss your meeting tomorrow for it. I know how important that is for you. Afterwards is fine.' I—Deb, I don't like this."

"Neither do I," I said grimly. "She never gave me any genealogy stuff to store. And she knows I wanted to go to that meeting about like I wanted to swallow a dose of castor oil. Harry, I'll call Millner *now*. If I can get a flight out tonight, can you meet me at the airport?"

Five

. . . .

"SO YOU THINK it's a snatch?" Captain Millner asked me, his voice only slightly distorted by the thousands of miles of telephone lines that separated us.

I was sitting at Ray's desk in a crowded and not very tidy squad room, with Ray in the adjacent chair looking at me with large brown eyes full of sympathy undimmed by all the surrounding bustle of activity. "I know damn well it's a snatch," I said. "You know Matilda, she wouldn't—"

"I know Matilda," Millner said. "And she'd be smart enough to try to get that kind of message across the way she did. But I'm damned if I know why in a situation like that she'd practically insist on having you go to that DAF meeting."

"I don't know either," I agreed, "but as clear as she made it, I'd better find a way to be there. Harry says whatever time I get a flight out he'll pick me up. I *do* wish you hadn't sent me here; there just wasn't any reason—"

"I thought you might find a reason when you got there. If you didn't, you didn't. It was a fishing trip. I'm sorry, but I did what looked best to me at the time. Don't worry any more about George Milton; I'll get that taken care of. What are you going to do about putting a genealogy chart in her mailbox, considering you don't have one?"

"I don't know, cobble up something from my own genealogy, I suppose. At least that'll be easier than making one up from scratch.

. . . . .

I don't know how far back Tutwiler was supposed to be searching any more than I know for whom. Anyway, she hasn't *got* an outdoor mailbox."

"Well, look, go on and get a plane reservation out, but let's not jump to any conclusions," Millner said. "I'll get a car en route to see if she's home. And—what time—you said she was holding a public meeting tonight, what time was that supposed to be?"

I had to think about that. "I think they're usually at seven. Has anybody found Tutwiler's car?"

"Time's real close, but I should be able to get hold of Sarah and send her out there in plain clothes. If Matilda's there, no harm done; Sarah'll just let us know there's nothing wrong. If Matilda's not there—well, Sarah can tell the people that Matilda had an emergency come up, and that way we don't get three dozen missing-person reports." Sudden dead silence. "Tutwiler's car?"

"Yeah, Tutwiler's car. You said Missing Persons was on the case—have they done anything about finding his car?"

"Deb," Captain Millner said carefully, "I didn't even know he *had* a car."

"Oh, shit," I muttered, and then startled even myself by bursting into tears. As Ray fetched me Kleenex I needed and coffee I didn't, and Millner tried to comfort me over the phone, I managed to get out, "Look, never mind me, just try to find that car. I don't know why I didn't tell you. I know he had one; his landlady said he drove off in it last Thursday, and I forgot to follow up. She'll know the color, and I'm sure you can get the make and license-plate number from the state computer. I don't know what finding it'll tell us, but the location of it might tell us *something*."

"I'll do that. And—hold out some good thoughts. Maybe Sarah'll just find her and tell us nothing's wrong."

"I wish. You believe that about as much as I do. Okay. I'll call back—should I call you at home again?" I had called him at home this time.

"You might as well."

· · · · ·

The earliest flight back to Fort Worth was at nearly eleven-thirty San Francisco time, which of course is one-thirty Fort Worth time; as it wasn't much past seven at this point, Ray had time to take me out to dinner. He knew how worried I was—any experienced cop understands these things fairly well—and he was trying to distract my attention, so he offered first to take me out for a drink or two or three.

"This missing woman, the probable snatch, she's a pretty good friend of yours, right?" he asked gently.

"Yeah," I said, "we've been friends for years. She's—different. She's not like everybody else. Totally individual."

"It's the ones like that the world needs most," Ray said. "I don't blame you for wanting to get her back. Look, you're through here"—which I was; as I had expected, there was no earthly need for me to go talk with any of Uncle George's relatives, and I continued to regard this trip as a complete waste of time—"Let's head for a nice bar. Maybe you can drown at least a few of your sorrows."

"I'm a Mormon," I said, more abruptly than I meant to because I was trying not to start crying again.

"Oh. . . . That means you don't drink, right?"

"Among other things."

"Well, then I've got a different idea. Come on. You get the vest-pocket tour of San Francisco."

In vain did I try to protest that I really didn't want to do anything but go to the airport and wait for my plane. "There's nothing you can do right now," he said, "and worrying about it will just make you sick."

"But I don't need you to baby-sit me—I'm sure you've got a family waiting for you. . . ."

"Nobody is waiting for me, and I'm not baby-sitting you. If I were in Fort Worth and I got very worried about a friend of mine at home, wouldn't you want to help me?"

"Yes, but—"

"Well, I feel that way too. We're going to go ride the cable cars."

"But—"

"We're going to go ride the cable cars. Would your friend, this Matilda Greenwood, would she want you to worry yourself into the ground when you are in a position where you can't do anything at all?"

"No, but—"

"So we're going to ride the cable cars. You'll see. It'll raise your morale. Let me just make one quick phone call."

Then, telling me where he was going at just about every turn and stoplight, he drove out to Fisherman's Wharf, parked the car, and set out, leaving me to follow him or sit in the car and sulk. Of course I followed, as he undoubtedly knew perfectly well I would, because he began talking as if to the air: "We're at the north end of the cable-car line. In just a bit we'll get to a sort of a turntable—that statue is of Saint Francis of Assisi, by the way; it's stainless steel, by Benny Buffano, and he's Italian. Was Italian. I don't know if he's still alive."

"It looks like something you'd see in New Mexico," I said.

"Yeah, I know. Nice and simple. I like simple lines in statuary, not like that grotesque piece of junk you saw earlier. Okay, at the turntable Muni employees actually turn the car around, while the riders have to wait outside because if they stayed on there would be too much weight. Then everybody runs to get on the car, and most tourists do it wrong."

"So you're going to tell me how to do it right."

"Sure," he said. "You don't want to sit down, because if you do you'll be side-on to the action and there'll be people all over the place blocking your view. Instead, you want to run to the front, as close to the front as you can get, and stand up; there are plenty of rails and things to hang on to, and you've got the wind. It's not fast, like a carnival ride, of course; it's kind of slow, but you're going up and down all these hills, and it's nice and windy and the driver keeps clanging the bell. There's an annual contest to see who's the best bell-ringer, and all the drivers practice for it year round. Okay, now this is Hyde Street, and if it was better weather there'd be all sorts of hippies out here with saxophones and guitars and everything. There, they're through turning—here we go!"

Caught up in the excitement, I raced with him to the front of the car, and he paid for both of us. The hills were incredibly steep, and except for the speed—which, as he said, was pretty slow—I'd have felt like I was on a roller coaster. As it was, the wind and rain in my face at least temporarily blew away the cobwebs from my mind. All too soon somebody was calling, "Everybody out!" and somebody stuffed a paper transfer into my hand.

As we scrambled off, Ray handed me his transfer. "We'll pay both ways," he said, "so you can have these to take home. People always want to keep them as souvenirs. Give them to your kids or something. Look at it, you can see the cable-car picture—well, it's too dark, you can't see it now, but you can look at it later. You know why they are called cable cars?"

"Uh-uh," I said, "because I don't see any kind of cable. I thought they would be like trollies."

"Nope. No, they ride on underground cables, and here's what's weird: The car always stays stationary in relation to the cable. It's the cable that moves; it's hauled around by all these great big pullies underground. By the way, we're on Market Street now, and if it was decent weather the streets'd be full of street preachers with bullhorns."

"You're kidding."

"Nope, and they're always warning about the wrath of God that's going to befall this city. Who knows, maybe it already befell, but anyway, when you come back with your husband, be sure you get out here in the daytime, because they're a sight to see. Okay, here we go again!"

This time we found ourselves standing right next to a rather large man with a mustache and beard, wearing a peacoat, an orange-and-blue watchcap, and a long, orange-and-blue scarf. He was declaiming Scottish ballads at the top of his lungs into the wind; as loud as he was, I was sure people two feet away couldn't even hear him over the wind and the bells.

By the time we arrived back at Fisherman's Wharf, I had not forgotten Matilda—because I couldn't possibly forget Matilda and my fears for her safety—but I had temporarily recovered my zest for life. "Now we're going to dinner," he said. "The Rusty Scupper. The best darn seafood house in the world, for my money. And I'm going to order for you, because you'd just want ordinary stuff," he explained. "Inlanders always do. But there's all kinds of good stuff you'd never even think to try."

I am very fond of good food. I will even eat shark and octopus, which the sampler plate had on it. But while waiting for the food to be served, I went and called Captain Millner again, asking, "What did Sarah learn?"

"Matilda was scheduled to be there, and she wasn't. That's all."

"Did Sarah check the apartment?"

"Yes. It was locked, but Sarah slipped the lock and went in—told me she knew it would be okay with Matilda for her to do that."

"She's right."

"I figured that too. She said there's no change from when she was there earlier except that the work area had been straightened a little. And she said to tell you she took the cat home with her, so you don't have to worry about that. Deb—you know I like Matilda."

"I know."

"But damn it, if she didn't play this Sister Eagle Feather game—"

"Captain," I interrupted, "if you think this has anything to do with Sister Eagle Feather, you're wrong. Haven't you read Sarah's reports?"

There was a brief silence before he said, "No."

"Then I suggest you read them. And the reports from the Keating burglary. And the reports from the Gaines burglary. Tutwiler was, among other things, a genealogical researcher. And he started researching somebody's ancestral line and my guess is he found something somebody was ready to kill to keep secret—something somebody *did* kill to keep secret. I don't know what, any more than I know who. But whoever it was about, that person or somebody close to that person killed Tutwiler and looked for the paperwork in Tutwiler's boardinghouse, and Tutwiler's estranged wife's house, and Tutwiler's ghostwriter's house, trying to find it, and then kidnapped the ghostwriter. Damn it, if she just hadn't told Gaines she was holding Tutwiler's papers hostage until he paid her. . . ."

"Did you put her up to that?"

"No, she thought it up herself. But I encouraged her."

"Nine times out of ten it would be a perfectly sensible response."

"That doesn't help this situation. If he's killed her—"

"Deb, I'll put everybody I can on the Tutwiler case. And remember this: She was still alive when she called Harry."

"Oh, I know. I guess I better go eat. I need the fuel."

"That you do." He hung up without saying good-bye.

I returned to my table to find that a couple had joined us. "Deb, I'd like you to meet Dorinda and Howard Everett," Ray told me. "Howard is George Milton's nephew." He was smiling like the Cheshire cat. Obviously he'd set this up and had dragged me all over San Francisco to give the Everetts time to get to the restaurant.

Well, that was okay, I guessed. Dorinda was a smiling, brown-haired woman about my age; her husband was a bluff, red-faced outdoorsman who looked much older but probably wasn't.

"Hello," Dorinda said. "Ray told us you found Uncle George, and I want you to know we're so very grateful."

"Actually my son-in-law found him," I muttered, feeling rather embarrassed. "But I'm glad we were able to identify him."

"Uncle George would say it doesn't matter," Howard said.

. . . . .

"Where a body is buried. He'd say it doesn't matter. But it matters to *me*." He wiped his eyes. "I'm gonna miss that old man. He never met an enemy in his life, at least not one who stayed an enemy."

"I met him a few times," I said.

"Oh, did you?"

"Yes, my husband is an Elk—"

"Ohhh, yes," Dorinda said feelingly. "You'd have met him. I'll bet every Elk and Elk's wife in this *country* met him."

"He enjoyed life," Howard said, and lapsed into silence as the waitress slid a plate heaped with interesting-looking, interesting-smelling food in front of me, following with similar plates for other people.

I started eating with gusto, but long before my plate was empty, Dorinda and Howard had excused themselves—Howard had, embarrassingly to him, started crying in the middle of dinner—and the exhilaration of the cable-car ride had worn off for me. I was exhausted, and after a while Ray seemed to realize that. "Had enough, huh?"

"It looks like it."

"Well, then let's go—no, never mind, the department is paying for this."

On the way to the airport, he pointed out a brilliantly floodlit building in the distance. "You're a Mormon," he said, "and there's the Oakland Temple. The way it's sitting, you can see it thirty miles away. When you come back, get your husband to take you there. The grounds are one beautiful garden."

"I hope my husband will take me there," I said, and nearly burst into tears, because in Mormondom a wife's being taken to the Temple by her husband has a very special meaning I wasn't about to try to explain here and now.

Ray pretended not to notice, but once we were inside the terminal he said, "Wait here for medicinal chocolate." He bounded off, returning with Ghirardelli chocolates, which I was quite sure the department had *not* paid for, and he stayed with me until I boarded

. . . . .

my plane, saying, "Take care of yourself. And I hope you find your friend all right. Deb? I hope you didn't think I was uncaring, hauling you all over the way I did."

"I figured it was to give time to the Everetts to get to the restaurant."

"It was partly that. And partly—I just wanted to distract your attention. But if you thought it meant I didn't care—"

"No, I didn't think that at all. I appreciate it, really—and I hope so too, that we find Matilda all right, and thank you," I told him.

At the last minute he slapped his business card, with his home phone number on it, into my hand, and said, "When you and your husband come out here, you call me and I'll take a couple of days off, all right?"

"Thanks," I said again, and headed into the loading chute. I managed to sleep part of the way back, so I wasn't totally drained when I stumbled off the plane at close to five-thirty in the morning. Harry drove me home through a dank, rainy, nasty predawn and I fell into bed again, sleeping until seven, when the telephone woke me.

Harry, in the living room, and I, in the bedroom, answered at the same time, and I came wide awake when Matilda said, "Deb?"

"Matilda, are you okay?"

"Of course, why wouldn't I be okay?" But I could hear the stress in her voice. "I'm just . . ." There were sounds in the background, and I could hear her say, over a partially covered telephone receiver, "I'm asking her right now!" Then she got back to me. "When can you get into the safe deposit box those papers are in?"

"Well, I guess anytime after ten," I temporized, realizing her captor might be listening. "But—"

"I'm—I'm visiting a friend, I spent the night here," Matilda said, "and she's really anxious to see the papers. But I told her you had this meeting you absolutely had to go to, because they were going to give you that important form to fill out, and you couldn't go pick my stuff up until after your meeting, but she—uh—needs to plan her day, so when does it let out, Deb, about two o'clock?"

"Something like that," I said, "and I'll go to the safe deposit box right after that. Where did you say you wanted me to leave the papers?"

"In my outdoor mailbox." She sounded much calmer, now that she knew I was playing along. "Then after my friend and I go over the papers I'll be *heading home.*"

There was a pleading in her voice when she said that, a tone that wouldn't be recognized except by somebody who knew her very well. She was trying to tell me something. Then I remembered: The record she'd played when I went over to her house after her burglary. Her comment on what it meant. No matter what her captor might have told her, her captor actually intended to kill her, and she was sure of that.

"I gotcha," I told her. "And I'll see you before you get home."

"You do that. But if not, I'll see you when I can. 'Bye, Deb." The little click told me she was no longer on the line.

What now? I hung up the handset, stared at the phone, and burst into tears as Harry came tearing into the bedroom to comfort me. My head against his shoulder, I sobbed, "Harry, why didn't we get Caller Identification as soon as it came out?"

"Because we didn't think we needed it. Honey—"

"You did, you wanted it, but I said it was just another gadget. . . ."

"And that's all it would have been. I didn't think we would really—"

"But if we'd had it I could have gotten Matilda back in half an hour, and now—now I don't even know where to look—and you heard what she said, they're going to kill her—"

"She didn't say that. Deb, calm down now."

I twisted away from him and grabbed blindly for tissues before I said, "Yes she did," and told him about the record.

Through the mist of my tears, I could see his face paling. Matilda was his friend too. But he said, reasonably calmly, "Then I guess we've just got to get her back before they have a chance, don't we?"

He knew as well as I did how unlikely that was. Throat aching with the need for more tears, I called Millner and told him what she had said and what she had meant, and he swore about six times and said, "I don't know what to tell you to do, Deb."

"I do. I've got to fiddle up something that looks like genealogical research, and then I've got to go to Aunt Darla's DAF meeting, though I'm darned if I know why. Who's on the case now? The murder of Tutwiler, I mean?"

"I haven't assigned it yet. He was identified so late last night. But we did put a lookout on his car, and Conner's been sitting on her apartment all night just in case . . . just in case. Livingston spelled him just before dawn."

David Conner and Bill Livingston are members of the Stakeout Squad, and I was glad to know somebody was watching Matilda's apartment, although I didn't expect that anybody would actually go there before two-thirty or so. I glanced at my watch. "I'll be in the office at eight."

"Okay, I'll see you then."

As I hung up the phone, Harry asked gruffly, "You want me to stay home today in case she calls again?"

"Oh, Harry, would you?"

"You bet. Let me just call the office. . . ."

"I don't like putting people on cases they're personally involved in," Captain Millner said, "but this time"—he half-smiled at me—"I have no doubt Deb would be on the case whether she's assigned to it or not. So Deb, you're heading the investigation of the kidnapping of Matilda Greenwood, and Dutch, you're heading the investigation of the murder of Marvin Tutwiler. Since it's certain that the two are connected, you'll have to coordinate pretty closely. Deb, you've got the floor."

The squad room contained almost the entire Major Case Unit,

not just the three of us; obviously Captain Millner assumed that one way or another, we were all likely to get our fingers into this one. He'd brought out the big easel with the chalkboard-size paper on it, and the big indelible markers we use when we're charting a complicated situation.

"Here's what we know," I began. "We know that whoever the perp is—and I'm saying perp even though there's more than one, because there's at least a ninety percent chance that the large man is retarded, which means the other person, probably though not certainly a woman, is heading the operation. If the lead perp isn't a woman then almost certainly there are three perps, but we don't have any reason to suspect there are more than two. So, we know that the perp has access to the back room of Mullins Brothers Mortuary; we know that because the body of George Milton was stolen Friday night from an already closed coffin, and the body of Marvin Tutwiler was placed in the coffin and then the coffin was reclosed and left where it had been placed for shipment Saturday morning to San Francisco. We know that the perp had a place to hide a body, because both medical evidence and the evidence of Tutwiler's fiancée indicate he was killed Thursday night, which means the body had to be stashed for at least twenty-four hours before it was placed in the coffin. We know that the perp knows knew—Marvin Tutwiler well enough to know a good bit of his history. Although the only places actually searched were his most recent past home, where his estranged wife Dora Gaines lives; his present home, a boardinghouse near the T and P depot; and the home of Matilda Greenwood, his hired ghostwriter, we know that several of his ex-wives and ex-fiancées were also telephoned, along with his current fiancées—"

"Wait a minute, Deb," Henry Tuckman objected, "what kind of a guy would have that many exes? And did you say his current *fiancées?*"

"A slip of the tongue," I said. "One current fiancée so far as I know."

. . . . .

95

"And as to what kind of guy," Nathan Drucker put in, "I'd say he was a busy one." He made at least a small effort to compose his features, which kept breaking into a grin.

"Anyway, how come you're dressed so fancy?" Wayne Carlsen demanded.

"Because I have to go to a ladies' luncheon," I said, with as much dignity as I could muster. It was perfectly true that the red-and-black dropped-waist dress, black beads, and black high-heeled shoes I was wearing did not comport well with my job. I was even on duty with my pistol in my bag instead of in a shoulder holster for the first time in longer than I could remember.

"For the benefit of those of you who don't know," Captain Millner said, "Matilda Greenwood, the kidnap victim, is a very close personal friend of Deb's." This put an abrupt end to the clowning, and Millner added, "Go on, Deb."

"To backtrack a little," I said, "the murder victim is Marvin Tutwiler." I was writing on a large sheet of paper as I spoke. "He wrote—or had ghostwritten—several books on genealogical research. He gave lectures on genealogy, and he did genealogical research for clients. My hypothesis—and I think it's accurate—is that he was doing genealogical research for someone, stumbled onto something that someone considered very threatening, and was murdered over it. He may have been killed just because he had the information, or he might have tried to blackmail somebody over it; that I don't know. I do think the killing of Tutwiler was probably manslaughter rather than murder, because from the looks of the body, it seems that he fell against something like the corner of a coffee table, though it would have had to be a very heavy one, and that's what Stein thinks too."

"Stein?" Dutch asked.

"Deputy coroner in San Francisco. He did the autopsy. This, as I said, probably happened last Thursday afternoon or evening, because Tutwiler was expecting to receive a good bit of money that day and was going to take his fiancée out to dinner. Apparently he and his client got into some sort of fight in which Tutwiler fell or was shoved against something that caved in the side of his skull. The medical examination indicates that although the wound wasn't instantly fatal, he died within minutes.

"So there the perp was, suddenly, with Tutwiler's body to hide, and on top of that, he or she didn't have the information and didn't know where it was, which meant it could easily fall into somebody else's hands.

"The first step was to get rid of the body, and that's the first place where we run into a quandary. We think, as I said, there were two perps, a large one, probably male, probably mentally retarded, and a small one, probably a woman, possibly the other one's sister or mother. Well, the big one was—is—certainly big enough to move the body, but how would he know where to move it to? They wound up having to stash it until the next night before actually getting rid of it."

"Any idea where?" Dutch asked.

"None at all," Millner said.

Then I went on, "But eventually they got to Mullins Brothers Mortuary. It was possibly serendipity that they found, in the mortuary, a coffin already packed for shipment to San Francisco, but the question still remains, how did they happen to pick *that specific* mortuary, and how were they able to get into a locked preparation room so easily that nobody ever knew anybody had broken in there, and how were they able to open, and close, the coffin so quickly? And could it be completely accidental that they just happened to pick a coffin in which there was a body bearing a superficial resemblance to Tutwiler? Well, I don't know, but I'm assuming that one or the other of the perps had, at some time in the past if not at present, had some connection with Mullins Brothers and might even have had some connection with George Milton, enough to know that Milton looked a lot like Tutwiler and that Milton's body would be shipped to San Francisco. And the only connection we know of that Milton had in Fort Worth was with

* * * * *

the Elks lodges, so the perp might have had some connection with one of them."

"Wait a minute," Dutch objected. "If the perps are a woman and a retarded man . . ."

"Maybe she's an Elk's wife or widow. Maybe she has a father or a brother who's an Elk. I don't know; I'm just telling what it looks like."

"Okay," Dutch said, and subsided.

"Anyhow, as I was about to say, exchanging the bodies in the coffins brought a new problem. The perp is now rid of Tutwiler's body, which gets rid of part of the risk, but he, she, or they still have to dispose of Milton's body. And that's far less of a risk, because so few people in Fort Worth knew George Milton that there's a good chance the body might have gone unrecognized permanently, especially if San Francisco had buried or cremated who they thought was Milton without ever opening the coffin. But the question now was how to get rid of Milton's body. It probably didn't matter to them whether Milton's body was found, because probably nobody would know of a connection between them and Milton, but they did have to dump it somewhere.

"Well, as you know, there's an experiment going on about how bodies decay when left in the open or in unusual containers. And here's the next problem—our next problem, I mean, not theirs: The perp managed to get a key that is totally unavailable to the general public, get inside the compound where the experiment is going on, and deposit the body there, all with nobody knowing or suspecting anything and all within a very narrow time frame, from the time Tara whatever-her-name-is checked the bodies late at night until the time Olead Baker checked the bodies in the middle of the morning. The best I can figure out, from the time Tara left till the time Olead got there was less than ten hours.

"Okay, at this point the perp is rid of both bodies and has delayed the investigation somewhat, because we have a missing person—Marvin Tutwiler—and we have an unknown corpse, but

. . . . .

the unknown corpse doesn't turn out to be Marvin Tutwiler.

"But the perp has another problem, and that's the problem of where are the missing papers, the missing genealogical research? The perp knows where Marvin lived during his last marriage, and first calls over there to try to get the papers. But the phone isn't answered at first, and the perp is afraid to leave a callback number. Then Dora Gaines turns off her answering machine and goes out of town for the weekend.

"The perp goes in and searches Dora's house, but Dora has not retained anything at all that belonged to Tutwiler. We don't know exactly when that house was burglarized, because Dora was gone for the weekend and didn't discover the burglary till she got home Monday. There was no rain to get in through the broken window, or anything else that would give us a time, and none of the neighbors saw or heard anything."

A collective "yeah" rose from the group at that point. It is very rare that neighbors see or hear anything, and even if they do, often they decide not to admit to having seen or heard. Nobody wants to get involved these days.

"The perp then—or at some point, let's put it that way, because we don't know the exact order all this happened in—goes and searches Tutwiler's boardinghouse room and the basement of the boardinghouse, where personal belongings that won't fit in the rooms are stored. I really think that the boardinghouse was searched first, before the Gaines house, and the perp had some intention of burying either Tutwiler's body, or Uncle George's body, in the basement of the boardinghouse, which has a dirt floor. There's evidence of digging there, but that's the next strange thing: The digging tools were kept in an inconspicuous, closed, but not locked, closet in the basement. And when I say inconspicuous I mean inconspicuous; I didn't spot it until it was pointed out to me. So I figure there's at least an even chance the perp had some sort of connection with the boardinghouse, to know where the tools were. But the dirt proved too hard-packed for the perp—either perp—to be able to make much progress in it, and that plan was abandoned.

"The perp, or a female accomplice of the perp, waits till Monday, and then starts calling not only Dora Gaines but also *all* of Tutwiler's ex-wives and ex-fiancées, as well as his present fiancée, asking them about the papers, but nobody admits to having them. Now this tells me that either the perp knew Tutwiler pretty well, to know all this about him, or that the perp copied Dora's address book and then Tutwiler's, because Dora didn't *have* all the names and numbers. We know Dora's address book wasn't stolen, because Dora gave me some information from it as recently as yesterday, but we didn't find one for Tutwiler, so my guess is they got it. Dora Gaines tells the perp that Matilda Greenwood has a lot of Tutwiler's papers. Both Dora Gaines and the perp call Matilda, and Matilda says she's holding Tutwiler's papers hostage. To Dora this just means that Matilda wants to be paid, but it's possible that to the perp, this suggests that Matilda might want to pick up the blackmailing—assuming there was some, and I think there was—right where Tutwiler left off.

"So first Matilda's house is searched, and then Matilda is kidnapped. Matilda, thinking fast, tells the perp she's left Tutwiler's genealogical research with a friend—me—and she doesn't tell the perp that I'm a police officer. Under duress, she makes the phone call that Harry got last night, and then, with the perp getting antsy, she makes the phone call that I got this morning.

"I know from the phone call that Matilda desperately wants me to go to a Daughters of the American Flag meeting I've been invited to. I don't know why she wants that, but I'm going. She specifically mentioned the important document I'm supposed to get there, but the only document I'm really supposed to get there is a membership application. I don't know why Matilda wants me to get that, but it must be very significant in this case, and she clearly *does not* want me to just go ask for it now; she seems to be afraid I'd spook somebody if I did that. I also know from the phone call that

Matilda expects the perp to kill her." At this point I nearly lost it again, and I spent what felt like two or three minutes, but probably was really only about fifteen or twenty seconds, gulping and sniffling before I could go on.

"Matilda asked me to bring the papers and put them in her outdoor mailbox. I don't have any papers, and Matilda doesn't have an outdoor mailbox. She gets her mail at a post-office box about two blocks from her house. So—Captain Millner, could you get somebody from the Stakeout Squad to locate a scroungy, used-looking outdoor mailbox, install it somewhere around Matilda's building, and then sit on it as invisibly as possible?"

"Will do," Millner promised, writing a note to himself. "Livingston can sit on it, since he's already there. I'll get somebody else to go out and install one."

"Wait a minute," Dutch objected. "We know the perp's been there once, since the place was searched the way it was, and most likely the perp's been there at least twice, because Matilda was probably taken from her home. So wouldn't the perp have noticed there isn't an outdoor mailbox?"

"Matilda knows she doesn't have an outdoor mailbox," I said. "But she told me to leave the papers in the outdoor mailbox. The only way I can do that is if somebody puts an outdoor mailbox there. So she must know that the perp *didn't* notice whether she had one or not."

Dutch shrugged. "Okay, I guess. Go on." He leaned back in his chair.

"So here are the things we know, or assume, about the perp: First, the main perp is probably female with a male accomplice who's probably no more than a tool. Second, either the main perp or the accomplice probably has worked at Mullins Brothers, and either the main perp or the accomplice probably has some sort of involvement with the medical examiner's office or the medical school. Third, one of the perps has had some sort of acquaintance with Mrs. Keating sufficient to know where the gardening tools are

. . . . .

kept. And fourth, one of the perps, almost certainly the female, has both the money and the interest to hire somebody to research her family tree."

When I stopped, Dutch added, "And fifth, that the perp wants to get into the DAF, or is already in the DAF, and Tutwiler found something that could endanger that membership."

I looked at him.

"Makes sense to me, anyway," he said. "Why else would Matilda want you to go to the DAF meeting?"

Dutch had departed for the medical school and the ME's office; I had decided to go and talk again to Mrs. Keating. But before I did that, I removed from my briefcase the mass of genealogical material I had stuffed in it this morning; Aunt Darla had given it to me several weeks ago, under the assumption that *of course* I would want to join her DAF group. Starting with two generations back from my own, in hopes that there would be no immediately recognizable names, I photocopied the mass of it on the police department photocopier, stuck Aunt Darla's originals in my briefcase for now, and headed out the door.

I found Mrs. Keating dressed in her best finery, weighted down with what looked like military medals and ribbons, each with a different name on it. She opened her door to me and led me into her parlor, which didn't look any better today than it had last time I'd seen it. "Oh, dear, I'm so sorry," she told me, "but I just don't have time to talk with you very long today, I'm about to leave for my DAR luncheon."

"You're in the DAR," I echoed, questioningly.

"Oh, dear, yes, I've been a member for forty years." She looked complacently at her medals and ribbons. "Every one of these represents a different ancestor, you know, and every one of them fought in the American Revolution. These"—she pointed to several different ribbons, one at a time—"each represent someone who actually *died* in the war. My ancestors were *most* valiant in the defense of liberty."

. . . . .

"I'm sure that's wonderful," I said, trying to sound far more enthusiastic than I felt. "Do you know anything about an organization called the Daughters of the American Flag?"

She fluttered her hand at me in an exaggerated gesture of dismissal. "Oh, those silly Daffies! You wouldn't want to get mixed up with *them*, would you?"

Personally I thought anybody with her chest full of ribbons representing ancestors was pretty silly, no matter what organization she saw fit to join, but I didn't dare say so. "My aunt is a member," I said, "and she wants me to join."

"Now, who is your aunt, dear?"

"Darla Slaughter."

"Oh, yes, I know Darla, she's just so easily led, you know."

I had always considered Aunt Darla as easily led as a mule with its heels dug in, but I encouraged Mrs. Keating to go on.

"Well, it happened about fifteen years ago," Mrs. Keating said, in a confiding tone that indicated she'd settled in for the next hour regardless of when her meeting was scheduled to begin. "Right here in Fort Worth, you know." She cocked her head, birdlike, and asked, "Or did you know?"

"I really don't know anything about it," I said, "and I'd be grateful for anything you could tell me."

I hoped it wouldn't occur to her to wonder why a police detective had come to ask her about the DAR and the DAF. Fortunately it didn't; she obviously assumed that *of course* anybody else would be as absorbed in these things as she was.

"Well, one DAR chapter here in Fort Worth—there are several, you know, I don't even *remember* how many—got mad at the national board for some official statements they had made," she began. "Now, I don't even remember what statements they *were*, and I very much doubt any of those silly Daffies remember either, but they got together and demanded that the statements be retracted and of course the national board refused, and then this entire chapter simply *defected* and a few people from several other chapters did too, and then they got some people from other chapters to join them, and practically before I knew it they had an entire national organization of Daffies! Can you believe it?"

"I'm afraid I can," I said. "Do you have any idea how many—uh—Daffies there are in Fort Worth now? Or even how many chapters?"

"Oh, there's still only one chapter," she answered. "I mean, of course anybody with any real *breeding* wants to join the DAR—oh, I'm sorry, dear, I don't mean to speak against your dear Aunt Darla, but you know she is so easily led—and she *was* in the DAR until that *awful* Gertrude Wallace simply *lured* her away. She *is* still in the same garden club I am, you know."

Six
· · ·

I SIMPLY STARED at her for a moment, beginning to put things together in my mind as I wondered whether I was going to have to arrest my own aunt for murder and if so, what my mother would say and do, though in fact Aunt Darla was on my father's side rather than my mother's. Finally finding my voice, I asked, "Are there many other women in your garden club who are also in the DAR or DAF?"

"Oh, yes, dear, virtually all of them," she said. "That's how we met each other, you know. It was well before the Daffies got started. We found out so many of our members were interested in gardening, and of course we couldn't discuss gardening at a DAR meeting, that we just decided to found our own gardening club. Oh, mercy, look at the time, I simply must run—"

"Mrs. Keating," I said hastily, "is there any way I can get a list of the people in your garden club?"

"Oh, dear, what would you want that for? Well, I suppose you could, I think Thelma Chipperly has one, but you see, she's on a tour right now. She's gone on a bus to Chiapas. I think that's in Mexico."

"It is," I agreed, thinking that a bus tour to Chiapas sounded rather interesting. Harry wouldn't want to go, but maybe Matilda could go with me. If we got Matilda back alive. "Would anybody else have one?"

"I shouldn't think so. Now, Im sorry, but I really must scurry.

· · · · ·

Please make yourself at home; if you need to look at anything else, go right ahead. And Mr. Wolverton and Mr. McBride are upstairs if you simply must speak to somebody, but Mr. Wolverton is an engineer and Mr. McBride is a brakeman and they didn't get in until four A.M., so it would be kind to let them sleep." And out the door she pattered, in her rust-colored jersey dress printed with autumn leaves, her chest nearly covered with ribbons and names, and her black silk brocade overcoat clutched around her.

After the door closed behind her I allowed myself to say a few words I do not normally say.

I did not see any sense in disturbing Mr. Wolverton and Mr. McBride. I simply went out the door and took a good look at Mrs. Keating's garden, which in November in the rain wasn't particularly impressive except for a redwood gazebo, its floor full of dead leaves and nothing else. Beside it were a few battered chrysanthemums still trying to bloom, and I could see the dusty green foliage of what would, in the spring, be a magnificent iris bed.

Unfortunately iris beds made me think of my trip to Salt Lake City early in the summer, which made me think of murder, which made me think of Matilda's voice saying she was heading home, which made me cry.

Which did no good whatsoever.

I went back inside the boardinghouse, went to the telephone in the parlor, looked in the telephone book for a number I had not memorized and had never expected to need to memorize, gritted my teeth, and telephoned Aunt Darla.

When I was seven years old, we went to Aunt Mary's birthday party. Aunt Mary, who actually was my father's mother's aunt, was one hundred years old, and though it was close to forty years ago I remember as if it were yesterday. Although the late May morning was beautiful, the gas space heater inside the old fireplace was on full blast. The room was stifling hot and far too full of people, and in the middle of the room in a chair that looked older than she was crouched Aunt Mary, leaning over a brass-headed cane and clutching it with both hands so as to remain as near as possible to upright. She wore a brilliant purple orchid pinned to the lavender housecoat she wore over a lavender nightgown, a tan cardigan sweater over the housecoat, and a white crocheted shawl over the cardigan; and her gnarled fingers were encased in purple lace mitts to keep the crusts of psoriasis from falling everywhere. Her eyes—glossy white with cataracts the doctors would not risk trying to remove, because in those days cataract surgery was not the in-and-out laser thing it is now but a weeks-long ordeal involving sandbags on both sides of the head to prevent movement for the first week—ceaselessly moved around as if trying to determine, through the deep, blurry fog of her wasted vision, who had come to disturb her, and her mouth, sans teeth, endlessly worked as if retasting food eaten before my mother's mother was ever born.

A white sheet cake trimmed in pink, blue, and orchid decorating frosting was perched on a piecrust table in front of her, near the yellow telegram bringing birthday greetings from the president of the United States, at which I had been unimpressed, suspecting—correctly, I think—that the telegram had not really come from the president at all. Aunt Mary's companion and younger sister, Aunt Lucy, a mere eighty-four years old, cut her a piece of the cake and fed it to her with a spoon, deftly capturing the falling crumbs as a mother catches the falling dribbles of a baby's first spoon-feeding. Aunt Lucy kept shouting to her, telling her who was there, reminding her again and again what the celebration was about, again and again waving in front of her the telegram that had probably been sent quite routinely by a presidential aide.

The whole thing appalled me then and still appalls me now; it was evident that Aunt Mary had overstayed her time upon the earth and there was no enjoyment left to her, no sight, no hearing, no taste, no smell, no comfort, no joy, nothing but a ceaseless struggle to keep warm in a world where she had outlived her children and grandchildren and even many of her great-grandchildren. The birthday party seemed to me a cruel celebration of decay and on-going, unfinal death.

The parlor had so many chairs and couches and tables and lamps and bright and glary and sharp and pointy things in it that I was almost afraid to try to walk through it; even now I cannot imagine how a near-blind, invalid old lady in a walker (she used the cane only for sitting) could maneuver her way through all those *things* several times a day.

The parlor had once, I think, been the dining room, back when the house had contained a happy, growing family. Across the hall from it was a family library, probably dating back before or just after the Civil War; Aunt Lucy had been lovingly tending it for at least the last seventy years. Floor-to-ceiling shelves on all four walls bulged with books; books were in stacks on the floor and on the library table, which itself was invisible under all the books. A stand held open a huge book, and I still don't know whether it was an unabridged dictionary or a pulpit Bible.

I wanted to go in that room. I didn't want to stay in the hot, stuffy, crowded parlor and eat any of the cake that I was sure would choke me, while all those books were singing to me from across the hall. But my mother insisted I stay right where I was; it would be disrespectful to Aunt Mary for me to go wandering off.

I didn't see why. Aunt Mary didn't know who I was; Aunt Mary didn't know whether I was in the room beside her or a million miles away. And the pink and blue and orchid decorating frosting had a bitter aftertaste to it that all the punch in the world couldn't wash away. I surreptitiously slipped the paper plate and wooden fork into the trash, along with most of the piece of cake, and asked again to go across the hall.

Refused, I drank punch, helped to care for the current baby (I couldn't even remember, now, which of my brothers and sisters that was), and sulked.

My mother promised later that one day she'd let me go into Aunt Mary's library.

She never did, even after Aunt Mary finally was buried and it became Aunt Lucy's library. I realize, now, that Aunt Lucy would have been delighted beyond measure to share with me the books that had been her life and joy, her husband and her children, all her life, but I didn't realize I could ask her to do so until after her death at ninety-six, when I was nineteen.

By some will, deal, arrangement, or bit of finagling, Aunt Darla, my father's aunt, had wound up with Aunt Mary's house. The library—which Aunt Darla today decided to show me—had been cleaned and garnished, and all the interesting books, the ones Aunt Lucy had bought and read and cherished, the Jules Verne, the Edgar Allan Poe, the *The Naulakha* edition of Kipling Aunt Lucy had twice shown me volumes of, had been sold or given away. What remained was the complete works of James Fenimore Cooper, bound in green cloth; a large collection of sermons, half-folio size and bound in crumbling black leather covers, by nineteenth-century Methodist ministers my father had been related to; a good bit of poetry by people I'd never heard of, bound as uninterestingly as possible (perhaps in hopes of keeping people from actually reading it); a lot of empty shelves embellished with small and very uninspired statuary; a computer table and computer in place of the dictionary or Bible stand; and all of Aunt Darla's genealogy books, every one of which she seemed determined to show me today, along with improving anecdotes about dozens and dozens of ancestors and collateral relatives of whom I had never heard.

Mormons are taught that tracing their genealogy, so that the eternal family relationships can be kept up in the next world, is a spiritual duty, and I tried very hard to concentrate on what Aunt Darla was telling me. But after I yawned the fifth time, Aunt Darla said acerbically, "Well, I can see that these matters hold no interest whatever to you."

"Actually they do," I said, "and I'm terribly sorry. The problem is I had to go to San Francisco on business yesterday, and I didn't get home till after five this morning. I hope you'll tell me about it all again later, when I'm more myself."

She opened her mouth to answer, and judging from her expres-

• • • • •

sion I expected her words would not be friendly. Fortunately for me, at that moment my beeper went off, and Captain Millner's voice said, "Call me in the office. We've found the car."

Aunt Darla might not—probably does not—approve of her grandniece's being a police officer—she believes the proper place for women is at home or at meetings of the DAR, DAF, Daughters of Texas, Daughters of the Confederacy, Garden Club, Bible Study Club, League of Women Voters, and so forth—but all the same she respects the law. She showed me her phone.

"It's in the parking terrace at the medical school," Captain Millner told me. "It probably was there all along and nobody paid any attention; it's got five parking tickets and a boot on it, and it was the wrecker operator the school called to tow it that recognized the license plate. I'll have it taken to the police pound, unless you want to see it first."

I couldn't decide whether to go look at the car myself or not. I couldn't see any reason why I should. I also couldn't see any reason why I shouldn't. I suspected I had no business being on the road anyway, as tired as I was. "Okay," I said, "let them take it to the pound. Thanks." And I hung up. "Aunt Darla," I said, "I really want to be alert for the DAF meeting, so do you have any place I could lie down for an hour or so? You could wake me when it's almost time to go."

Aunt Darla did not want to be considered churlish, and I expect that even she could see how tired I was. She showed me into the room Aunt Mary had slept in during the twenty years she had used a walker and could not manage the stairs. There was Aunt Mary's bed where she'd spent the last three years of her life before dying at a hundred and four. The wood was waxed, the high-centered mattress was covered with a white crocheted cotton spread over a white wool blanket, the pillows—every one encased in a pillowcase embroidered with raised purple flowers, which were sure to leave their outline on a sleeper's face—were piled high; the chair-commode sat beside the bed, and the piano across the room had its

. . . . .

lid open to show yellow keys that I had banged on when I was three years old. Aunt Mary could have been out only for a couple of hours to go to the doctor, rather than in the ground for more than thirty years. Why Aunt Darla had chosen to keep this room as a shrine I could not imagine, as to the best of my knowledge she and Aunt Mary, to whom she was scarcely more closely related than I was, had never been particularly close.

"I don't want to mess up that beautiful spread," I said lamely, and Aunt Darla, her lips set in a tight line, turned the bed back for me before leaving and closing the door behind her with an emphatic little click. I meekly slipped off my dress, draped it over a chair, and went to bed in my slip.

It probably had been almost forty years since anybody had slept in this bed. But judging from its condition, Aunt Darla still washed and changed the sheets weekly. And for once I was grateful for her nitpickiness. I was asleep in seconds.

In my dreams I could see Matilda. She was trying to tell me something, but I couldn't tell what. She was lying across a map of Texas. Her feet were in East Texas. There was something important there that she was trying to get through to me. She brought the map closer to me. I was looking at the area around Daingerfield, Linden, Kildare, Pittsburg, Hughes Springs, Marshall—Lone Star Steel, Lake O' the Pines, Caddo Lake—but her head was in the Hill Country, Austin, Fredericksburg, where so many Germans settled. *What was she trying to tell me?*

I wasn't to find out, at least not then, because my beeper went off again, and Captain Millner sounded grim even for him as he said, "Call me in the office right now, because I'm on my way out."

That's a message that can waken me out of sleep no matter how deep; I got up, reached for the old-fashioned dial phone on the bedside table where it had remained for forty-odd years at least, and dialed the police station.

He gave me an address. I recognized it, and I told him I was en route.

. . . . .

It took me approximately thirty seconds to slide on my dress and hook the back, another thirty seconds to find Aunt Darla and tell her I had to take off, and fifteen minutes to drive to the address.

A patrol officer let me through the barricade, past the batteries of news cameras and microphones. Another patrol officer opened the front door to a small entry area and closed it firmly again behind me. Before the door closed I could hear the flies, could smell what I always want never to have to smell again.

From the foyer with its hall table and the mirror above it reflecting a bowl of wilted bronze chrysanthemums, I entered a formal living room where a woman perhaps five years older than I sat on the blue printed chintz couch, her face blotched with weeping, looking drained despite her perky white blouse printed with a scattering of flying butterflies. She wasn't crying right now, but clearly she had been and would be again; for the moment, her eyes were fixed straight ahead of her, clearly seeing nothing at all. "This is Mrs. Malone," Captain Millner told me. "She was worried because she hadn't been able to reach her daughter by telephone for a couple of days, and came over and found her. Mrs. Malone, this is Detective Ralston; she'll be handling the investigation."

Mrs. Malone started slightly and then looked at me, moving her eyes only instead of turning her head. "You look competent," she said in a very thin voice. "But I don't understand—who'd have wanted to kill my daughter—Janet never hurt anybody in her life—I just don't."

This wasn't the right time to tell her that almost surely her daughter had been killed not because of anything she had or hadn't done, not even because of someone's hatred or jealousy of her, but because of someone else's crime. All I could say was, "Mrs. Malone, I don't know either, but I can tell you I'll do everything I can to find out who did it and bring that person to justice."

"Yes," she said. "But that won't bring Janet back, will it?"

What could I say? "No, it won't. I'm so sorry."

She returned to staring at nothing at all. I went past her into the

· · · · ·

hall then, and followed Captain Millner to the kitchen, a lovely, sunny yellow room on the east side of the house, sheltered from the wind by a brick fence enclosing a small patio where a hot tub bubbled and steamed, with a blaze of red and yellow climbing roses still in bloom, even in November, on a white trellis just outside the window. The room had been planned to be so bright and cheerful that anyone in it could forget even the worst rain and chill.

But it wasn't lovely, bright, or cheerful now.

The death of Marvin Tutwiler might have been an accident, followed by a very elaborate attempt at concealing the body, at least long enough to prevent identification.

The death of Janet Malone was no accident, though it was almost certainly unpremeditated. Our perp was getting desperate.

Janet Malone lay facedown in front of a sliding glass door, open as it must have been since before her murder. The heavy cast-iron frying pan, enameled black inside and yellow outside, that had been used to kill her still lay on top of her crushed skull, mercifully hiding some of the damage, but her brains were spattered, along with her blood, all over the yellow textured vinyl floor, the yellow tile walls, the stark white appliances, the clear glass table with the daisy place mats on it, and the glass and screen of the open door where rain had puddled on the floor and flowed over the dried blood without mixing with it. Even in November the room was full of darting, buzzing flies, and white balls of maggots seethed in the vast open wound.

Nobody, now, was going to have to tell Janet Malone that her fiancé was dead, or that her fiancé had largely lived off women and had probably been a blackmailer.

I would rather she had been alive to find out. She'd have gotten over that.

It was now ten-thirty Wednesday morning. I had seen her early Monday afternoon; I had talked with her on the phone about 5 P.M. Monday. And from the looks of the body, my guess was she'd been killed very shortly thereafter.

. . . . .

113

And this had happened *before* Matilda was kidnapped, *before* Matilda's house was burglarized.

So our perp had gone from manslaughter to burglary to murder. Whoever she was, she wouldn't think twice about disposing of Matilda.

After checking to be sure Crime Scene was through with the telephone, I dialed a number I had inadvertently memorized because I had called it so many times over the last few days. Dora Gaines answered, and I identified myself and asked, "That woman who called wanting Marvin's papers, did you tell her how to reach Janet Malone?"

"Why, yes, shouldn't I have? She was quite anxious, and I told her that if Ms. Greenwood didn't have them and Ms. Malone didn't have them, I was quite sure I didn't know where they were, and then she asked me how to reach Ms. Greenwood and Ms. Malone."

"I see," I said.

"Shouldn't I have?" she asked again, anxiously.

"I don't know, Mrs. Gaines," I said. "They'd probably have found out some other way anyhow."

She asked me what I meant. I didn't want to tell her, but maybe it was better she learn it from me than from the news. She was crying when I hung up, crying and promising to get the phone numbers she didn't have and call the rest of the "wives-in-law" and warn them all, and call me back at Janet's number if there was a single one of them not where she ought to be at this time of day on a Wednesday morning.

Then I looked at my watch. I had to go fairly soon if I was to get to the DAF meeting that seemed to be my only hope of getting Matilda back alive, but first. . . .

"Has she signed a consent-search?" I asked Captain Millner.

He glanced at me. "Not yet. I haven't asked. I don't even know whether she has the authority—but if you want to find out. . . ." He opened his briefcase and handed me a form from one of the many manila file folders.

. . . . .

I went into the living room and sat down beside Mrs. Malone. "I'm sorry you had to see that," I said.

She nodded, her lips set tight.

"Could I call anybody for you?"

She shook her head.

"Your clergyman, maybe?"

"We don't go to church." Her voice was heavy as lead. "I never did believe in God. And if I did I wouldn't now. If there was a God, how could He let anything happen like this?"

"Because people have their agency," I said softly.

"What does that mean?"

"It means God doesn't want humanity composed of robots. People, to be people, have to be allowed to make their own decisions. And some of the decisions people make are horrible ones—like this. I'm sorry, Mrs. Malone, I shouldn't be trying to preach to you. . . ."

"It's okay," she said thinly. "Times like this, I wish I *did* believe in God."

She began weeping again, and I held her hands silently until this spasm of weeping was over and she began to reach blindly for tissue. Then I put a couple of tissues into her hands and retreated slightly, sitting near her but not too near, so that she wouldn't feel I was crowding her.

After wiping her eyes and blowing her nose a couple of times, she asked, "What do you do, to investigate a murder?"

"A lot of things," I said. "For one thing, we're about a hundred percent certain this is tied up with a case that's already under investigation."

For the first time she looked closely at me.

"You're upset too," she said. "Why would you be that upset about my daughter? You didn't know her, did you?"

"I knew her slightly," I said. "And murder always upsets me. But, besides that, they—whoever killed your daughter—they've kidnapped one of my closest friends. And if I can't find her soon they'll kill her too, if they haven't already."

· · · · ·

115

"Your friend, is she married?"

"No," I said, "but she has parents, and brothers and sisters. And people who depend on her for help. She's a psychologist."

"This is about that awful man Janet was engaged to, isn't it?" Mrs. Malone asked.

"Yes, I think so."

"She wouldn't really have married him. . . . She had better sense than that. . . . She was just sorry for him. How can I help?"

"Is it all right if I ask you a few questions?"

She sighed deeply, wiped her eyes again, and said, "I guess it has to be. Yes, if it will help get your friend back—and find out who did this to Janet. . . ."

"Some of them will sound rather rude, and I'm sorry, but there are things we have to know. First, I had the impression Janet was rather well-off financially. Is that correct?"

"She would have been," Mrs. Malone said. "Her grandfather was big in the pioneer oil business in East Texas, and he left her quite a large trust fund, but she wasn't to have access to the principal until she was thirty. In the meantime she had a very good income from it, you understand, she didn't have to work or anything like that, but she did receive it by the month, just some of the interest, not in any kind of lump sum."

"About how much per month did she receive?"

"About ten thousand dollars."

I didn't even try to estimate in my head how big a wad the trust fund was if "just some of the interest" added up to a hundred and twenty thousand dollars a year. Certainly it was more money than I'd ever see—but unlike Janet, I had a life. "So who will it go to now? Will it be divided among her brothers and sisters?"

"Janet was an only child." Quite suddenly Mrs. Malone's voice sounded very distant, very shocky. "I have no other children. And my husband's been dead three years." She didn't weep, this time, but her face had gone chalk white.

I got up, stepped to the door, and said to the patrol officer there, "Call an ambulance."

· · · · ·

Then I went back in and sat down beside her again, mentally reciting the little rhyme from my first-aid book: "Face is pale, raise the tail; face is red, raise the head." Initially she resisted my attempts to lay her down on the couch, but then she quit fighting and lay back, and I slid a pillow under her feet and covered her with a crocheted afghan. For the life of me I couldn't remember what else to do for shock, though it didn't cross my mind to wonder, then, whether I too might be partly in shock. (But I was cold, so cold even in my warm, lined jacket, and I wished someone would close the kitchen door, only of course they wouldn't until Irene Loukas or Bob Castle or whoever had come out from Ident said Ident was through with the crime scene and they weren't yet, not by a long shot.)

Keep her talking, keep her talking, even if she doesn't like what she's talking about. If I can just keep her talking until the ambulance gets here, maybe I can stave off complete shutdown a little longer. "Who will inherit this house, do you know?"

"Janet didn't own it," she answered, sounding even more distant. "It's in my name."

Yes, I asked her to sign the consent-search form, and yes, she signed it, using my pen, with me holding the form on a clipboard in front of her face and Captain Millner as witness. If I had been searching for evidence of criminality she had committed, it wouldn't have held up in court for a second, given the state she was in, but I knew she would back me up later even if she didn't actually remember signing. Then I kept her talking, talking, about Janet as a child, about her own childhood, about her widowhood and her hopes for Janet to find a good husband, her dreams of grandchildren to carry her and her husband's genes on to the future, and inwardly I raged at the cruelty that had stolen all this from her, from Janet, and I couldn't help thinking about poor Aunt Mary, living past all that makes life life, and contrasting her woe of age to Janet Malone's early death and all that had been taken from her, until finally the ambulance came and an emergency medical technician

. . . . .

checked Mrs. Malone's blood pressure, called the hospital, gave her a shot, and took her away on a stretcher.

Only then did I begin to walk through the house, to look at the rooms, the neatly made bed in what seemed to have been Janet's own room, the neatly made beds in the guest rooms she must have hoped someday to put her children in, the complete and sadly familiar disorder, like that I had seen in three places before, in the room where her books and papers had been kept.

Bob Castle from Ident was taking pictures in the kitchen; I told him what I needed from the rest of the house, and then—awake again after the flow of adrenaline—I drove home, to change clothes and wash my hair. I couldn't possibly go to the DAF luncheon, or anywhere else, smelling like this. Harry was sitting in the living room reading. He looked up at me and said, "Luncheon over already? I hope you didn't eat any, if it smelled like that."

"Corpse," I said briefly. "Several days old. I've got to hurry."

I was in and out of the shower in about five minutes, and Harry had abandoned the magazine and was in the bedroom fiddling with my computer as I hastily threw on clean clothes and combed my hair, fortunately short, into some semblance of order.

The telephone rang, and with a glance at me, he pushed the speakerphone button. I dashed toward the phone as I heard Matilda's voice. "Harry?" she was saying. "My—the person I'm staying with—she said to tell Deb that she'd pick up the genealogy sheets at three-thirty. Will they be there by that time?"

"I'm here," I said, "and I'll have them there. Matilda, are you okay?"

"Sure, why wouldn't I be, Harry? And I'm glad Deb went on to her meeting." Her voice was as thin and reedy as Mrs. Malone's, but she still had her wits about her. With very few words she had told me that although her captors could hear what she said, they couldn't hear what I said, and she had reminded me again that I *had* to go to the DAF meeting.

"We found Janet. Did you know about that?"

"Yeah, sure," she said, with highly forced cheerfulness. "Got to go, now." She hung up before I could say anything else.

The moment the dial tone took the place of her voice, Harry reached out and pushed three buttons on the phone: Star-six-nine. He glanced triumphantly at me—and a voice said, "Private number. Push the star for call back."

"What the heck!" He looked around frantically. "That's supposed to give me the phone number of the last person who called." He dialed it again and got the same disembodied voice with the same chilling message. This time he pushed the star button, and we both listened to the phone ring at the other end. I don't know if Harry counted the rings. I did. It rang, unanswered, thirty-six times before Harry pushed the cut-off button. Then he dialed a regular number, and after a while somebody from the telephone company came on the line.

"I thought you told me that star-six-nine would get me the number of the person who called me!" he shouted.

"Who is this please?" the woman asked.

Clearly raging but managing to keep his temper at least to a mild extent, he identified himself and then repeated the question, making it more clearly a question this time.

"Yes, that's what it does," the woman asked.

"But it *didn't*," he said, succeeding once more in not yelling. "It said 'Private number.' "

"Yes, that's what happens when the calling party has blocked Caller ID."

"Then what's the good of having Caller ID at all?" Harry demanded. "Is there any way you can get around it? I mean, like if you're getting phone calls you *have* to trace?"

"Why would you have to trace them? The service will call the number back for you, if it's the last party who called you."

His face looked like he was going to start swearing, but he said, very precisely, "My wife is a police officer. A close friend of hers has been kidnapped. She has received three phone calls here from the kidnap victim, almost certainly made from the kidnapper's house. We *did* call back, and we didn't get an answer. Now how does she get that phone number? Are you telling me it can't be done?"

"No, sir, not at all," the woman said. "She just has to notify me officially, and then we set up star-five-seven, and that will trace the call."

"How long does that take? And how do we get the number?"

"Well, once it's set up, it takes about fifteen minutes. The number goes to Telephone Security and the police department gets it from Telephone Security with a court order. I assume your wife can get one?"

"A *court order*?" he yelled, and then lowered his voice. "Okay, can we dial star-five-seven while Deb gets the court order?"

"I'm sorry, sir, but that has to be set up in advance."

"In *advance*?"

That was when I stepped forward. "I'm Detective Deb Ralston of the Fort Worth Police Department," I said briskly. "Are you telling me that there is *no way* that I can get the telephone number of the call that was placed to my number about five minutes ago?"

"I'm very sorry," the woman began, sounding close to tears, "but—yes. It's impossible, now. Do you think they might call back?"

If it was impossible, it was impossible. "I doubt it," I said. "But set up star-five-seven service for my number, 555-6347, immediately. We'll get a court order to Telephone Security within an hour."

"It'll be on in five minutes," she promised. "And I'll alert Security. I'm so sorry—if your husband had just told whoever he talked with earlier today what it was needed for . . ."

After she hung up, I telephoned my office. Captain Millner was out, of course, but I talked with Dutch Van Flagg and he promised to get the court order and hand-carry it over. We'd be able to find her, now. If it wasn't too late. If she called again.

. . . . .

If it wasn't too late. If she called again.

After I got off the phone, Harry asked, "Why didn't you know about that?"

"Because the kind of cases I've been working lately, I haven't needed to know it," I answered. "Last time I had a case that needed to trace a phone call it was two years ago and we still had to get it done through the switching office. And—I don't know why I didn't think of that as soon as we got the first phone call—but we didn't expect the first call, and after the first we didn't expect the second, and then we certainly didn't expect the third. *I'm just so tired, Harry. . . .*" I bit my lip to keep from crying, because I still had to get somewhere looking decent to find the information that might be my last hope for finding Matilda alive.

"No more sleep than you've had in the last three days; it's a wonder you can think at all," he said.

But he didn't offer to drive me to the DAF luncheon.

He couldn't.

He had to stay home and mind the telephone.

Seven

· · · · ·

THE LUNCHEON WAS in the basement fellowship hall of a large downtown Presbyterian church, and after all that had happened I was totally amazed to find that I was early. Aunt Darla, who of course had been even earlier, met me in the foyer before I got into the hall and looked me over with a gimlet eye before apparently deciding that I passed her muster—barely. "Why did you change your clothes?" she demanded. "The dress was nicer."

"You don't want to know," I told her. "Police business gets unpleasant at times."

She sniffed. "Surely your husband can make the living and let you stay home with those poor neglected children of yours. And that suit seems sort of—*bunchy*—around the shoulders."

"Oddly enough, Aunt Darla," I began, keeping my voice much calmer than my body felt, "I'm very good at my work, and I'm performing a valuable service for the people of Fort Worth. My suit is bunchy around the shoulders because I'm wearing a shoulder holster." She opened her mouth to say something at that point, but I didn't give her time. "And my children are scarcely neglected. In case you haven't heard, Vicky and Becky are married with children of their own, and Hal is in Nevada—"

"What in the world is he doing *there*? Gambling? All Chinese gamble. It's in the blood, you know."

"No, I don't know any such thing. And anyway Hal never was Chinese; he was Korean. And he's in Nevada on his mission."

· · · · ·

She sniffed again. "Oh, yes, that *cult* you're in. I'll be glad when you get over that."

"Don't hold your breath. Anyway, Cameron is the only child I have at home right now, him and Lori—"

"Who is *Lori*? Surely to goodness you haven't adopted *another* Indian"

"It would be none of your business if I adopted every orphan child in the whole Cherokee Nation, Creek Nation, and Comanche Nation combined. But no, Lori is Hal's girlfriend. Her parents are dead and she's living with us now."

Aunt Darla had her mouth open to say something else, probably even more hateful, when the outside door opened again and three women came in. Immediately assuming a huge smile, she said, "Why *hello,* Mrs. Thomas, Mrs. Edgely, Mrs. Hughes."

Right behind Mrs. Thomas, Mrs. Edgely, and Mrs. Hughes came Aunt Alicia, the very nicest of my grandaunts—as hard as it is to believe, she is Aunt Darla's sister—and I picked the moment to escape into the main hall along with her, but of course Aunt Darla quickly abandoned Mrs. Thomas, Mrs. Edgely, and Mrs. Hughes and caught up with me. I suppose she was afraid of what I might say if she didn't keep an eye on me. Deftly taking me away from Aunt Alicia, she began to introduce me, as her beloved grandniece, to everybody she could think of. As there were fifty-seven women there, all of them wearing heavy twill red-white-and-blue-striped sashes, diplomatic style, with ribbons, medals, and names on them, information overload set in quickly, and I was utterly confused by the time we all sat down to eat lunch. I tried to sit with Aunt Alicia, but Aunt Darla instantly corralled me again and hauled me off as an honored guest to the head table, which like the others was covered with a crisp white cloth and crowned with a red-white-and-blue floral arrangement.

By this time I couldn't connect names to faces of a one of them other than my own relatives and the officers, most of whom *were* my relatives: Aunt Darla was the general; one Lucinda Meredith, who (I was informed) was Aunt Brume's cousin but on the other side of the family from my mother, was the colonel; and my grand-aunt Brume, my mother's mother's youngest sister, was the adjutant. I took those titles to mean president, vice president, and secretary-treasurer. I have no idea whether the DAR is organized the same way, though I think it probably isn't. This looked like something Aunt Darla would have thought up.

Or maybe Aunt Brume, and please don't ask me where the name came from because I haven't the slightest idea. But I wasn't at all surprised to find her in what had started out as a dissident branch of the DAR. Aunt Brume, a vigorous woman in her eighties by now, didn't look much past sixty. She was famous in the family as the one who had seceded from the Daughters of the Confederacy because it has become too liberal. Her stopover in the League of Women Voters had been quite brief, for that organization was also too liberal. At one point she had been part of the Dixiecrats, a breakaway southern branch of the Democratic Party, and then she joined the John Birch Society some years before deciding to campaign for George Wallace for president. She followed that debacle by becoming a Republican, until she decided the GOP was too liberal, and later a Perot follower, before deciding Perot was too liberal. The last I had heard from my mother, Aunt Brume had decided Rush Limbaugh was far too liberal (which, from Aunt Brume's point of view, he is) and was now listening only to G. Gordon Liddy on the radio. I had no idea whom she was politicking for now, as Liddy is (I believe) ineligible for public office. But I had no doubt she was politicking for somebody, and whoever it was, it was probably someone I wouldn't like.

She looked at me severely. If she had had a lorgnette she would have looked at me through the lorgnette, but in the last decade of the twentieth century not even Aunt Brume could get away with that. "Well, Deborah," she said, "it is quite a surprise to find *you* at our little *soirée*."

My name is not Deborah. It is Debra. And I was really quite

· · · · ·

surprised to find that Aunt Brume seemed to be speaking to me today. She had stopped speaking to me except to chew me out when—and because—I married Harry, who is about one-eighth Cherokee, and she had stopped speaking even to chew me out when we adopted the first of our two part–Native American daughters. I didn't even want to guess what she had said to the rest of the family later, when we adopted Hal. The last thing she had said to me, approximately twenty-three years ago, was, "Really, Deborah, you have *no idea* what you are getting into. Of course she's *illegitimate,* you know, and you know what *that* means." (I did not, and to this day do not, know what she meant by that.) "And *goodness knows* what her background is—skinny, sickly, little thing, and I do believe she has *fleas.*"

Of course if Aunt Brume had spoken to me again after that, it is highly doubtful that I would have listened. And if I had listened my replies would have been unlikely to be polite. (Skinny and sickly Vicky certainly had been—which was all the more reason she needed parents of her own—but she did *not* have fleas. Allergies, yes, a lot of them. But not fleas. And if she *had* had fleas I would simply have de-flead her.)

Aunt Brume and Aunt Darla must have had some really delightful conversations about me since then. I pitied Aunt Alicia, who had probably had to listen to most of them.

But to get Matilda back alive I was willing, for the moment at least, to listen even to Aunt Brume, who looked now at Aunt Darla and said, "Am I to suppose you have begun to bring this child to her senses?"

I wasn't even angry at that. To be called a child when one is nearly fifty is more comical than annoying.

"As much as is possible," Aunt Darla said. She looked at me with a mournful expression that would have been more suitable on a basset hound.

"It is *far* too late to do any good; divorce is more unsuitable than miscegenation, at least when it is not *obvious by sight,* and one can-

· · · · ·

not unadopt unsuitable children. I suppose *I* shall be called upon to cosponsor her," Aunt Brume said icily.

"I find my husband and children quite suitable," I said angrily.

Both of them ignored me as Aunt Darla said, "I had thought of asking Amabel—"

"Nonsense," Aunt Brume said. "No relation at all. We must put *the best face* on these things and *keep them in the family.*" No mention, of course, of the fact that she and Aunt Darla were related only by the marriage of my parents.

With the deliberate intent of creating mischief, I asked, "What about Aunt Alicia?"

Aunt Brume and Aunt Darla both looked at me with virtually identical expressions. "She would be *quite unsuitable,*" Aunt Brume said. I was rapidly deciding that *unsuitable* was now her favorite word. "No offense, Darla," she added.

"None taken," Aunt Darla said, shaking her head mournfully. "I am aware of my sister's shortcomings."

"Anyway I haven't decided for sure I want to join," I added. "I mean, as much as you two dislike me, I can't imagine why you *want* me to join."

"Nonsense. Of course we like you, you're *family* after all, which means you have the *obligation to do good for the country and the community*"—*like joining the Daughters of the American Flag,* I thought, *but not being a police officer*—"and of course you shall join," Aunt Darla said, glancing around in hopes that nobody had heard what I said. I admired the precision of her vocabulary as she rummaged in her capacious purse and handed me a form to fill out. I remembered from junior high that "I shall" and "you will" express simple futurity; "you shall" expresses great determination on the part of the speaker. "I have already given my genealogy to you; I suppose you can fill in the few remaining blanks connecting your father and yourself to my own dear father," she told me. "You may mail the forms to me, or bring them to the next meeting."

"And of course I shall give you my genealogy also," Aunt Brume added grudgingly.

. . . . .

126

Then she and Aunt Darla looked at each other, both faces some-what hostile. That must have been the moment at which they both realized that if I combined Aunt Brume's genealogy, from my mother's side of the family, and Aunt Darla's genealogy, from my father's side of the family, I would be entitled to wear twice as many little bronze name tags on my sash as either of them.

I might as well mention now that I had already made up my mind I wouldn't be caught dead in a sash with dozens of bronze cenotaph-markers on it. Presumably the ancestors these women were so proudly touting had been able to find other things to do than brag about *their* ancestors; well, I had plenty of other things to do also.

Someone from the luncheon committee brought around medium-size bowls of unimaginative chef salad (iceberg lettuce, chopped tomatoes, sliced cheese and chicken, and two slices per plate of boiled egg, with a dollop of mayonnaise sprinkled with very mild paprika) and plates of rolls (white flour, of course) about that time. My inclination to eat was absolutely nil, as I lose my appetite when I am worried. But Matilda wouldn't be helped by my starving myself into even worse mental confusion. Reminding myself of that, I concentrated on eating, letting Aunt Darla and Aunt Brume argue over my head. I scarcely even noticed that I was being addressed until Aunt Brume said, "Deborah! I have asked you three times to *pass the butter.*"

"I'm sorry," I said, and handed her the butter. "I'm not all here; I haven't had enough sleep in the last few days."

"I suppose you are still in that *unfortunate and unsuitable occupation,*" she said.

"If you mean to ask whether I'm still a police officer, yes, I am."

All conversation at the head table ceased at once as about eight pairs of eyes fixed themselves on me. "Oh really," a woman said faintly; her name tag said she was Amabel Gray. "Do you help schoolchildren across the street?"

"No," I said, determined to be just as rude as they were being, "crossing guards do that. I investigate murders." As a member of the Major Case Unit, I investigate other things a lot more often than I do murder. But I might as well go for maximum shock value.

"Oh dear," Genevieve Anderson (I knew from her name tag) said, "are you investigating anything right now?"

"At this precise moment, you mean? No," I said untruthfully, "but I was earlier today, and I will return to it later this afternoon." I deliberately did not say "shall." I can be as precise in my word usage as my aunts can, when I set my mind to it.

"What are you investigating?" Lucinda Meredith inquired, with what sounded like a small spark of real interest.

"I'm not sure I should discuss it at the table," I said.

"Well, we wouldn't want the *details* of course," a small, dark-haired, bird-boned woman named Kitty Pringle said, "but it does sound like such an *interesting* thing for a woman to do."

Five pairs of eyes fixed her sternly, and she shrank in her seat. "Well, it does," she said faintly.

For Kitty Pringle's sake, and perhaps for Lucinda Meredith's, I answered. "Yes, I'm afraid I'm investigating several things, including a rather nasty murder. A young woman who, so far as I know, had never done a thing in her life to harm anyone, was killed by someone who wanted to take from her something she didn't even have."

"Do you have any clues?" Kitty Pringle asked eagerly.

"I'm afraid I can't discuss that. Let's say we're nowhere near ready to make an arrest. But the poor woman's mother is in shock; the victim was an only child, and her mother is a widow."

"How sad," Lucinda Meredith said briskly. "Amabel, dear, are you having any luck getting rid of that awful bindweed in your garden?" She looked at me with a half-smile, as if apologizing for the change in subject, and added, "Amabel ordered a load of what was supposed to be *sterilized* compost from a dairy farm, and it turned out to be loaded with bindweed. And that's *so* hard to get rid of."

I tried to ignore the ensuing discussion of the various merits of three different weed-killers. If Matilda had been able to give me even the ghost of an idea what it was I was supposed to learn here, I would be a lot happier. As it was, I had to listen to everything, look at everybody. But unfortunately nobody looked at all suspicious; with the exception of Aunt Darla and Aunt Brume, everybody seemed quite charming and friendly, though it was obvious they and I did not live in the same world. Or if we did, we certainly didn't live in the same century.

After the seemingly interminable meal finally concluded, by which time I had eaten all my salad, two dinner rolls, and four buttered crackers and was being stared at reproachfully by Aunt Darla (that "You are disgracing the family" look again), the speaker was introduced.

I had to force myself to stay awake, as the speaker—whom I recognized from church as Sister Dorothy Rose, who was in charge of our ward's part of the international genealogical effort called Name Extraction—nattered on interminably about the uses of something called an Ahnentafel Chart, which I gathered had something to do with genealogy. I didn't know what one was, and I was pretty sure I didn't *want* to know what one was. My aunts might call my church a cult, but apparently they had no objection to accepting its help in genealogical research.

Sister Rose emphasized that although an Ahnentafel Chart looks quite simple, it is actually far more complicated and useful than people think at first.

Everybody else seemed quite rapt.

I would have ignored Sister Rose—not because I dislike her, which I do not—but because I simply could not understand what she was talking about. I started to, on the grounds that whatever it was Matilda wanted me to notice, it wouldn't be someone who was making a speech on genealogical charts. But I reminded myself once again that I didn't know what Matilda wanted me to notice. So I didn't dare not listen.

Listening did me no good whatsoever, though I supposed

· · · · ·

that sooner or later I was going to have to get a computer program—Personal Ancestor File was the one Sister Rose recommended—and get Harry's and my genealogy in order, from all those Ahnentafel Charts and other things Aunt Darla and Aunt Brume were giving me and from the records kept by Harry's family and by the Cherokee Nation.

Sister Rose concluded her talk to a small patter of applause and the presentation of a gift in lieu of an honorarium.

As everybody got up to leave, with me still totally in the dark as to what Matilda had meant me to notice, Aunt Alicia rushed up to me. "Debra, dear, I was so *happy* to see you today, I keep meaning to visit you but you seem so *busy* I hate to intrude. I *do* want to get together with you one day and hear all about your family and your work; you haven't visited me in three years; but are you really certain this organization would suit you? I'm just a teensy bit afraid—"

"I'm a teensy bit afraid you're right," I said, "but Aunt Darla wanted me to come and Mom kind of pushed me into it."

"Well, don't let them push you around," she said. "I didn't learn that until too late, and look where I am today." She grimaced. "I feel like Lizzie Borden's sister."

"Aunt Alicia, wherever you are, you're a darling," I said, "and if you are Lizzie Borden's sister, what does that make Aunt Darla?"

"Quite outraged, I'm sure, if she heard this discussion," Aunt Alicia said. "But you know, if Mother and Father hadn't given her everything she wanted I'm sure she would have found a way to *take* it anyway. Oh, here I am taking up your time, and I know you're in a hurry—"

"I really am," I admitted. "I'm sorry I don't have time to stay and talk with you. Let's plan on getting together soon. . . ."

It took me only ten more minutes to escape, and the truth was that if I hadn't had Matilda to worry about I'd have carried Aunt Alicia off for a long visit someplace where we could get some real food. Outside, I leaned my forehead on the cool steering wheel for a moment before starting the car and driving directly home. I did not stop by the day-care center to pick up Cameron; he'd be taking his nap right now, and I knew I would have to rush right back out again anyway.

Harry was asleep on the couch. He'd have been awake, waiting for me, if he'd heard from Matilda again, or more likely Captain Millner would have paged me in the middle of the luncheon. But just in case, I checked the answering machine for messages.

There were none.

So much for that.

I dialed the number for my office, and when Dutch Van Flagg answered I asked for Captain Millner. "Let me go look for him," Dutch said. "I just got in myself."

As I waited, I reached for the closest reading material, which happened to be the DAF membership form I had been handed. I was amused to notice that although the form itself was a photocopy of a printed piece, the word *Flag* had been neatly hand-lettered in place of a longer word. Obviously, in flagrant disregard of all copyright laws, the Daughters of the American Flag had used a DAR membership form, only marking out *Revolution* and inserting *Flag* in its place before photocopying. In fact, if I looked closely I could see the marked-out word bleeding through the Wite-Out that had been put on the original before the new word was entered.

Dutch came back to the phone. "He's not here," he said. "He's out at the medical school parking terrace again. That murder victim's car turned up there."

"That which murder victim?" I asked, confused. "Because if it's Tutwiler's car, they found it there hours ago and it's supposed to have been hauled to the pound."

"No, this was some woman. I think her name was Janice Malone. Or maybe Janet. Something like that, anyway."

"Wow," I said.

"What does that mean?" Dutch asked.

"Just that it's firm now, we've got a connection with the medical school. Because Tutwiler and Janet Malone were killed by the same person."

"You sure of that?"

"As sure as I ever am of anything before I'm ready to make an arrest. Look, have the captain call me, would you?"

"Sure thing," Dutch said amiably.

I sat waiting for the call and reading the membership form. And then, suddenly, I stiffened. That clause. If this was Utah—but it's Texas.

If this was Utah I'd know why Marvin Tutwiler had been killed. But—

Something Hal said one day, as he rushed in from Early Morning Seminary the year they were studying Church history—

That map of Texas Matilda had been trying to show me in her dream—

I got up and went searching for the books Hal had kept from his four years of Early Morning Seminary, both textbooks and the supplementary books we'd allowed him to purchase at Deseret Books near the Dallas Temple.

It took a while; he'd stored his possessions in his usual scatterbrained fashion, and although some of the boxes in the small cubicle that was one of the maze of small rooms Harry had transformed our former garage into were labeled, most were not. Of course the one I wanted was one of the unlabeled ones. That meant that I had to open a good many boxes. But I finally found what I was looking for.

I was right.

And now I knew why Marvin Tutwiler had been killed, and what the killer had been looking for, and why Janet Malone had been killed, and why my friend Matilda Greenwood might yet be killed.

But it was such a petty reason for murder—to preserve somebody's vanity, to preserve somebody's social position.

Murder is more often committed for petty reasons than grand

ones, but this—I shook my head, took the book out of the small cubicle, and headed for my room.

"Whatcha doing, Deb?" Harry asked sleepily.

"Working," I said briefly.

"I'll take you out to dinner tonight."

"I don't know if I'll have time to eat."

He sat up. "Deb, I know you're worried about Matilda. But— you know she wouldn't want you to kill yourself over this."

"I'm not killing myself. I'm just working. I had lunch, Harry, honest."

"But not breakfast."

"I wasn't hungry." I was opening the phone book.

"And you won't be hungry for dinner."

"Maybe not," I said, knowing quite well he was right.

"I'll take you out to dinner," he repeated. "We'll figure out a time later."

"Okay." I dialed a number, praying she'd be home.

She was.

"Aunt Darla," I said, "is there any way I can get the names of the people who were at that meeting?"

"Well, yes, I suppose so," Aunt Darla said. "But why do you need them?"

"I'd rather not say. But I need them badly." No, of course I was not going to tell Aunt Darla that I suspected one of her friends of murder.

"Brume will have them."

Oh, great, I thought but did not say. Of all the people I did *not* want to talk with again today, Aunt Brume was fairly near the head of the list.

"What about the membership list for your chapter?" I asked.

"Brume will have that, too."

"How big is the national organization? Or is there one?"

"Oh, my, yes, we have forty-seven chapters now, and it takes at least ten people to win a charter. So at least four hundred and seventy people, but most chapters have more than ten people—it could be as many as two thousand or more people by now."

"And who would have *that* list?"

"Brume," Aunt Darla said. "We're the founding chapter, you see, so we have all the records. And Brume takes care of them."

I thanked Aunt Darla and then, teeth gritted, I hung up and dialed again.

At first glance I found Aunt Brume's house, which I had not entered in at least twenty-seven years, as unpleasant as I found her. Although everything was tidy and dust free, carpet vacuumed, showroom-floor furniture showroom-floor clean, one important piece of bric-a-brac and no books in sight—clearly she had the gift of elegance, which I totally lack—it all seemed completely sterile. Although I knew she had three children and ten grandchildren and probably by now anywhere from six to twelve great-grandchildren, I could not bring myself to imagine a child ever romping around this room.

She met me at the door, invited me to wait in the parlor for a moment, refused to listen to my explanation of what I was doing there, and stalked out. In a moment I could hear a printer chattering. In one way I admired her: I've met a good many people, men and women both, much younger than she who are absolutely terrified of computers. Obviously she had decided to master them and had promptly done so. But couldn't she be intelligent and efficient without being hateful?

I looked around, finding myself full of an overwhelming longing for my own home, as messy as it often is, with newspapers on the coffee table and Cameron's toys strewn here and there as they usually are until he puts them away at bedtime, and all of Harry's hobbies all over the place, and Lori's homework and books and letters from Hal, and sometimes Vicky and Don, and Becky and Olead over visiting, and the grandchildren romping around with Cameron or playing video games, and Margaret Scratcher and Rags bringing in dead mice and live garter snakes (and Rags, my first long-haired cat, shedding enough fur around the house that I could knit another cat at least once a month out of my vacuum cleaner bag), and Ivory, the cocker spaniel who somehow was becoming an indoors dog at least half the time, bouncing around chasing moths, and Pat, half pit bull, who felt (not unreasonably) that if Ivory could come indoors so could he, galumphing around trying to find and kiss Cameron—no, my house would never look this elegant.

But nobody, in my house, would ever try to sit lightly for fear of leaving a seat-print on brocade.

Nobody, in my house, was going to feel suffocated. Overwhelmed, maybe, but never suffocated.

Aunt Brume stalked back in ten minutes later to hand over computer printouts of genealogy charts, including the dreaded Ahnentafel Chart, which turned out to be simply a list with my mother in the first position, followed by her parents, followed by their parents, and so forth, with a few dates and place names. "Now you have what you came for, so you may depart," she said. "And although I did promise to give it to you, it would have been *courteous* to wait a day or two for me to get it together."

"Thank you, but that's not what I came for," I said. "I need— "

"You need a switch taken to you. Miscegenation! That my *own grandniece* would be guilty of miscegenation . . ."

"You have a very nasty mind. You make it sound like a crime for me to have married Harry."

"Before government lost all decency miscegenation *was* a crime. And I don't care if he's only one-eighth or one-tenth or whatever it was you said, he's an Indian! One drop of Indian blood—one drop of Nigger blood—this country is going to the dogs and I know why!"

"That's the silliest thing I ever heard of. And that is a very offensive word."

"Why, only last week in the grocery store I saw a young woman, blond hair, blue eyes, married to a *buck Nigger* and they had a baby in the shopping cart, a little half-breed—all dressed in pink, she was, awful little thing, neither fish nor fowl—and I suppose you wouldn't even mind if your son, your *own* son if you had the decency to have one, not that nasty half-breed Chinese you adopted, *married* her!"

"As I've said before, Hal is Korean, not Chinese, as if that made any difference. And I do have a son I gave birth to. And you're right. I wouldn't mind in the least if he—Hal *or* Cameron—married a mixed-race woman. I find your opinions even more objectionable than you find mine. And I don't have all day. Aunt Brume, I need . . ."

Aunt Brume did not see why she should give me any DAF records, from the meeting today or from her chapter or from the national organization.

"Aunt Brume," I said, "I have tried as hard as I could to avoid saying this, but it's time you knew. Those records are relevant to the investigation of two murders and a kidnapping—"

"How dare you—"

"And I mean to have them one way or another—"

"You little snip—"

"And you have the choice of handing them over to me now—"

"And I was going to cosponsor you! Well, see if I don't blackball you—"

"Or handing them over to me when I return with a court order."

"Well, I never!"

"I quite believe that. I'm sorry, Aunt Brume—"

"You dare accuse ME—"

"I am not accusing you of anything. Frankly, by now I wish I could, but you don't fit the profile. But I am telling you that I have every reason to believe that a member of your organization is guilty of two murders and a kidnapping, and that the kidnap victim is in immediate danger of being murdered. And furthermore, the kidnap victim is a very close friend of mine, so if you think I feel like messing around with your nonsense you had better think again." I was breathing a bit hard but feeling elated. I had spent more than forty years biting my tongue and not answering back when Aunt Brume was at her nastiest, which was most of the time. It felt great to bite back.

She had run out of sputter. "What profile?" she asked weakly.

"The profile we have created of the murderer, based on a number of witness accounts and other pieces of information. Do you know a Mrs. Keating, who runs a boardinghouse?"

"Not a boardinghouse," Aunt Brume said. "Mrs. Keating is a lady. She simply provides lodging for a few paying guests."

"Providing lodging in a private home for paying guests is called running a boardinghouse. I see you know her. Are you a member of her garden club?"

"Certainly, though I don't consider it hers. Have you any objection to my membership?"

"None whatsoever."

"Surely you do not mean to imply that Mrs. Keating is a murderess. Mrs. Keating is a lady."

"So was Elizabeth Báthory," I said.

"I haven't the slightest idea whom you are talking about."

"She was a countess," I said. "And one of the biggest mass murderers in history."

"And you think that *Mrs. Keating*—"

"No, I do not," I said. "I'm sure Mrs. Keating is quite innocent. But the murderess, if you insist on a gendered word, is almost certainly both a member of the DAF and a member of the same garden club to which Mrs. Keating belongs."

It occurred to me, as Aunt Brume glared silently at me, that to anyone who didn't know the South very well—and much of Fort Worth is the South—the same women being in so many different organizations together would be hard to believe. But I had grown up here, and I was well aware that in Aunt Brume's generation and

. . . . .

culture, exactly the same set of women would be in the DAR, Daughters of the Confederacy, the Daughters of Texas, the Garden Club, the Bible Study Club, and probably two or three other clubs if they could think up enough of them. I spent many hours of my preschool life playing with a doll behind my grandmother's chair when she was at all her meetings. It was a special doll I was allowed to play with only at "parties" so I wouldn't get bored with it. In fact I still have it, though I'll be giving it to my daughter Becky as a Christmas present this year because she has begun a doll collection.

Aunt Brume was still staring at me. Finally, in icy tones, she said, "Mrs. Keating has not yet been accepted into membership of the DAF."

I had to stifle laughter, remembering Mrs. Keating's characterization of the "Daffies." My own opinion was that she would be accepted into membership three days after hell froze over, that being the day on which she would apply. But the laughter vanished as quickly as it had come, as I thought again of Matilda. "You're wasting my time and yours, Aunt Brume," I said. "Do I get the lists now, or do I have to go and get a court order while somebody murders my friend because I can't rescue her because you're stalling? Because I warn you, if I have to do that and Matilda is killed, despite the respect due your age I might give serious thought to charging you as an accessory."

It took a while longer—time I did not have to waste—but eventually Aunt Brume printed out, and turned over to me, the names of the members of her chapter and the nationwide organization. She told me she couldn't give me the names of the people at today's meeting because she had not yet transcribed them.

I told her I would return the register, or a photocopy of it.

She protested *pro forma* and handed it over.

As I headed for the door, she called after me, "You may return the records to Darla. You are never to enter my house again."

"That suits me just fine," I said. "But thank you for the records anyway. Would you like your genealogy back?"

. . . . .

"You may keep it," she said, "so that in the future, when you come to realize the enormity of your conduct, it may remind you from what heights you have fallen."

She slammed the door.

I shrugged and headed for the car.

Eight
. . . . .

"I THOUGHT YOU wanted me to call you," Captain Millner said. As usual, he was not in his own office, which he uses only for questioning people and for chewing out subordinates. He was in Dutch's desk chair, leaning back with his feet on the desk and a rather annoyed look on his face.

"Oh, yeah," I said, feeling a trifle embarrassed.

"I think oh, yeah. I tried, three times. The first and second times Harry said you were out and he didn't know when you'd be back. The third time Harry asked me not to call again because he didn't want the line tied up in case Matilda got another chance to call. That made sense to me, so I just came on in here and waited for you."

"I'm really sorry, I forgot all about it," I said.

"I gathered that. You want to tell me why?"

"I just had an idea about Matilda that looked so good I wanted to check it out, and I forgot all about everything else." I set my purse on top of my desk and started dragging out paper, beginning to sort it into several stacks that might make some frail amount of sense to me later.

"Were you searching crime scenes by yourself again?" Millner demanded, sitting up. "Because I damn well meant it when I told you I was putting you on suspension if you did."

"I was just visiting my grandaunt," I said with as much dignity as I could muster. I grabbed a handful of empty manila folders from my desk drawer and started shoving papers into folders and scrawling quick headings onto them.

"Visiting your grandaunt is an idea about a crime?"

"This time, yes." Hastily I changed the subject. "Dutch said you found Janet Malone's car at the medical school."

"Yep. Parked three stalls away from where Tutwiler's car was. We'd have found it the same time we found Tutwiler's if we'd known to look for it. Just like his, it already had a boot on it. Uniform division ran the tag when they found Tutwiler's car and got the owner's name but couldn't get hold of the owner, and we didn't have any reports about Malone then. Of course. Somebody remembered it as soon as her name got on the air."

I sat down rather limply in my own chair. "So it's one hundred percent sure we've got a link with the medical school."

"I would say so."

"Well, it just about was anyway. Did you find anything in it that looked usable?"

He shook his head. "Too soon to tell. A few good latents that aren't hers. They were on the rearview mirror so chances are they belong to the last person to drive the car. Small prints, considerably creased, smelled like Jergens hand lotion—I'd say an older woman. And Irene already ran them, and they're not in Texas files. She'll have the FBI run them overnight. But you know what I guess?"

"The same thing I guess. That they're not on file."

"Got it in one. So what was this idea you had about Matilda?" Millner asked. "And why did you need to visit your aunt to check it out? And what do all those files you're creating have to do with it?" He leaned back with his feet on the desk again; he's having back trouble lately, and that's about the only position in which he's even halfway comfortable. Since he habitually uses the desk of absolutely anybody who is not at that given moment using his or her own desk, we've all learned to keep small or fragile things at the extreme back so as to be out of the way of his feet.

I snatched the Daughters of the American Flag membership form

· · · · ·

141

out from one of the files, shoved it under his nose, and said, "Read this."

Still semireclining, he read it, with some puzzlement visible on his face. Then he sat up, laid it on Dutch's desk, adjusted his glasses, read it again, and looked at me. "Okay, so what was I supposed to see?"

"There's one class of people who would otherwise be eligible who cannot join," I said. "Didn't you notice that?"

He looked down at the form again. "There are a number of classes of people who would otherwise be eligible who can't join, and some of this I know because my mother was in the DAR, not because it's on this form. Convicted felons—"

"But there's one special class."

He browsed through the form again. "You mean people who are descended from polygamous marriages? Deb, they're not talking about the wife dies and the husband remarries, and you know as well as I do that bigamy is not that common a crime."

"Who's talking about bigamy, at least the fraudulent kind, or about the wife dies and the husband remarries? They're talking about a specific, and quite large, class of people."

"Oh, come on, Deb, I don't see how there could be very many people in the United States descended from polygamous marriages, at least not people whose ancestors would have fought in the Revolution, so I don't see—"

"There are many thousands of them," I interrupted. "The LDS—Mormon—church began in New York and spread over a good bit of the northeastern part of the country before it started moving west. Which means that there are thousands of women who would otherwise be eligible for the Daughters of the American Revolution, or Daughters of the American Flag, who are descended from polygamous marriages that took place in the second half of the nineteenth century, and who therefore are not eligible for membership. That's religious discrimination. That's an anti-Mormon clause, Captain Millner, and not a thing in the world else."

· · · · ·

He took off his glasses and rubbed the bridge of his nose. "Even granted that that's true—and I suppose it is—that doesn't mean this clause has anything to do with the case. Deb, just because you've become a Mormon you see Mormons, or anti-Mormons, coming out of the woodwork."

"Then why do *you* think Matilda, with her life at stake, told me *three times* to go to that meeting?"

"Maybe the person who kidnapped her was going to the meeting."

"Oh, I expect she was there, or at least she intended to be there. But there were fifty-six women there besides me. The kidnapper could be any one of those fifty-six, or she could have intended to go and didn't make it, or she could belong to another chapter—there are several others in the area." Without waiting for him to answer, I dashed into my explanation. "Imagine you have a socially ambitious woman who doesn't *do* anything, not anything she can derive any kind of prestige or status from. Her only sources of status are her husband, her children, and her ancestors. Such a woman is likely to be a joiner: She joins the DAR, she joins the DAF, she joins the Daughters of the Confederacy, she joins the Daughters of Texas, maybe she joins the Junior League—I don't know what all she might join because I'm not a joiner. Now, think about this."

I stood up, grabbed my chair and turned it sideways, and sat in it. "To join the DAF you have to prove descent from at least one person who fought in the American Revolution, but you cannot be descended from a plural marriage. Now certainly many, if not most, of the first members of the LDS Church were people who were children or grandchildren or even great-grandchildren of Revolutionary soldiers."

"You said that," Millner muttered, taking off his glasses and rubbing the bridge of his nose again.

"No, I just implied it. Now I'm saying it. And although the main body of the Church moved to Utah in eighteen forty-seven, a sizable chunk of it wound up in Texas, in two different colonies, the first of which arrived here in eighteen forty-four, with Lyman

. . . . .

Wight, and settled near Fredericksburg. I'm pretty sure there was one in East Texas too but I haven't found the exact date or location yet. I've got in my head it was Gilmer but that may not be right—it's somewhere near Gilmer, anyway."

"Fredericksburg started out mostly German. You're not telling me Germans—"

"I didn't say *in* Fredericksburg, I said *near* Fredericksburg. A little town named Zodiac, of all things, and it couldn't have been the Mormon colonists who named it that. It's so small it's not even on the map anymore."

"But—"

"Just a minute, let me finish. Now, there have been a good many generations since the eighteen-forties, and not all people stay in the same church their parents were in. So, just suppose. I know you don't agree with me but for the moment just pretend you do. We've got this hypothetical woman; well, I guess she's not so hypothetical, because we've got all kinds of evidence that a woman committed, or aided in committing, these crimes. So hypothetically let's assume our perp knows through family tradition that she's descended from Revolutionary soldiers—that's something people would go on bragging about. But she doesn't know she's descended from a polygamous marriage, because her branch of the family left the church and that was something nobody wanted to talk about. So she hired a genealogist and—"

"Deb."

"Yeah?"

"There's one thing you're forgetting," Captain Millner pointed out. "If you're right about this in any way, your perp is *already* in the DAF. So how'd she get in the DAF if she's just now hiring a genealogist?"

"Maybe she'd already traced her descent from one ancestor who fought in the Revolutionary War and now she wants to trace it to another. You don't know these people. . . ."

"I know these people. I told you my mother was in the DAR."

. . . . .

144

"I don't know about the DAR, but in the DAF they wear all these little bronze name tags for their ancestors who fought in the Revolution and apparently they get some sort of Brownie points for how many little bronze name tags they get. So maybe she got greedy. She didn't have enough little bronze name tags from one line, and she'd run into a dead end on the next line, so she hired a pro to follow it."

"That still doesn't prove your theory," Millner said patiently. "I mean, look, Deb, I grant you that if a genealogist was murdered, well, killed anyway whether or not it was deliberate murder, and this much effort has been expended to get whatever paperwork he had, he was probably blackmailing her over something in her family background. But what says it has to be this? Maybe she also wants to join the Daughters of the Confederacy and he found out that this Confederate ancestor she was so proud of met her female ancestor at the Quadroons' Ball in New Orleans."

"I haven't the faintest idea what you're talking about."

Millner grinned. "Now, see what you've missed by not having a mother who was in the DAR *and* the Daughters of the Confederacy *and* the Daughters of Texas?"

I could feel myself blushing. "I didn't mean—"

"Oh yes you did, and whether you were right in all cases I don't know, but you were certainly right in my mother's case. She didn't have anything else to be proud of, so she was very, very proud of her ancestors. And there was a big row in her Daughters of the Confederacy chapter because this woman tried to join, and she had documented evidence of her descent from a Confederate soldier, but there seemed to be something funny about the marriage situation because somebody else in the same chapter had the same ancestor with a different wife at the same time. So the officers in her chapter got to checking up on things and found out the woman who was trying to join was descended from a mistress rather than a wife, and that was when my mother's chapter found out about the Quadroons' Ball, and I heard about nearly nothing else for the next

. . . . .

six months. You know what a Quadroon is?"

"I think it was the old word for somebody one-fourth Black and three-fourths White."

"Yep. You know what a Quadroon looks like?"

I thought about it. "Maybe like Sarah in Ident? Well, maybe not, she told me she's Black and White and Chinese and Native American. Or maybe like O. J. Simpson's children? He looks part White, so those children might be about Quadroons, and they are beautiful. Poor kids."

Captain Millner heaved a deep sigh. "The next person who mentions O. J. Simpson to me is going to spend six months walking a beat in the stockyards. A lot of Quadroon women, depending on who their ancestors, Black and White both, are, are knockout gorgeous. Fair skin, just a little coffee with a lot of rich cream, with curly red hair and the most brilliant emerald green eyes you ever saw. The Quadroons' Ball was a major social event in New Orleans both before and after the Civil War, only it was one all the high-class women pretended not to know about, because it was at the Quadroons' Ball that the planters, and the planters' sons, selected their mistresses. Before the Civil War they out-and-out bought them. After—well, I suppose things had to be arranged a little more tactfully."

I don't know how long I sat with my mouth open before I said, "Oh." And then—I couldn't help it—I burst out laughing.

"What's so funny?" Captain Millner demanded, rather annoyed.

"If you'd heard my Aunt Brume today—talking about miscegenation—looks like it's okay as long as it's men doing it and not women, and as long as he doesn't actually *marry* the woman—"

"All you've got to do is look around you to know that," Captain Millner said. "This country, and just about every other country, is full of mixed-raced babies. And most of the time they got that way because White men were fooling around, to put it as mildly as possible, not because other men were. But historically it hasn't been considered all right. The father might be at the top of society, but his mixed-race children were usually treated like dirt by both races. Ever hear of Sally Hemings?"

"Thomas Jefferson's mistress," I said. "And the mother of a lot of his children." My laughter died away, as I remembered Aunt Brume's savage denunciation of the "nasty little half-breed," as if it were the baby's fault it was of mixed races, or as if there were something wrong with that, anyway. "Okay, it's an interesting story, and I'm glad you told me about it. You're right, of course, it could be something like that. But if it was, why would Matilda have sent me to this DAF meeting?"

"Maybe because it was the only way she had of pointing you toward the perp," Captain Millner said. "You weren't trying to join the Daughters of the Confederacy so she couldn't send you there. There could be any number of genealogical reasons, Deb. Maybe this person is descended from Santa Anna and trying to join the Daughters of Texas, but you're not trying to join the Daughters of Texas so Matilda couldn't send you there. You're assuming she wanted you to see that anti-Mormon clause because that affects you—"

"Not me personally," I interrupted. "You know perfectly well I'm the first person in my family to be a Mormon, except for Hal of course, and I'm older than he is. But some of my friends. It affects them."

"Okay, some of your friends. But you said it yourself. There were other things happening at that meeting besides your getting that form."

"That's true," I said, "but Matilda specifically emphasized over the phone that the papers I was going to get at the meeting were important."

"So they're important. Hell, Deb, the perp might just be descended from a common criminal like Sam Bass or Jesse James."

"There are people who will pay genealogists to prove they *are* descended from Sam Bass and Jesse James," I pointed out morosely. "Not too long ago they dug up Jesse James to see if he was really

. . . . .

him, because some people were claiming he'd lived a long time after he was supposed to be dead and had another family, but I lost track of how they thought they were going to prove it was or wasn't him."

"DNA, obviously, from the bones and known living descendants. Also superimposing known photos over the skull. It's an old technique, and it really was Jesse James, not that I was surprised by that. Deb, will you stay on the subject?" Millner demanded, and I felt my eyes fill with tears of worry and exhaustion. "Hell, Deb, I'm sorry," he said.

"No, you were right. I just—I don't want to *think* right now because every time I think, I think about Matilda and I get so scared—but I've got to think if we're ever going to get Matilda back. . . ."

"But I could have remembered you're out on your feet. And you've got to face the fact that no matter how hard you or I or anybody else thinks, we might *not* get Matilda back alive. And Deb, no matter what happens, you've got to get some sleep."

"You want to tell me how?" I asked, hearing the anger in my voice—anger not at him, but at the situation and at the unknown perp.

"I was reading *Life 101* the other day and it's a pretty good instruction book, but I guess I haven't got to that page in it yet," he muttered.

"Well, neither have I. I'll sleep when we get Matilda back."

He nodded. "Okay, there were people there. At the meeting, I mean. I don't suppose there's any way you could get a list of who was in attendance?"

"I've got one," I said, and produced it.

He looked at it gloomily. "How many names?"

"I told you, fifty-seven counting me. And I've also got"—I produced them one by one as I spoke—"a list of all the women in this chapter, and a list of all the members nationwide."

"Great," he said. "Now I guess the next question is, What are we going to do about it?"

. . . . .

Nathan Drucker breezed in about that time. There is about ninety pounds less of him than there used to be; ever since missing six months of work after a heart attack he'd been steadily losing weight, and he now looked about twenty years younger than he had looked five years ago.

"What are you on right now, Nate?" Captain Millner asked him.

"That Frost thing," Drucker answered. "Why?"

"Shelve it for a few days," Millner said, "and help Deb. She's got two murders and a kidnapping all tied together, kidnap victim still missing and a close friend of hers."

Nate looked at me sympathetically, pulled his chair over so that he was sitting near me, and said, "Same thing we met about the other day? Tell me what's new."

I did—nonstop—while the minute hand crept slowly around the clock. At one point Millner got up, walked across the room, and brought back the large easel with a tablet of huge paper on it, turned back the sheet of paper we'd used in the earlier meeting, and put a couple of brightly colored indelible markers in the chalk tray.

This huge tablet is an important tool in any complicated investigation. Yes, certainly we could now do the same thing on computer, but having the tablet up and constantly in sight of everybody coming in and out of the squad room keeps people's minds on the case, and the officer mainly responsible for a case may come in after being out of the office for an hour or two and find new ideas written in somebody else's hand.

This time I started the writing. "Here's what we know," I said. "We know—or at least we're so close to certain that we might as well say we know—that there are two people involved. One of them is a woman, probably about my age or older and quite possibly somewhere near my size, or at least her hands are about the size of my hands. The other is a much younger male, possibly her son, possibly mentally retarded."

On the tablet I wrote: *Perp 1, White (?) female, @50 years old,*

· · · · ·

small hands. Perp 2, White male, @18–25, large, possible mental deficiency.

I went on, "We know there's some connection with the medical school, for two reasons: First, anyone not in some way connected with the medical school would be unlikely to know about the experiment, because it hasn't been widely publicized here; and second, the automobiles of two of the victims wound up in the medical-school parking terrace."

On the tablet I wrote: *Probable connection to medical school.*

"Where's the kidnap victim's car?" Nate asked.

I looked at Millner, who said, "Parked beside her church."

"They probably couldn't get it started," I said. "If you knew Matilda's car like I know Matilda's car—never mind. Okay, this person, the main perp, also has some sort of connection with either the funeral home or Uncle George; otherwise she wouldn't have known about Uncle George. But the connection is probably with the funeral home, because otherwise even if she knew about Uncle George she wouldn't have been able to get in to get him."

On the tablet I wrote: *Probable connection to funeral home. Connection to Uncle George also?*

"We know that the secondary perp is quite large and strong; otherwise he wouldn't be able to manhandle bodies: Uncle George and Marvin Tutwiler were both pretty good–size men, and furthermore he wouldn't have been able to kidnap Matilda, at least not unless he took her entirely by surprise, because she's a lot tougher than she looks."

Nate nodded, and Captain Millner stood up and took the blue marker from my hand. "I'll add a little more to this," he said. "We have the final autopsy reports on Tutwiler now; they were faxed to us earlier today, and they back up everything Deb brought home with her. He died of a depressed skull fracture, and there's bruising on his back and side consistent with a fall. The ME thinks he probably fell heavily against something like a solid wood end table. The ME says the wound isn't deep enough to have been something

. . . . .

fixed, like the corner of a raised hearth; it had to be something that would give, maybe slide, at least a little when Tutwiler hit it. My own reconstruction, he was off balance for some reason, maybe in the process of standing up or sitting down, and somebody either shoved or struck him. He fell, hit his head against the corner of an end table, the corner dug into his head and then retreated as the table slid back from the force of the fall. I called the ME and asked, and he said yes, an angry woman could have hit him hard enough to make him fall like that if he was off balance to begin with. Or— this is the ME's idea—maybe he was standing on a throw rug without a nonskid backing."

He wrote some of that on the chart and then said, "I wish I had more people I could haul off other cases."

He didn't. Fort Worth, like just about every other major city, is seriously underpoliced, and the investigative branch is constantly as busy as a cat with two tails. Nate could leave what he was doing because the Frost case involved a blackmailer who had already gotten his comeuppance: The former victim who had become his killer was now in jail, and all we were trying to do now was track down the rest of his victims. That was important but not urgent, in terms of a time-management system I'd been reading about with considerable interest: Any intended action can be important and urgent, important but not urgent, urgent but not important, or not urgent and not important. Retrieving Matilda alive was both important and urgent.

Millner strode out of the office with the guest list from today's meeting, coming back in moments later to return the original to me and divide the photocopy between himself and Nate. "Let's go check them out," he said.

"What'll Deb be doing?" Nate asked.

"She's got to fake some sort of genealogical form," Millner replied, and glanced at me. "You got everything you need to do that?"

"Yes," I said. Aunt Darla had at some point in the past given me several whole packages of pedigree forms and family group sheets, and I had put them in my capacious purse-briefcase-holster before leaving the house the second time this morning, even though I had returned my pistol to its usual shoulder holster. I just couldn't feel comfortable with it anywhere else. It's too easy to take a purse away from just about any woman.

I sat down with Aunt Brume's genealogical information. I had originally intended to use Aunt Darla's, but I'd absent-mindedly hauled home even the photocopies I made, and then left them all on my dresser. So—what could I get away with doing, in terms of faking genealogy?

Aunt Brume had begun hers with my mother's mother, leaving me to fill in between. How far back would this perp be likely to know?

My mother was born in 1920. Her mother was born in 1898, her father in 1896. All four of their parents were born not long after the Civil War; their parents in turn were born before the Civil War. That was the end of this chart—I don't know what you call it; it's the one I think of as a regular family tree. Before going on to the next one of those forms, I started looking at family group sheets. The one for my grandparents, showing my mother as one of their eight children, again showed the birth dates of my grandparents, as well as birthplaces, marriage dates, death dates and places.

Next was the sheet for my grandmother's mother and father, showing my grandmother as the third of their six children and Aunt Brume as the youngest. My great-grandmother was born in 1873, my great-grandfather in 1869. Next family group sheet, my great-great-grandmother was born in 1845, my great-great-grandfather in 1840. And then . . .

The next family group sheet showed my great-great-grandmother as the youngest of seven children. Amos Gridley, born in 1800 in Vermont, was father on that sheet; Amanda Sutherland, born in 1810, also in Vermont, was shown as mother. She had died in 1847.

. . . . .

I turned over the next page and blinked. There was a second family group sheet showing Amos Gridley as father. On this one Rachel Kelley, born in 1823 in Illinois, was shown as mother, and they had three children, born in 1844, 1847, and 1850. In the section for notes someone—presumably Aunt Brume—had written, *This record, from the middle pages of a family Bible, is obviously erroneous. Ggf Amos clearly married Rachel after the death of Amanda, and two of Amanda's children were erroneously written up as being those of Rachel because she raised them after their mother's death.*

I looked at one more thing: the marriage date and place for Amos and Rachel.

Amos and Rachel were married in 1843 in Nauvoo, Illinois, the city the Mormons had carved out of a swamp, the city where Joseph Smith had lived when he first recorded the polygamy doctrine.

I wasn't the first Mormon in the family.

And Aunt Brume wasn't even eligible for membership in the organization she had founded.

Nine

. . . . .

Why in the world had Aunt Brume given me this?

Why had she even saved it? Although she's not a certified genealogist, she knows genealogy well enough that she could certify anytime she wanted to, she and Aunt Darla both. And anybody capable of becoming a certified genealogist would know enough about nineteenth-century Mormon polygamy not to mistake the marriage date of Rachel Kelley and Amos Gridley for an error, at least not in view of the marriage place. She wasn't fooling herself; she was fooling, and possibly really deceiving, her children and grandchildren, to whom this record had probably been given. But I couldn't see how she could possibly have expected to deceive me in view of my change in religion, which she knew about and deprecated.

She was descended from the first marriage, the one she (and the DAF) would, I suppose, consider the legitimate marriage—not that I could tell from the paperwork whether the DAF considered the first marriage, or none of the marriages in a polygamous family, legitimate. So records on the second marriage weren't necessary to prove her line of descent, or for that matter mine. And I couldn't convince myself for a second that Aunt Brume had saved, much less turned over to me, what she would consider highly damning information out of innate honesty.

So the only reason for her to have saved the information about the second marriage was that the Bible containing the information belonged to somebody else. Other people would have access to it, and eventually somebody, somewhere, who knew the scope of her search and knew she would have seen the Bible, would challenge her honesty if her records didn't include this—to her—damning record. So she must have kept it so she could not later be accused of falsifying records.

But even so, she certainly wouldn't have given it to me deliberately.

She had been angry while she was printing this stuff out—so angry that she had mistakenly given me something she didn't mean to give me?

That was the only possible answer. If she had realized by now what she gave me, she would probably be having a fit and trying to decide whether she should call me and ask me to return it, in hopes that I hadn't read it yet, or whether she should just keep her mouth shut and hope like crazy I took her word on that informational note she had added.

For a moment I entertained the notion of the possibility of Aunt Brume as the murderer/kidnapper—but only for a moment, because not only did her age mitigate against that, but furthermore I could imagine no way at all she could have gotten hold of the young male accomplice we knew about both from our one semi-witness and from the fingerprint record at the crime scenes.

But I could be grateful for one thing: Aunt Brume had given me the information I needed to put in Matilda's mailbox. All I had to do was copy it; I wouldn't have to make something up.

Because on whatever ancestral line our unknown female murderer was looking, if she needed to hire a genealogist there was a very good chance she had not gotten as far back as the 1840s.

Very carefully, using pencil and making occasional deliberate strike-outs as if I were working from original documents that were difficult to read, I copied Amos Gridley's two family group sheets onto blank family group sheet forms, using pink work sheets rather than white final sheets. I photocopied the result, so there'd be no

· · · · ·

question, later, when I went in with a search warrant, as to whether the sheets I found were the sheets I had made. Then I went over to the Sex Crimes office and got Margie Herrera, so it would be in a different handwriting, to write a note: *I know you kidnapped Matilda Greenwood. This is all you get until I get Matilda back alive and unharmed. Then I'll leave the rest anywhere you want. I don't care about your secrets. I just don't want my friend hurt.*

It might not do any good, but then it might. At least it was worth trying.

And it wasn't completely untruthful. I didn't care about the perp's secrets. I just cared—a whole lot—about what she had done to protect her secrets.

What to do next . . . I couldn't risk the least possibility that the perp might be watching Matilda's place by now and might realize it was a police officer who put the three sheets of paper in the mailbox. Of course I wasn't in uniform, but my big holster-bag might be spotted, and the bunched-up left underarm of my jacket concealing my shoulder holster might also be spotted. I had no idea how alert, how knowledgeable, our perp might be.

That meant that right now I'd better take off my holster and put my pistol and hand radio in my bag, and when I got out of the car, if I got out of the car at all, I'd have to put my bag in the trunk and just carry my billfold and car keys with me. I had to look like just another housewife now—a housewife dressed for a luncheon meeting, because the perp knew I'd been to a luncheon meeting, but definitely nothing other than a housewife.

No, come to think of it, I'd have to put the bag in the trunk earlier than that. If she was watching, and she certainly might be, she couldn't miss seeing me do it after I parked. I'd have to do it as soon as I left the building. . . .

That wouldn't work either. I wanted to use my radio as long as possible.

Fatigue and worry were sapping my brainpower. The answer was perfectly obvious. I wouldn't park at Matilda's "church" if I decided to go there any longer than it would take to jump out of the car and stick papers in the mailbox and jump back into the car. I would park somewhere else, somewhere nearby, and walk there.

But even doing that, I felt that I had to use my personal car rather than a police car, and that my radio had to be shut off two blocks before I reached Matilda's "church." It, too, had to be hidden in my bag in the trunk if I got out of the car. And I was going to get out of the car, because even as I was thinking of these things I was also thinking of exactly how I was going to approach this situation.

Of course I had to hope like crazy that if the murderer was watching Matilda's place she hadn't gotten close enough to me at the DAF luncheon to recognize me by my clothes. I certainly didn't have time to go home and change again. I also had to hope she wouldn't be close enough to spot my face, if she'd been introduced to me at the luncheon.

Had Matilda ever used my name over the telephone? I didn't think so. She'd called me Deb—she'd also called Harry Deb, as a signal to let him know that only her side of the conversation had been monitored—but there must be a lot of people who are called Deb. Anyway Aunt Brume had introduced me as Deborah, not as Deb.

I checked my watch; Matilda had let me know that she expected me to reach the mailbox between two and three o'clock. Even now, after all that had happened today, it was just barely two. I couldn't believe the way time was crawling—but it wouldn't matter, surely, if I got the papers there early. Late might matter, but not early. I let Millie know what I was doing, and then I called Dispatch and said, "I'm going to be ten-six the next hour. Please don't try to raise me; I'll have the radio off most of the time." Then I went down to the parking lot, got my car, and headed out Belknap, turning off it a few blocks later.

My throat felt tight as I drove past the familiar parking lot with its ramshackle sign without stopping or even slowing, to park two blocks away beside a boarded-up convenience store with graffiti scrawled all over the plywood. I ignored the the conflicting claims of territory and the messages about who from which gang was or was not going to kill whom from which gang; most of the time the threats are never carried through anyway, and I had other things on my mind. I swallowed back the lump, swung the door open, got out, and headed for the building, walking the two blocks somewhat less confidently than I would have walked if I'd had my pistol or even my radio.

I had to admire the artistry of the Stakeout Squad. The rusty white mailbox, nailed to the lowest post of the outside staircase, looked as if it had sat right there for years; whoever put it there had even managed to find old, dull nails rather than new, shiny ones. One side, where the name and/or address should be painted, had been sprayed with white enamel and then artistically sprinkled with sand, dust, and a little bit of what looked like cat hair to make the enamel look old rather than new. I could tell it was new only because I got close enough to glimpse a couple of tiny spots where the enamel had gone on too thick and wasn't quite dry yet. GREEN-WOOD had been hand-lettered over the enamel, using glossy black paint and a fairly narrow brush. That paint, too, had been carefully aged, probably by use of Ident's heat lamp as well as dust, sand, and cat hair.

Then, with a start, I recognized the mailbox and realized why it had been necessary to paint over the side. It used to have a different name on it. Somebody had raided the evidence room. This was the second kidnapping case this mailbox had figured in. The first was the abduction of a Dallas schoolgirl, who had died of asthma and panic in the trunk of the kidnapper's car.

I try not to be superstitious. But I didn't like the omen.

And I didn't like the stillness all around me.

Bill Livingston was supposed to be watching this mailbox. Livingston was a good stakeout man; he wouldn't have driven his car here. He'd either been dropped off by someone who'd left quickly, or he'd parked his car—a ten-year-old Ford sedan seized in a drug raid and kept licensed as a personal automobile rather than a government vehicle—several blocks away and walked over here, just as I did. He'd have taken care not to be seen.

But something just didn't look right, didn't feel right. I pivoted slowly, looking at the parking lot, looking at the so-called church, looking at the flaking gray asbestos siding of the side wall and the peeling white paint of the outside stairs up to the apartment where Matilda lived. And then I realized what it was that was bothering me. I should have spotted it instantly. The telephone wires had been yanked free of their junction box under the stairs.

Trying to look as natural as possible, as if I were a normal visitor and didn't know Matilda was missing, I turned and headed up the stairs, calling, "Matilda? Are you here? Matilda?"

I stopped short at the top of the stairs.

The door, which should have been closed and locked, stood partly open. There was a dreadful silence inside.

I pushed it on open, using the toe of my shoe almost at the bottom of the door so as to avoid messing up any fingerprints that might be where a door would normally be touched by anyone but the smallest child.

The apartment had been tossed again, even more thoroughly than the first time. But this time I had eyes only for the middle of the floor, where Bill Livingston lay stretched facedown, his right arm extended with his pistol—like so many other officers, he'd gone to a semiautomatic years ago, but it hadn't done him any more good than the old revolver I still used would have done —still clutched tightly in his hand. A red puddle had spread in all directions from his torso, but it was drying and darkening now.

He'd been shot in the back. He'd had his pistol out, facing one enemy, but another had come up behind him.

Gingerly avoiding damage to the blood and the bloody footprints, I crouched nearby and touched my hand to his face.

He was already cold, and now I could see the purple staining of hypostasis—postmortem staining—in the lower part of his face and

. . . . .

arms. This must have happened very soon after he arrived this morning.

My search for his radio was brief but thorough. As I had thought as soon as I saw him, it was gone.

I didn't know why they hadn't taken his pistol, until I tried to take it myself.

Usually, in death, all muscles relax. But in some rare situations, usually involving very sudden violent death, the muscles tighten into what is called cadaveric spasm, which is indistinguishable from normal rigor mortis except that it isn't preceded by that stage of relaxation during which anything the person might be holding drops from his grasp. In that case, it can often take two or three strong men to pry loose whatever the person had in his hands at the time of death.

I didn't have two or three strong men, and I had to have his pistol. Because in the time it took me to find the body and realize the radio was gone, I'd already decided what I was going to do. It wasn't standard police procedure; it would infuriate Captain Millner and probably earn me a three-day suspension. But it might work. And it was absolutely the only thing I could think of right now that stood a chance of working.

If Livingston had been alive I would have gotten to the closest telephone to call for an ambulance. But he wasn't. Nothing was going to help him now. My choices were to get Crime Scene out here right now, blowing any possible chance of getting Matilda back alive as well as making Livingston's sacrifice totally useless— because he had died in the effort to get Matilda back alive, to catch this killer before she killed again—or to leave him lying here in his own blood while I finished his assignment.

I knew which he'd prefer that someone (not necessarily me, because like a lot of the men, he'd still had a little tendency to want to protect policewomen) would do. Because he, like me, had been tracking the crimes, observing the increase in seriousness and deliberateness. Our perp had started with what could have been, probably was, accidental death—manslaughter at the worst. Janet Malone's death had been murder, but it wasn't planned. Nobody I know of plans a murder that uses a frying pan as a weapon. But this was premeditated. She'd come here looking for the stakeout officer she knew must be here, she'd come here with a gun, and she'd come here to kill. I've heard that after the first murder, murder gets easier every time. I'm not sure that's always true. In my experience, a lot of murderers never kill again. But it was obvious that this time it was true.

So I wasn't going to go find a phone, or go get my radio, and get help over here right away. I was going to take over Livingston's post. I was going to see who picked up those papers I'd put in the mailbox, and I was going to find out where she'd stowed Matilda, and I was going to get Matilda back, and then I was going to do everything I could to make sure this murderer paid for the rest of her life.

Yes, of course I was crying as I continued to struggle to pry the pistol out of Livingston's hand. But then, after the pistol came loose with a sickening snap, I stood up, went to the bathroom and wiped my face with toilet paper, and stopped crying. I couldn't see if I was crying. And I couldn't hear very well, either.

I wiped my face again, blew my nose as quietly as possible, and pulled out the clip to check it. Yes, he'd fired—more than once, probably three times. There were five rounds in the clip, and this pistol held nine rounds, eight in the clip and one in the chamber. That meant there were six shots left. As many as I would have if I had my own pistol.

I wasn't comfortable with anyone else's pistol, because I hadn't sighted it in myself and I didn't know exactly what its quirks were. But I was a lot more comfortable with it than I would be with no pistol at all.

Gun in hand, I walked over to examine the wall and door he'd have been facing. Nothing. Either the door had been open, in which case all three slugs could be anywhere within a half mile or so from the door, or he'd hit somebody three times.

And by golly, there was a little bit of blood here. Not much, but a little. He had hit somebody at least once. Somebody might even have gone to the hospital with a bullet wound. I'd check on that later. And I'd ask the lab to collect blood samples. DNA analysis takes at least two weeks, and right now we didn't have anybody to compare it with, but if we got somebody. . . .

Of course the person he'd hit had been in front of him and the person who killed him had been behind him. But the two were together. And one of them would tell us where the other was.

Then I went and partially closed the door, so that it was in exactly the same position the murderer had left it. A person peeking in without opening the door wouldn't see anything unusual, but when the door was opened Livingston's body would be visible.

I wasn't tall enough to stand and look out the window Livingston had been using, so I went to the kitchen and got the high footstool Matilda kept there to reach upper shelves, and I carried it over to the window.

And now I saw why Matilda had wanted to be sure the perp tried to pick up the papers at, or after, two. She'd guessed the only place a mailbox could be put without looking new. She'd guessed where somebody would have to be to watch that mailbox. The way the sun—yes, the rain was finally over at least for now—was hitting this window I had no glare in my eyes because the glare was passing over my head, but anybody getting something out of that mailbox would not be able to see me at all, no matter how suspicious she was, no matter how hard she stared, because glare would reflect from the window.

But then I started getting jumpy. That open door wasn't quite at my back, but it was out of my sight to my left side, and somebody who walked quietly enough could get up the stairs without me knowing it, could even get inside the apartment without me knowing she was here.

How *had* they gotten to Bill Livingston?

. . . . .

But I could guess that fairly easily. They'd both come up the stairs. The big young man had probably created a distraction, had probably looked like the threat; Livingston would have concentrated on him, would have let a middle-aged woman who probably looked pretty harmless get behind him if he couldn't watch both of them at once.

He'd made a judgment call. And it had turned out to be the wrong one.

I had made my own judgment call, in deciding to stay here without calling for help. How mine would turn out remained to be seen.

I have had better hours than the one I spent then, wrapped in my jacket and a blanket I'd grabbed from Matilda's bed (because the heat was off, the door was open, and after all it was November), shivering with cold and shock, sitting on the high stool looking out the window, holding the bloody pistol in both hands, watching and listening with equal intentness, watching for someone entering the parking lot, watching for someone approaching the mailbox, watching for someone coming across the front of the building and up the stairs far enough toward the inside wall that I couldn't see her, listening for the slightest creak or whisper from the staircase or the parking lot or anywhere else. All the time Bill Livingston's body was stiffening in the living room less than fifteen feet from where I was sitting.

And no, I hadn't covered it with anything. Anything that I could cover it with would leave trace fragments to confuse the laboratory, might conceivably take away trace evidence that could have clarified the situation.

I was thankful it was November. There weren't any flies.

But, as I waited, I should have guessed that eventually someone, probably Captain Millner, would wonder where I was, would ask Millie, would ask Dispatch, would try to raise me by radio, and then would get rather excited.

It was exactly three-twenty-two by my watch when two things

began to happen almost simultaneously. A rather elegant gray Saturn pulled into the parking lot, a husky young man with no visible bandages got out of the passenger's seat, the driver looked out her window and shouted at him to come back, he did so (before reaching the mailbox), they took off hell-for-leather, and another car, this one a dark blue Plymouth, pulled into the parking lot moments later.

Nathan Drucker was talking into his radio as he parked the Plymouth.

And of course the perp had the radio she'd stolen from Livingston. By tomorrow she wouldn't be able to use it; the batteries would have run down; but she certainly heard Drucker announcing his approach.

She wouldn't be back.

And I had only part of a license-plate number. DNA 6 . . . 6 what? There should be two more digits, but I hadn't had time to see them.

How many possible comibnations are there?

Let's see, DNA 60 zero, one, two, three, four, five, six, seven, eight, nine. That was ten, and the number after the 6 could be anything from 0 to 9, so ten times ten, well, that was just a hundred plates. That shouldn't take too long to track down, at least not on the computer. Assuming the computer wasn't down, which it sometimes was.

Shouldn't take too long . . . but the perp knew the police were almost on her. How long did Matilda have to live? Or was she dead already?

While I was thinking I was running down the stairs, regardless of their dilapidated condition, while Drucker was getting out of his car. "Damn you, Nathan," I screamed through tears of rage and frustration, "you scared her away before I got the plate!"

"Scared *who* away?" Drucker demanded, heading toward me. I don't cry easily and I never cry on duty, so he knew something was badly wrong.

"*Her!* The murderer! That was her, in the Saturn!"

Drucker pivoted on his heel, staring at the now empty street. "Damn," he said. "Damn—and she's sure as hell gone now, but how did *I* scare her away? She left before I got here."

"She heard you, when you started to go ten-six and gave the address. She's got Livingston's radio."

"How in the hell did she get Livingston's radio?" Color was draining from his face; like me, he knew only one way that someone could get a cop's radio and prevent that cop—in a heavily peopled area like this—from finding a telephone and calling in. He knew, but he didn't want to know.

"Livingston is dead!" I screamed at him. "She killed Livingston hours ago! He was stone cold by the time I got here! She killed him and took his radio. When I found him—I figured the best thing to do was . . ."

I was talking to empty air. Drucker was going up the stairs two steps at a time.

It wasn't until that moment that I remembered that Livingston's wife was Drucker's oldest daughter.

That it had been Drucker who'd convinced Livingston that police work was pretty interesting for somebody who didn't mind working odd hours, and while nobody honest would get rich doing it, it paid well enough compared to other wages in the area.

That I had picked a damned lousy way of letting Drucker know that his daughter was now a widow and his advice to his son-in-law had sucked.

I followed him up the stairs, somewhat more slowly. I didn't know how many more pounding footsteps this rickety staircase would take.

Drucker wasn't crying. His face seemed set in stone; he was on the radio, asking for Captain Millner, asking for the medical examiner. "Stand by," he said to Dispatch, and then to me he said, "What's the number?"

"What?"

"The license-plate number. How much of it did you get?"

· · · · ·

I gave it to him and he relayed it, adding, "The vehicle's a gray Saturn. Year unknown. Stand by for further from Detective Ralston."

I took the radio out of his hand and said, "Check with all the hospitals. At least one of the perps was hit at least once, probably the male. Driver is White female, middle-aged, gray or blond hair, wearing olive green clothing, further description unknown. Passenger is White male, about twenty-five, about six-two, a hundred and ninety to two hundred pounds, brown neck-length hair, eye color unknown, wearing charcoal chino trousers, white sneakers, and a blue ski jacket, may have minor bullet wound. Consider armed and extremely dangerous. And when you get the list of possibles on that license plate, put it in my E-mail box."

"Ten-four," said the voice at the other end of the radio. He sounded as matter-of-fact as possible, but I could tell from overtones and undertones I could hear even over the radio that he was shaken.

Cops don't like cop killers. And our nice lady perp, in her willingness to kill to retain her "nice lady" status, had crossed the line.

I heard a screech outside as of a car peeling out, and ran out the door onto the landing just in time to see the gray Saturn pulling out again. I ran down the stairs as fast as I could with Drucker right behind me, undoubtedly seething because he couldn't pass me, and opened the mailbox. "She got them!" I heard my own voice shouting incredulously. "The bitch came back for the charts!"

If I hadn't seen her myself I absolutely would not have believed it. *Knowing* that at least one police officer was on the scene, she still had come back for the mailbox contents. Whatever Tutwiler had on her must be maximum explosive. That must have been when I began to wonder whether I was wrong about what Tutwiler had. Could *anybody* be that frantic to maintain her membership in the Daughters of the American Flag, to preserve what she saw as her good name and social status?

I'm not sure Drucker even heard me; thrusting his walkie-talkie into my hand, he pelted toward his car, slung the door open, and peeled out while he was still closing his door. "All units ten-three your traffic!" the dispatcher said, and over the radio in my hand I could hear Drucker shouting very nearly incoherently about where the gray Saturn might have gone.

I sat down on the steps, feeling completely numb, to wait for more units to arrive so I could hand the crime scene over to them. Captain Millner arrived first, and I stood up, walked over to him, and said, "Chew me out later, okay? I've got to go back to the office." I handed him Livingston's pistol. "He was still holding it when I found him. I had to pry it out of his hand. I needed it."

"Where's yours?"

"In the car. I didn't want to look like a cop. And—I didn't expect to find this."

"You think Livingston winged one of them?"

"I'm sure he did. I didn't mess up any evidence except the pistol. You'll see it yourself."

"Where's Livingston?"

I nodded toward the staircase. "Upstairs. You won't have any trouble finding him."

"No, I don't guess I will." He walked past me toward the stairs, patting me lightly on the shoulder.

He hadn't reached them when Drucker drove back in, leaped out of the car, and pounded on the hood with his fist. "I lost her!" he yelled hoarsely. "I lost the fucking bitch—I lost her——" He leaned over the hood and began to sob, loudly, convulsively.

Millner walked toward him. He glanced briefly at me, made a "get lost" gesture at me. I nodded and left the two men alone.

I walked the two blocks to where I had left my car, got my bag out of the trunk, put my shoulder holster back on and put my pistol back into it, and drove back to the office.

I've always made a lot of jokes about the in-baskets; we all do, because the truth is that if the City of Fort Worth expected any detective to actually read the entire contents of his or her in-basket, they'd have to hire somebody else to do the detecting, because the typical morning in-basket is about as thick as a Russian novel, only it's 8½-by-11-inch paper, usually single-spaced and double-sided.

The coming of the electronic mailbox hasn't greatly reduced the paper load. It's just added to the overall load. The only difference is that nobody can tell whether you've read the contents of your electronic mailbox or just deleted it unread—well, come to think of it, they also can't tell whether you've read your paper in-box or just initialed it unread.

The problem always is that the one thing you *don't* read is likely to turn out to be the thing you needed most, to save your own hide or that of somebody else, so you have to at least skim everything.

But this time I was glad to get my electronic mail. I skipped over most of it to get to the most recent thing added, the download from the state computer. The list of names and addresses of people who had license plates beginning with DNA 6.

Two-thirds of the way down the list I came to a name I recognized. Lucinda Meredith. She'd been at the head table at the DAF luncheon. She was a relative of Aunt Brume but not a relative of me, or so Aunt Brume said.

That meant she wasn't descended from either of the marriages of Amos Gridley, because if she was descended from Amos Gridley she was related to me.

I think.

I'm not what I'd want to call an expert in genealogy, and the more tired I am the more confused I get.

But according to the state of Texas she owned a Saturn, which might or might not be gray, and she had been at the DAF meeting.

That wasn't enough to arrest her on. I had insufficient probable cause. But it was certainly enough for me to go out and talk with her. A nice, long, probably unfriendly talk . . . except that since I now definitely considered her a suspect, I had to give her a Miranda warning, and she had the right to refuse to talk with me.

If she was the perp, that was a right she would definitely employ.

. . . . .

I went on through the rest of the list, but not only were there no more names I recognized, there were only three more Saturns with license-plate numbers beginning DNA 6. Of course this record didn't tell me the colors of the cars.

But just to be on the safe side, I wrote down those three names, and then got out my own copies of the list of women who'd been at the luncheon, the list of women in that DAF chapter, and the list of women in the entire DAF organization.

None of the last names matched.

Lucinda Meredith was the only woman in Texas who drove a Saturn, had a license plate beginning with DNA 6, and was a member of the DAF.

It was just about 100 percent certain that Lucinda Meredith, with whatever assistance she'd had from the young man who might or might not be her son, had killed Marvin Tutwiler, Janet Malone, and Bill Livingston, and had kidnapped Matilda Greenwood.

At this moment I didn't stand the chance of a snowball in hades of proving it. And I still didn't know *why* and wasn't sure I'd ever know.

$\mathcal{T}\varepsilon n$
. . . .

IN MY OPINION, I had enough to get a search warrant. A judge might not agree, but it was worth trying. Not bothering with Millie, who was busy typing somebody else's report, I called up the forms on my computer terminal and began with the affidavit. A list of items I expected to find: *A police radio.* I needed brand and serial number, so I called and got those from the Stakeout Squad office and added them. *Two family group sheets, pink, in my own handwriting (see photocopies, attached). A firearm, make, caliber, and model unknown, used to kill Corporal William Livingston.* I wiped tears from my face, resolutely, and went on typing. *Ammunition for a firearm. Evidence that someone sustained a bullet wound and was taken to the house for first aid. The reasons for believing these items may be found at this location are as follows:*

I specifically mentioned my intention to search all vehicles, described the gray Saturn we expected to find there, and noted that there were probably other vehicles as well, and mentioned my intention to search all outbuildings, including garages and garden sheds.

I took the time and space to explain thoroughly, and then I called a judge.

The only major inconvenience resulting from the move of the police station about ten years ago is the fact that the courts are no longer next door. They're within possible walking distance, but not practical walking distance: far enough away that unless a person has

. . . .

all the time in the world, it's easier to drive or, if you're sure you won't get any emergency calls until after you get back, hop on one of the city buses that run about every ten minutes. So if you're sensible, as I try to be, you call first.

I got Judge Eamon Reilly, who would have been my first choice, if I'd had a choice, for two reasons: He likes police, and he listens long enough to get a full explanation instead of cutting people off at their second sentence. I explained the situation, reading from the affidavit, and he asked, "Let me be sure I understand this. You *saw* her take papers from the mailbox?"

"Not really. I saw the car pull up near the mailbox—and if state records are up to date, and they usually are, this has got to be the right car—and then the young man got out and approached the mailbox and then she called to him and he ran back to the car. Then later the car, at least I'm assuming it was the same car, came back, and when I checked immediately afterwards the papers were gone. And I can say no other person, to the best of my knowledge, came near the mailbox during the time the papers were in it."

"And you had your eyes on the mailbox all the time."

"No," I said patiently, "I didn't. I told you that. I found Livingston's body and I spent some time coping with that."

"How much time?"

"I don't know, maybe five minutes. It felt like a lot longer, but you know, something like that always does. Thinking about how long it would take to do the things that I did, five minutes max."

"Do you think you would have heard if another car had arrived in the parking lot during that time?"

"I think I would." I stopped and thought about it. "I probably would, unless it was extremely quiet, quieter than most cars. My nerves were on edge and I was listening for just about anything. But I wouldn't have heard a person on foot, probably."

"But you saw this gray Saturn come into the parking lot. A person in it tried to get to the mailbox but was foiled, apparently, by the arrival of a police car; the same car later returned—"

. . . . .

"A gray Saturn," I said, "but I didn't see the license-plate number the second time. All I saw was the car on the road after I heard it peeling out, and Drucker, when he tried to chase it, never got close enough to see the license plate. I think it was the same car. In my own mind I'm sure it was the same car. But I can't swear to it in court."

"But you had probable cause to believe it was the same car?"

"Yes. I already told you that."

"And you saw a woman driving the car, and you believe it was Lucinda Meredith but you weren't close enough to see her face."

"Yes."

"You had met Lucinda Meredith earlier in the day."

"Yes." This was sounding like cross-examination, but he had to know what was going on if he was going to give me the legal authority to search the house. Search warrants are challenged in court every day, and it was possible a defense attorney would someday ask me exactly the same questions.

"What was Lucinda Meredith wearing when you met her?"

I had to stop and think about that. Could I remember? Yes. "She was wearing an olive green suit. That sounds unattractive but it was perfect with her coloring."

"And when you put the lookout on the car, you said the driver was wearing something green."

I had to stop and think again. "Yes, I did. How'd you know that?"

"I have a police scanner in my office. What shade of green?"

"Olive green."

"But you couldn't make out her face."

"No. Not in the car. It was just too far away."

"So earlier in the day you met Lucinda Meredith and she was wearing an olive green suit. Later in the day you saw a woman drive up in a gray Saturn, and you saw a young man get out of the car and approach the mailbox, but he didn't reach it because he was called back to the car. The driver of the car, whose face you could

. . . . .

not make out, was wearing something olive green. You got a partial license-plate number and you later found that Lucinda Meredith owns the only Saturn listed on the state computer with that partial license plate number. Later the same, or a similar-looking, car entered the area again and attracted your attention by a noisy, and very fast, exit. At that time you checked the mailbox and the papers were gone. A tidy chain of evidence. You have probable cause."

"I have probable cause for assuming that was Lucinda Meredith," I agreed. "I already knew that. But do I have probable cause to get a search warrant?"

"Taking anything from a mailbox that you're not the authorized user of is a federal crime. I'll authorize your search warrant. And while you're about it, write an arrest warrant too," he said. "I think you can prove it—and if you get to her house and find out her Saturn is bright red, then you don't have to serve the warrants. But this way you'll have them with you to serve if the Saturn is gray, and I think it's going to be. How soon can you get here? I'll be leaving fairly soon, and I want to get these signed before I go."

"You're not a federal judge," I said. "Mail theft is a federal crime. And she didn't steal the mail anyway. She took—she could legitimately argue that what she took was put in the mailbox for her to get."

"You let me worry about that. If necessary you can argue about it in court, but you've got to get to court first. You wrote on the warrant that you were searching for items that were taken from a mailbox? That's fine. Put theft from mailbox on the arrest warrant. Remember, this isn't the final charge. It's just to hold her until you're ready to make final charges. Now, can you get this to me fast?"

"You bet," I said, and hung up and started typing.

I admit I wasn't thinking straight. Neither was the judge, but he had a better excuse: He didn't know what I knew. I had probable cause to charge Lucinda Meredith with kidnapping, and I was so

. . . . .

fuzz-brained from stress, shock, and lack of sleep that I didn't even think of it.

Arrest warrants go faster than search warrants do. About ten minutes later I looked around for a backup. Admittedly I'm not always as careful as I ought to be about taking along a backup, but in the first place this woman had probably killed three times, and in the second place I didn't want to run the slightest risk of her walking because I searched by myself without somebody else to witness anything I found. As a result of some highly publicized trials, juries tend to be a lot more sophisticated than they used to be about such things.

When I had first gotten into the office to check the computer, Wayne Carlsen was sitting at his desk studying a document—I didn't know what—enclosed in a thick plastic sleeve. At this moment Carlsen was still studying the document. The slightly glazed look in his eyes told me he was thinking so hard he hadn't heard my telephone conversation with the judge, probably wasn't even fully aware that I was in the room.

"Have you got time to go with me to get a couple of warrants signed and then lean on a suspect?" I asked, loudly enough to snap him out of his near-trance.

"Not really," he said after a moment, "but what did he do?"

"*She* killed Bill Livingston, but I can't prove it yet."

Wayne stared at me, his mouth open and horror growing in his eyes. "Killed—not our Bill Livingston?"

"You mean you hadn't heard? I'm sorry, Wayne, I'm dropping bricks right and left—I even forgot he was Nathan's son-in-law."

"I haven't heard anything, Deb. Are you saying—?"

"Our Bill Livingston," I confirmed bleakly. "He was shot early this morning, probably right after he took over the post from whoever had it all night. I found him a little after two o'clock this afternoon."

"And you're sure about this suspect?"

"Let's say she fits all the criteria I can tell about so far, and the best I can tell, she's the only person in Texas who does."

Wayne stood up, dropped the paper on the desk. "For that I have time," he said. "Just let me go empty something first."

I decided to call Harry while I was waiting for Wayne to get back from the rest room, in view of the fact that it was now past four o'clock, which was officially my quitting time. He answered on the first ring and sounded rather disappointed that the caller was me instead of Matilda. It was pretty obvious he wasn't expecting me to get home anytime soon. But when I mentioned serving a search warrant, he instantly demanded, "Who's going with you?"

He's getting absolutely paranoid lately about being sure I don't serve search warrants by myself. I don't know why; it's not that I make a habit of doing it.

Well, actually, I guess I do know why. Although I don't make a habit of doing it, it seems that pretty often when I do it I get in trouble. But this time I was able to assure him that Carlsen was going with me.

"Okay," he said. "I know Wayne. He won't let you get into too much trouble."

"What's going on at home?" I asked.

"I sent Lori to get Cameron, and when she gets back I'll send out for pizza. I'm still staying by the phone."

"But Matilda hasn't called again."

"No, Deb. Matilda hasn't called again. I'd have let you know if she had. Take care of yourself."

"I will," I said, and laid down the receiver, feeling sick.

I hadn't expected Matilda to call again. But I had hoped I would be wrong.

Millie, of course, had left for the day. I called Dispatch and told the woman who answered—I didn't know who she was; it seems like we're always getting new people in Dispatch and I can't keep track of who they are—where we were going and what we were doing, and asked for radio silence about the trip and told her why. Normally we could just switch to a different radio channel, one that most scanners don't pick up, but this time we couldn't because of the stolen radio.

Wayne caught up with me at the elevator. "We're taking my car," he told me firmly. "You look like hell."

I wasn't the least bit surprised. I also felt like hell.

The house looked like about three hundred thousand dollars' worth of real estate, the kind that Publisher's Clearing House might portray in its advertising as the potential residence of somebody who won their ten-million-dollar prize. Gray brick, Tudor-style architecture with fake half-timbering and about an acre of lawn and shrubbery with a few very large trees. Even in November the lawn remained green, and it was obvious that a dandelion or stray leaf wouldn't dare show its face there. The annual flowers were gone now, but pansies still made a brave show in raised, manicured planting beds.

The gray Saturn was sitting at the curb; she hadn't even bothered to hide it in the garage. I couldn't decide whether she was unbelievably stupid or completely confident she'd never be suspected.

Carlsen parked behind it and I got out and felt the hood. Despite November's chill, it was still quite warm. This car had run hot and fast fairly recently, hot enough that even in this chill weather it hadn't fully cooled off.

"I'll take the back," Carlsen said. "Be careful, you're between her and her wheels."

I nodded. "And you watch out for the male subject," I said, "because from what I saw of him, he looks to me like he could eat a telephone pole and spit out splinters, and he may not have many inhibitions." I took my gun out of my holster and slung my bag over my left shoulder, leaving my right hand free to shoot fast and accurately if necessary.

"Gotcha," Carlsen said, drawing his own weapon. Unlike me, he also had gone to a semiautomatic. Sooner or later I was going to have to do the same, but I didn't like the idea. I trust a revolver. A semiautomatic doesn't seem quite predictable to me, mainly because the only one I ever owned, a .22 target pistol, had jammed on the third shot of every second clip no matter how many new clips I bought it.

Carlsen disappeared around the corner of the house. Although I knew that Mrs. Meredith—or somebody in the house—knew we were here, because I had seen the elegant heavy gold brocade draperies twitch from someone standing behind them and looking out, I waited until I was sure Carlsen had time to get into place before I walked to the front door, stood back against the wall (though not as far back as I would have liked to stand, because the doorway was enclosed in a little roofed alcove) so a shot fired through the door would be unlikely to hit me, and rang the doorbell.

Mrs. Meredith answered immediately. She was still in the olive green suit and dark brown high-heeled shoes she'd worn to the luncheon, and her first words made it clear she'd decided to try to brazen it out. "Why, Mrs. Ralston, what a surprise to see you— and my word, what *are* you doing with that pistol?"

"Arresting you," I said grimly.

She tried to close the door on me, but not without difficulty— she was both taller and heavier than I, and about the same age—I wedged it open with my knee and shoved my way in, over her physical as well as oral objections. I was almost all the way in when Carlsen appeared in the living room from the back of the house where the kitchen door had obviously been unlocked. He strode steadily to her, dragged her off me, and handcuffed her.

"You're under arrest for theft from a mailbox," I said, panting slightly. "You have the right to remain silent. . . ."

She looked at me unbelievingly, as well she might in view of what she had really done, and then burst into laughter. "Theft from a *mailbox*?" she repeated, tears of unfeigned laughter running down her face. "You are out of your mind. I did take something from a mailbox an hour or so ago, but it was mine. The owner of the mailbox had arranged to have it left there for me to pick up."

. . . . .

"Do you waive your right to remain silent?" I asked.

"Oh, of course. This is perfectly ridiculous," she said.

Carlsen took the handcuffs off, so that she could sign the rights waiver, and she started to sit down in a richly polished rock maple chair upholstered in a subdued orange-and-green plaid. "Wait a minute," he said, and she watched with an amused smirk as he lifted the cushion out of the chair and felt down into the upholstery before backing off. "Now you can sit down."

Even then he kept his eyes on her as she sat composedly and leaned over a heavy maple coffee table to sign the form. In front of her, atop a highly polished wood parquet floor, was a braided throw rug. Beside her was a heavy maple end table, one corner of which appeared stained and somehow frayed—that's not the right word but I can't think of one that fits exactly—despite its polished finish. I had little doubt I was looking at the spot where Marvin Tutwiler had died, and almost certainly I would never be able to prove it.

"There," she said, handing the pen and the form to Carlsen. Then she automatically reached for her purse.

"Negative," I said, and picked it up and began looking through it. It was obvious at a glance, from its size, that it did not contain a gun or a police radio, but it was big enough to contain the family group sheets.

"Don't you have to have a warrant to do that?" she asked pointedly.

"Wayne, hand her the search warrant," I said. "Would you like to tell me what all this is?" I held out the two family group sheets and the note I'd had Marge write.

"I told you, it was left in the mailbox for me to pick up," she said, her voice perfectly even. "Don't tell me—oh, my goodness! Mrs. Greenwood"—she pronounced Mrs. *Mizziz,* so there was no possibility of misunderstanding what she said—"was talking to someone named Deb—and Brume told me that your name is Deborah. Don't tell me it was you! Oh, what a silly contretemps! You mean it was *you* who wrote that silly letter about kidnapping? Oh,

Mrs. Ralston, my goodness! How could you think such a thing? Mrs. Greenwood just wanted you to leave the forms in the mailbox for me, that's all."

"I see. And where is Miss Greenwood now?" I asked. Of course I didn't tell her that Matilda had never left any forms with me. I had no intention of telling her that. Let her find out in court.

"Why, I'm sure I don't know," she said. "She spent the last two nights with me, because her roof was leaking. . . ."

(It was perfectly true that Matilda's roof leaked in a couple of places, but it had done so for as long as I had known her. She would just put large buckets under the leaks and go on about her business. And whoever tossed her house certainly knew about the leaks; it would have been impossible to miss them in rainy weather.)

". . . but she left several hours ago and I have *no idea* where she went."

"How did she leave?" I asked.

"What do you mean, how did she leave?"

"Was she driving?"

"Why, no, I don't believe she was."

"I don't believe so either," I said, "because her car is still at her home."

"Then she must have taken a taxi," Mrs. Meredith said. "That's right, she asked me to call her a taxi."

"What taxi company?"

"I beg your pardon?"

"What taxi company did you call? We'll check its waybills and find out who the driver was."

"Do you know, I don't even remember."

"That's fine," I said, "we'll check the waybills of every taxi company in town, and you know as well as I do what we'll find out."

"Well, my dear, I can't be blamed if some driver neglects to write down his fares. I suppose all those drivers steal from the company all the time."

"The driver has to account for all the mileage on his odometer

. . . . .

179

from the time he gets the taxi until the time he turns it in. And even if he decided not to report a short downtown trip when somebody hailed him, he'd certainly report a pickup that was dispatched to him. The dispatchers also keep logs."

"Well, then, in that case I'm sure you'll find the driver, and he'll know where he took Mrs. Greenwood."

"Did she take a taxi to your house also?"

"Why, no, she telephoned me right after it started to rain and told me her roof was leaking and she needed a place to stay, and I picked her up. Such a nasty day, and with that awful leak." She paused and examined the beginning of the search warrant. "Do you intend to search my entire house?"

"I most assuredly do."

"Then I believe I had better call my attorney."

"You do that," Carlsen drawled to her, and then spoke to his radio. "Detectives two–seven–six and two–four–five are ten–six at . . ." He gave the address. "Get somebody from uniform division out here to baby-sit a White female subject."

"Ten-four," said a voice in Dispatch that I recognized as Reuben Dakle. "Is that subject juvenile?"

"Negatory, adult."

"Ten-four, I'll get a female officer en route."

He moved away from the telephone stool and bowed ironically to Mrs. Meredith, gesturing her to the telephone.

Mrs. Meredith sat down beside the phone, dialed, murmured into the mouthpiece. I didn't try to hear and neither did Carlsen. This was a privileged discussion. Eventually she hung up and said, "My attorney will be here presently."

Then Carlsen, Mrs. Meredith, and I sat in a far from companionable silence for a while. Carlsen and I couldn't begin searching because we had to be together when we searched, and we didn't want to haul Mrs. Meredith along with us from room to room. And considering what we suspected her of, what I at least was sure she had done, we certainly didn't want to leave her to her own devices, even handcuffed, which at the moment she wasn't.

After a while she said, "You're not going to find anything here that shouldn't be here."

"That may be true," Carlsen said without moving.

"Because there's nothing to find."

Neither of us answered her, this time. But if she was that sure, probably she was right.

She waited until past time for an answer, and then added, "I already told you that Mrs. Greenwood was here, so there's no question about that. So it doesn't matter if you find her fingerprints or something like that. And it happens that I overheard her every time she called you. Really, you know, even if you had tape-recorded everything she said, there would be nothing at all to incriminate me. I'm sure you'll find her soon, and she won't have a bad word to say about me."

And it was perfectly true that nothing Matilda said would sound incriminating to a jury. Mrs. Meredith had been very careful in what she had allowed Matilda to say. But if she was that sure I would find Matilda soon, and that sure Matilda wouldn't have a bad word to say about her—I couldn't help looking at her then.

"Really. She won't." Mrs. Meredith's expression wasn't far short of a smirk again.

"Mrs. Meredith," I said, "I know Matilda Greenwood very well. You don't."

"She was a guest in my home."

"I'm sure she was. I'm sure you made her an offer she couldn't refuse. But if you knew her very well you'd know she is Miss Greenwood or Ms. Greenwood. Not Mizziz Greenwood. And you'd also know that there are some things she says that mean one thing to a person who knows her well and another to a person who doesn't. So don't bother to go on lying. I don't want to listen to you."

"Can you prove I'm lying?" Her voice didn't even bother to be contemptuous. It was quite matter-of-fact.

. . . . .

"Not yet," I said. "But I will." I opened her purse again, fished out her keys. "Let's go outside," I said.

She shrugged and stood up, Carlsen staying right with her, and they followed me out to the Saturn. I opened its trunk.

Matilda was not in the trunk.

I had not expected her to be. I had only hoped it.

If Mrs. Meredith was this certain that Matilda would have nothing bad to say about her, then she knew that Matilda would say nothing at all. About her or anybody or anything else. To me or anybody else.

Matilda was dead.

Mrs. Meredith had told me, in effect, that the body would be found soon.

And there wasn't one damn thing I could do about it.

Officer Arielle Thompson arrived and took over baby-sitting Mrs. Meredith, and Carlsen and I started searching.

Matilda's favorite bracelet—the one I'd never seen her without—was on the floor behind the headboard of the bed in the guest bedroom. That would mean something, if Mrs. Meredith had said Matilda was never here. But she'd been smarter than that. So it meant nothing at all. Matilda had been here. Matilda had left her bracelet here. So what? she would say.

Matilda never took that bracelet off; she had told me once that she even bathed and swam in it, and I'd seen her wearing it in full ceremonial dress. She'd taken it off now in hopes that I would find it, if I ever got this far. And I had.

But there would never be a way I could convince a jury that I knew she never took that bracelet off.

Matilda lived alone, had lived alone for at least ten years. If a defense attorney asked me, or anybody else, if she might have taken the bracelet off when she slept, if she might have absentmindedly left it behind after misplacing it in a guest bedroom, there would be no way at all that I could prove otherwise.

What I knew didn't count in court. The only thing that counted in court was what I could prove.

. . . . .

Wayne and I completely tore that room apart looking for anything else. There wasn't anything else there to find, not anything that was evidentiary in the least.

We could look just about anywhere. One of the things that was missing was a police radio, and it was small enough to be placed in a drawer, on a shelf, between the mattress and springs.

That's the important thing in writing a search warrant, to list the smallest thing it is reasonable to think you might find in the search. Because you can't look in any place too small to hold the smallest thing you listed. If all you listed was a stolen refrigerator, and you opened a kitchen drawer and found the pistol used to kill your closest friend, you couldn't even present that pistol in court, because the refrigerator couldn't fit in that drawer.

But if the smallest thing you listed was a postage stamp, anyplace where a postage stamp might fit was fair game. And the pistol would be admissible evidence.

A police radio is pretty small.

But we didn't find it.

We also didn't find a gun, and we didn't find evidence that a young man lived in that house. Of course we hadn't put that on the search warrant, but we looked anyway.

We searched all three bathrooms for evidence of first aid involving a bloody wound. We searched every trash can in the house and every trash can outside.

We searched the garage. We searched the garden shed.

We did not find Matilda. We did not find evidence that a young man lived in that house. We did not find a gun or a police radio or even a box of ammunition, which people frequently forget to get rid of when they get rid of a gun. The only bandage material we found clearly had never been opened.

When Carlsen and I went back into the living room, attorney Sam Brannan was sitting there. He looked at us, not particularly hostilely, and asked, "Are you taking anything?"

"Yeah," I said. "If you'll advise your client to return her copy of the search warrant to me, I'll list what I'm taking."

. . . . .

"I have to ask something," Mrs. Meredith said.

Brannan looked at her and nodded.

"On this piece of paper, this search warrant, it says the family group sheets are in your handwriting."

"That's right."

"So where are the originals?"

"That's my business."

"You read my personal papers—"

"Did I?" But despite my distress over Matilda, a small glow of satisfaction was beginning inside of me. I'd guessed right.

"You know you did! These are my personal papers! I paid—"

She stopped suddenly, probably aware that she was heading into very dangerous territory.

"You paid whom, Mrs. Meredith? You paid a genealogist? You paid Marvin Tutwiler, and then he started blackmailing you?"

"You're out of your mind!" she shouted. "Nobody was blackmailing me! These papers are lies, all lies! I'm descended from Amos Gridley, but he *didn't* have two wives. Only one, only Rachel Kelley, and I don't know where you got the idea—or where anybody else got the idea—and you had *no right*—"

"Well whoop-ti-doo, Cousin Lucinda," I said. "So Aunt Brume was wrong. She told me she was related to you but I'm not, and she was wrong. Which doesn't make my day. I'm descended from Amos Gridley and Amanda Sutherland. This information, these group sheets, came from my genealogy, not yours. Amos Gridley did have two wives at the same time. And if you were half the woman either Amanda Sutherland or Rachel Kelley was, three people, maybe four, wouldn't be dead right now and I wouldn't be here right now and you wouldn't be under arrest."

"You lied to me!" She vaulted out of her chair like a cyclone, heading for me with hands twisted into claws, and Brannan, as well as Carlsen and Thompson, grabbed her just before she could reach me. The three of them shoved her back down into a chair. "I suggest," Brannan said, his voice icy, "that you sit down and shut

up, if you want me to continue to represent you."

He picked up the now-crumpled search warrant and handed it to me, and I put it on top of the other two copies on my clipboard and began to write.

The affidavit had been in duplicate; one copy had stayed with the judge at the time it was filed, and the other copy had stayed in our case files. The warrant itself was in triplicate: All items seized must be listed on all three copies, and one copy must be left with the person controlling the area searched (or in a conspicuous place, if the person wasn't home at the time of the search), one copy must be filed with the court within ten days after issuance of the warrant (that's as long as a search warrant is good, because the law assumes that information more than ten days old is stale when it comes to the location of any kind of contraband), and one copy must be placed in the case files.

For this we still use carbon paper and a hard-tipped ballpoint pen, because the soft-tipped pens we use now for most things won't work with two layers of carbon and three sheets of paper.

I listed the two family group sheets, the note, and the bracelet, and handed Mrs. Meredith's copy of the warrant to Brannan. We hadn't found anything else to take.

"I may return and search again on the same warrant," I told Brannan.

"I can't permit that," he said remotely, his eyes fixed carefully on a section of blank wall. I've often wondered what defense attorneys think when they know darn well their client is guilty. Whatever it was, he was clearly thinking it now.

"Fine, I'll get a new warrant."

"I doubt you have probable cause. Are you arresting Mrs. Meredith?"

I had to make a fast decision. I didn't have enough evidence to convict; he'd have her out on bail or, more likely, on habeas corpus inside of two hours. But dammit, I wanted her to see the inside of a cell at least a little while.

. . . . .

"Yes," I said. "Here's the arrest warrant, for theft from a mailbox. We'll be adding another for resisting arrest. Officer Thompson, will you transport the subject?"

I started crying in the car, in the dark, and Carlsen said, "I sort of know how you feel."

"Yeah?" I sniffled.

"My first partner got killed. I was there."

I went on crying, hardly noticing where Carlsen was driving until I realized he had pulled up in my driveway. "Hey," I protested.

"You've got to get some sleep," he said gently. "I know what you think about your friend, and you're probably right. But you can't help her, or Bill Livingston, by killing yourself on the highway. You're not fit to drive and you're sure not up to working. Let some of us who got a little sleep last night take over for now."

He went in the house with me, where Harry was watching a videotape of *The X-Files* (he has religiously videotaped every episode, so that when Hal gets home from his mission, during which he is not allowed to watch television, he can catch up on them), and I stumbled through the living room into Harry's and my bedroom, to throw myself facedown flat on the bed while Carlsen told Harry the situation.

Cameron came in and lay down beside me. "I missed you, Mommy," he said.

I hugged him. "I missed you too."

"Daddy says something happened to Matilda."

"Yeah."

"What happened?"

"We don't know yet."

"Won't she tell you? I told you when the vole bited me."

That was entirely true. He had told me, after some persuasion. Originally, he had run inside howling, trailing blood, and yelling "A *thing* bited me!" With visions of rattlesnakes in mind, I had rushed him to the bathroom to wash the bleeding thumb and examine it closely; it was only after careful questioning that he had revealed that he had tried to help Margaret Scratcher catch a vole (he thought it was a mouse) and the vole had bitten him. We were able to identify it as a vole only after Margaret Scratcher brought it in to present to him as a gift, and it was only after a telephone call to a veterinarian, who assured me that there has never been a known case of a vole carrying rabies, that I quit worrying.

But he had indeed told me. "We can't find her to ask," I explained.

"Do you think a vole bited her?"

"I hope not." But my head at once was filled with mental pictures of the chewed body of Uncle George, out at the compound, and tears once more welled up in my eyes.

"Oh." He was silent, digesting that information, watching me. What can a four-year-old say to comfort a weeping mother? Finally he said, "That sounds pretty bad."

"It is pretty bad."

He cuddled for a while longer and then said, "I guess I'll let you sleep. Maybe you can find Matilda tomorrow. Good night."

"Thank you," I told him, "and good night to you. I'm glad you came to talk to me."

He tiptoed out and closed the door carefully behind him, and I crawled under the blankets and pulled a pillow over my head. After a while Rags came in, curled up beside me with her head on my hand, and started purring, and I began crying again as quietly as I could.

Harry came in later, to rub my back gently. "You did the best you could," he told me.

"But it wasn't good enough."

"Sometimes it isn't. And you can't do anything about that. I—I don't tell war stories. And I'm not going to now. But believe me, I know. Sometimes the best any of us can do isn't good enough to keep a friend alive. But if it's the best we can do it's the best we can do. And that's just the way it is."

Harry had spent three years in Vietnam. He knew. I knew he knew.

But I still went on weeping.

. . . . .

Eleven
· · · · · ·

SOMETIME MUCH LATER in the night, the telephone rang again. I heard Harry answer it in the living room, but for a moment I lay somnolent, too drowsy to remember anything and therefore too drowsy to move. Then I heard him say, "I'll tell her when she wakes up."

Then I remembered everything. "Harry," I called, "I'm awake. What happened? Did they find Matilda?"

He came on into the bedroom but didn't turn on the light as he sat down on the bed. "Not yet," he said, "but Millner and Carlsen decided that in view of your testimony they had enough to charge Meredith with kidnapping. And then Sarah Collins checked the fingerprints from the burglaries and made her on them, so that's three more charges."

"But nothing on the killings?"

"Nobody can prove yet where Tutwiler was killed. None of the fingerprints from Malone's house match up, and there weren't any prints that could be tied directly to Livingston's murder."

"What about the fingerprints on Malone's rearview mirror?"

"They haven't gotten to them yet. Sarah got called out on something. She'll compare them as soon as she gets back in."

"Has she said anything about Matilda? Meredith, I mean, not Sarah."

"She still insists that Matilda visited her by her own choice and left this afternoon by taxi and she doesn't know where. Nobody has told her how we know that's not true."

· · · · ·

"Nobody's going to," I said.

"Right. Which means ultimately, in court, it'll come down to who is more convincing, you or her."

"Which means whose lawyer is more convincing, hers or the state's."

"Maybe," Harry said patiently.

"Which means she hires the right dream team and she walks."

Harry didn't say anything for a moment. Then, carefully, he changed the subject slightly. "Millner told me to tell you that she's being held without bond and you're to get a decent night's sleep before coming in tomorrow."

"I'm not sleepy," I said. "I'm hungry."

"There's leftover pizza."

"I don't want cold pizza. I'm sorry, Harry, I'm not trying to be disagreeable. Anyway, isn't this the second night in a row you guys have had pizza?"

"No, just the second in three nights. Lori cooked something last night."

"What?"

"I don't know, some kind of a thing with macaroni and tuna and cheese soup and peas. I don't think she has a name for it."

By now I was sitting cross-legged on the bed with the blanket draped over my shoulders; I had at some point yanked it free at the bottom, and clearly I was going to have to remake the bed before Harry got in it.

And Rags, after leaping disgustedly out of bed, had sneezed twice, sat in the middle of the floor and washed her ears, and gone out the cat door onto the patio. I could hear Ivory snuffling outside the door. It drives him crazy, how the cats can get in and out and he can't. But that's the difference between a four-pound cat and a forty-pound cocker spaniel. Pat, at close to eighty pounds, has long since given up trying to find a way through.

"Want me to go out and get you a hamburger?" Harry asked patiently.

. . . . .

"It's too late."

"Deb," Harry said, "it's not even nine o'clock."

By this time Lori, too, had crowded into the bedroom. "I could make you something," she offered.

"I don't want you to have to cook this late at night," I protested.

"So what it boils down to," Harry said drily, "is that you're hungry but you don't want leftover pizza, you don't want Lori to cook anything, I'm sure you don't want to cook anything yourself, you don't want me to go out and get you something, and I'll bet you also don't want to get dressed and let me take you out."

"I guess so," I said. "But when you put it that way it sounds awful."

"Not awful. Just cranky. Like a fractious two-year-old."

I promptly stuck my thumb in my mouth like a binky, and Harry and Lori both laughed. "You're cool," Harry said, in the slang of our long-ago young years, and Lori looked slightly puzzled.

Then she went back to looking distressed. I wasn't the only one worrying about Matilda. She had been kind to Lori before we knew of the psychological warfare Lori's aunt was subjecting her to, and Lori adored her. Impulsively I held out my arms to her, and she threw herself into them and burst into tears.

Harry stood and looked very troubled, as well a man might when all the womenfolk in his household are crying and there's nothing at all he can do to solve the problem.

Finally he ambled off, returning twenty minutes later with a large hamburger, fries, and a chocolate shake for each of us. Cameron, of course, was long since asleep. I went out into the living room long enough to eat, and then I went right back to sleep, waking at my usual time when Lori banged the door on her way out to Seminary. As Harry has a new truck, his old one having two months earlier been parked (by me, unknowingly) directly above a bomb attached to a gas main, the roar of the truck no longer wakes the neighborhood, but like most teenagers Lori is pretty well allergic to closing doors quietly.

· · · · ·

I got up and immediately called my office. Nobody was there. That was not a surprise; usually nobody is there until eight. But I was too restless to wait; I called Millner at home.

"I thought I'd be hearing from you about now," he said. "No, we still don't know anything about Matilda. Sarah did make the print from Malone's rearview mirror, though, and I talked with an assistant DA last night late. We'll be charging her with Janet Malone's murder this morning. We don't have enough yet to charge her on Livingston."

"But we've now got her on theft from a mailbox, resisting arrest, kidnapping, and murder."

"That's right. I thought about dropping the theft from mailbox, but that would have left me with no arrest for her to resist and I wanted to keep that one."

"It'll give the DA a chip if it gets into plea bargaining," I agreed. "Has she said anything about her accomplice?"

"She now refuses to talk with us at all."

And we couldn't make her talk with us if she didn't want to. That is the law.

"I'll just head on up there—"

"You'll get a decent breakfast and arrive late," Captain Millner interrupted. "Dan Phelps from the DA's office will be there at ten, and we're going to consult with him about further search and arrest warrants and see what we still need to build a case. Nothing else is going to happen until then, and I want you rested, fed, and thinking straight."

I surrendered meekly enough, having no real choice in the matter, and after attending to small matters such as teeth and face, I wandered into the kitchen, to stand in silent contemplation of a small can of blueberries until Harry came and asked me what I was doing.

"I'm making blueberry muffins," I said.

"You sure? Because it looked to me like you were going to sleep standing up."

. . . . .

"No, I'm making blueberry muffins."

As usual, I began by opening the canister of white flour, deciding it looked completely icky, putting it away, and opening the canister of whole wheat flour. Today it didn't look much better. I shrugged, got out my collection of biscuit-mix recipes, and dragged out the canister of homemade biscuit mix, half white flour and half whole wheat. I use that stuff for everything. It took about two minutes to mix up the muffins, pour them into the sprayed muffin pans, and get the pans into the almost preheated oven. Then I went in the living room, sat down, and began to look at the paper. I wasn't sure what day the paper was for; several days' worth seemed to be strewn around the living room, and I remained so tired I didn't even think of looking at the dateline. If I could manage to read the comics and the advice columns I'd be doing well.

Come to think of it, I also wasn't sure what day this was. I had totally lost track of time.

I decided not to ask. I wasn't sure I *wanted* to know what day this was, unless I had to write another search warrant, and if Dan Phelps was coming over he (or his secretary, who undoubtedly would come with him) would write the warrants and I wouldn't have to worry about them.

The muffins came out perfectly, and I was sure I would choke if I had to eat a bite of one, though no such compunctions seemed to trouble Harry, Lori, and Cameron, all of whom were quite delighted with the novelty of anything other than cereal on a weekday. I tossed milk, frozen orange juice, vanilla, sugar, a raw egg, and a handful of wheat germ into the blender and drank the result while I was dressing.

Of course I got to work early.

That gave me time to read the contents of my in-basket, which I had been neglecting entirely.

I read with much more absorption than usual. When I was reading I couldn't think about Matilda. That was the theory, but of course I thought about her anyway, and I was grateful for the box of Kleenex I keep in my desk drawer and for the extra backup box in my locker. I had a hunch I was going to be into the backup box before this day was through.

"Desecration of a corpse," Phelps said. "Theft of a corpse. Burglary of a funeral home; we don't know how or when she got in but we know she had to have gotten in to switch corpses. Improper disposal of a corpse. We'll start with all that. The corpse of—look, I can't write Uncle George down on a warrant."

"George Milton," Captain Millner said.

"Okay, so we want to find the connection between Meredith and this Milton, if any. There are too many *m*'s in this case. And what funeral home did you say it was stolen out of?"

"Mullins Brothers."

"*More m*'s. Why do you want to do this to me? Never mind, never mind. So we want to find some connection between her and Mullins Brothers Mortuary. And we've got to find out who that young lunk was that was with her. Never mind that, I'm getting out of order again. Let's see, what's next? Well, we don't know if it's first or next. The Gaines burglary. That was probably first, actually, unless it was third. It couldn't have been second, I don't think, though, because Tutwiler was almost certainly a manslaughter, would have been called accidental death if she'd just *reported* it, and then she had a body to get rid of and that's when she went and stole Uncle George—damn, you've got me doing it now. But you've got to collect that throw rug you think he slid on, Tutwiler I mean, not Uncle George, and that end table he might have knocked his head on. Lucy, that will need to go in the search warrant."

"Right," Lucy said, making fast and, to me, unintelligible pothooks on her notebook.

Clearly, Dan Phelps was enjoying this case, I thought sourly. I had never worked with him before. He was very tall, very heavy, very black, and at the moment, very pleased with himself. But why shouldn't he be? I might have enjoyed the case myself, in some ways, if it hadn't been Matilda missing and probably dead.

"Okay, so we've got the Gaines burglary, the burglary of Mrs. Keating's boardinghouse, the burglary of Marvin Tutwiler's room *in* Mrs. Keating's boardinghouse—you have that as two separate counts, why?"

"Because Tutwiler controlled his room, which he rented from Mrs. Keating, but Mrs. Keating controlled the basement, which was used as a common storage area," Millner said.

"Oh, of course, I see."

"And then—"

"I just thought of something," I interrupted him.

Everybody turned to look at me. "What?" Phelps asked.

"Well—she was looking for whatever work Tutwiler had done on her genealogy. We're sure of that, now. She tossed all those places looking for it but she never did find it—we know that because she was so frantic to get it that she snatched that stuff out of the mailbox with Carlsen and me right there. Tutwiler had done a real good job of threatening her with it, and he couldn't have threatened her with it if he didn't have some information to give her. So it really did exist. And she never found it. And we never found it. So where is it?"

"Have you talked with *all* the wives-in-law?" Millner asked, and added, "I like that word, by the way."

"Every one of them," I confirmed. "But I never asked if—oh, rats, I *know* he had children, because one or two of them mentioned child support. But did he have any *grown* children? The age he was, you'd think he would."

"Why do you need to find this now?" Phelps asked.

"I don't know if I need to find it or not," I said, probably not very coherently. "I won't know if I need it until after I get it. But I'm thinking if he had something he wanted to store secretly he might have stored it with one of his children, because his clients wouldn't likely have known how to find his children."

Phelps shrugged. "We'll wait while you make telephone calls."

. . . . .

195

It took me five minutes, and three telephone calls I should have made at least four days ago, to reach Amaranth Tutwiler Chavez and ascertain that her father had three weeks earlier left with her a sealed manila envelope he had told her to keep safe and not open, because it might be worth a lot of money.

Yes, of course she'd be glad to bring the envelope to the police station, if it might help police determine who had killed her father. "Not that I'm surprised somebody killed him," she told me candidly. "I'm just surprised it wasn't over a woman."

When I got back to the conference, the topic of discussion was whether Mrs. Meredith's fingerprints on Janet Malone's rearview mirror constituted sufficient probable cause to charge her with that murder. The consensus seemed to be that it was.

That left the murder of Livingston, on which there was really no evidence, and the kidnapping of Matilda—not that they couldn't charge her with that (they already had), but we still didn't know where Matilda was.

By now my head was spinning. The best that I could figure out, both from what had been said at this conference and what hadn't, was we still needed to find at least the following things:

a connection between Meredith and George Milton;
a connection between Meredith and Mullins Brothers Mortuary;
a connection between Meredith and the medical school;
evidence of exactly how Tutwiler had died;
the husky young man both Victoria Hardage and I had seen;
the gun with which Livingston had been shot;
Livingston's police radio;
and, of course, Matilda, alive or dead but preferably alive.

I didn't have much hope, now, of finding her alive.

Phelps finally decided that we could charge Meredith with all the burglaries (which we already had done), with desecration and improper disposal of the bodies of both George Milton and Marvin Tutwiler, with the murder of Janet Malone, and with the kidnapping of Matilda Greenwood. We could not, yet, charge her with the murder or manslaughter of Marvin Tutwiler because we didn't yet have enough evidence as to how he had died, and we could not charge her with the murder of Bill Livingston because we had insufficient evidence to indicate that she had done it. After all, Phelps pointed out, we couldn't *prove* that some drug-hunting gang of punks hadn't broken in there and killed him, which meant there was sufficient reasonable doubt and there was no sense bringing the charge at this point.

But he agreed that we did have sufficient evidence to get another search warrant, and he wrote it himself (well, dictated it) to make certain that it was exactly right.

I stayed in the office while Phelps and Millner took the warrants to get them signed. It was fortunate I did, because Amaranth—I had trouble believing that anybody, even Marvin Tutwiler, would name a child Amaranth—showed up while they were gone.

The desk officer called me, asking if I wanted him to send her up or if I wanted to come down and get her. I decided I had better come down and get her.

The envelope she was holding looked about fourteen by ten inches, and it was over an inch thick. I wrote her out a receipt for it and asked, "When your dad gave it to you, did he tell you anything about it?"

"No," she said, "just to hold on to it and not to open it."

"Did he tell you anything else?"

She grinned wryly. "Catch him telling me anything. As far as he was concerned I was still six years old. 'Course I thought the same thing about him, by the time I was eight. You know I don't even *know* how many brothers and sisters I have? That's why I married Manuel. He's full-blooded Aztec so he couldn't possibly be my brother. Just kidding, of course I fell in love with him, but knowing

. . . . .

he wasn't my brother was a plus. My dad was a *dork*."

But then she turned her head away from me, her eyes suddenly full of tears, and bit on her left knuckles, silently, for a minute or two. Then she shook her head. "Sorry," she said, her voice slightly muffled. "I thought I was cried out. I just—you know—laughing to keep from crying. You know."

"I know," I said.

"I always wanted a dad with good sense, you know? I figured out a long time ago he was like that T-shirt you see in ads—I might grow old but I'll never grow up—but I kept on hoping someday he really would. You know, like he'd marry the right woman and she'd know how to make him behave and he'd start acting like a man instead of some irresponsible kid. But I guess I knew he wouldn't. And now he's dead so he can't. He tried to be a decent dad. At least I guess he tried. I keep telling myself that anyhow. I'm sorry for bawling at you."

"That's okay."

I thanked her again for bringing the envelope, took it upstairs, and began to look through it.

It contained one Ahnentafel chart, tracing the direct ancestry of Lucinda Harrison (presumably Lucinda Meredith's maiden name) back only two or three generations on some lines, twenty to forty on other lines, and about sixty family group sheets.

No wonder Tutwiler had been able to blackmail Meredith over the contents of this envelope. The children of Amos Gridley and Amanda Sutherland had scattered around Texas and adjacent states; most of them had only one marriage or more than one in normal succession. But the children of Amos Gridley and Rachel Kelley had moved to a Mormon colony in Mexico, and one woman listed on the Ahnentafel chart as a direct ancestor of Meredith was the sixth simultaneous wife of her husband. Although one of her ancestral families was back in Texas in time for the husband to fight for the Confederacy in the Civil War, the last plural marriage recorded on any of these family group sheets was in 1883, only a very few years before Wilford Woodruff's Manifesto put a halt to plural marriage among real Mormons. (I am quite aware that there are splinter organizations in which polygamy continues to this day, mainly in Arizona, Utah, and Idaho.)

I did not know how the Daughters of Texas and the Daughters of the Confederacy, for which Meredith was otherwise eligible, viewed these things. But there was no possible doubt that release of these documents would get her thrown out of both the DAR, if she still belonged to it, and the DAF.

And I felt a moment of intense bitterness, that the religious prejudice of a couple of so-called patriotic organizations, the social climbing of one woman, and the criminal bent of one blackmailing man could have cost as many lives and caused as much misery as these documents had done. But then Phelps and the others returned, and I didn't have time to sit and brood. I took off with the rest of the group.

Lucinda Meredith's house comprised more than four thousand square feet. Despite the intensity of our search, Carlsen and I had barely scratched the surface, although we had been able to rule out any possibility that Matilda was in or near the house unless there was some hidden room, which I didn't really believe was likely. This time, Captain Millner called six detectives off what they were doing, and they, along with him, Carlsen, me, and Phelps himself, and Irene and Bob from Ident to take charge of physical evidence and do photography, went to the Meredith house in convoy.

Phelps immediately, and personally, ordered Irene to seize the end table on which I had speculated Tutwiler had landed, along with the throw rug on which he might have slipped, and to get it to the state crime lab as soon as possible.

While everybody else fanned out searching, I headed for the room Meredith had apparently used as an office. Before, I had looked through it only quickly enough to find something the size of a gun, a box of ammo, or a police radio. This time, I began by scanning the walls—interesting, she had a degree in computer pro-

. . . . .

gramming—and then I sat down and started to go through paper files.

Then I had a better idea. I've learned enough about a computer to be able to find out what files are in it, and to get at all unlocked files. Since she lived alone (we'd ascertained that she was a widow) I doubted she'd have any locked files. Our search warrant covered computer files; Phelps had thought of that possibility and listed them specifically. I booted up her computer.

Good. It went straight into Windows, where I feel much more at home than I do in DOS. I went to Main, went to File Manager, and started reading the names of files.

She'd never added a full-scale word processing program; she'd just worked in the scaled-down Word that came with the computer. That told me she probably hadn't worked very heavily with text files.

She had a genealogy program I'd never heard of, but from the subfiles in it I judged that it was a good one.

She had a text file called *genlibs,* which, when I looked at it, seemed to be a very comprehensive listing of names and addresses of every genealogical library in the country, from the biggest of all, the LDS Family History Library, through smaller but authoritative ones such as the DAR Genealogical Library and the genealogical divisions of various public libraries, including the one in Fort Worth, to a complete list of every LDS stake-center Family History Library in the world. I couldn't imagine what she had wanted them for; surely she must know that the information in one of them would be in all the others, so she really needed only one.

She had a time-management program. Ah, there was her address book! I started through it and was momentarily puzzled to find the names Dorinda and Howard Everett. They sounded extremely familiar, but where could I have met—the address was in San Francisco, and then I remembered. The Rusty Scupper. A San Francisco police inspector with worried, sympathetic eyes introducing me to Uncle George's nephew Howard, Howard and Dorinda

. . . . .

thanking me for what I had done to help get Uncle George where he belonged.

That was very interesting.

Using my own telephone charge card——the department would reimburse me later, and I wasn't sure I had the authority to put long-distance charges on a suspect's telephone bill—I called the Everetts, using the address from the computerized address book and doubtful whether I would find anybody at home at this time of day.

"Hello?" The voice was almost, but not quite, familiar. But then I'd only met her once, at a time when I was dreadfully upset.

"Dorinda Everett?" I asked.

"Yes, who is this?"

"Deb Ralston. We met——"

"Oh, of course, yes, I remember you! Are you back in San Francisco? What can I do for you?"

"No, I'm in Fort Worth. And the news I have might not be good. What is your relationship to Lucinda Meredith?" I was pretty sure I had already guessed, from the similarity in names.

"She's my twin sister, why?"

"But you're not identical twins."

"Oh, no, we never were that much alike. Is something wrong?"

If I didn't tell her the truth I would feel like a rat, because she'd been very kind to me and I had no reason to suspect she knew anything about this case.

If I did tell her the truth I would feel like a rat, because I might blow my chances of finding out things I needed to know.

If I didn't tell her the truth I would probably blow my chances of being able to use, in or out of court, anything she might tell me.

I took a deep breath. "Yes, I'm afraid so. I hate to tell you this, but we suspect Lucinda of murder."

"I see." Her voice was shaking slightly. "That—the man that got here in Uncle George's coffin? That man?"

"Among others, one of them a police officer, one a perfectly harmless young woman. And what's worse is, we have reason to

· · · · ·

believe she has kidnapped a friend of mine who might still be alive and might not be killed if we can reach her soon enough."

"Kidnapped—that Comanche psychologist you were worrying about that night?"

"Yes."

"I'll answer your questions. I—I'm not very happy about it, but I'll do it." She sounded uneasy now; I didn't blame her.

"Do you happen to know why Mullins Brothers Mortuary was selected to ship Unc—Mr. Milton's body back to San Francisco?"

A little bit of a laugh. "Oh, do go on and call him Uncle George, everybody always does. Why Mullins Brothers was selected? Well, I really don't know, except that Arnie used to work there before he got the job at the medical school."

I couldn't believe things were falling into my lap so fast. "Who is Arnie?"

"Didn't Lucinda tell you that?"

"Lucinda is not in a mood to tell me anything. And of course I can't force her to."

"Of course not, I didn't think of that," she said in a shaky voice. "I wish I could tell you I was surprised by all this."

"But you aren't?"

"No. I'm not. Except that she could be so stupid. I mean—it was a hundred and fifty years ago, and okay, those people followed the customs of their religion and their community, so what's wrong with that anyway?"

"I don't think she cared whether it was wrong," I said. "It was those DAF rules."

"Oh, yes, I know. Those clubs have been the be-all and end-all of her existence for the last twenty-five years. She only had the one child, you know. After Arnie was born and he had, you know, those *problems,* she never wanted to take the chance of having another child."

"Which brings us back to Arnie. He's her son?"

"Yes, and he's—oh, I forget what they call it now, there's some

. . . . .

fancy term, but they used to call him trainably retarded. You know, they had all these categories, I don't remember all of them, but a trainable retarded person could learn to perform simple tasks but couldn't learn to read or write and would have to live in a group home, and an educable retarded person could learn to read and write and could live alone under fairly sheltered circumstances."

"And Arnie is twenty-five and he's trainably retarded, and he works at the medical school and he used to work for Mullins Brothers Mortuary," I said. "Is that an accurate summary of what you just said?"

"That's right. And there's something else you ought to know, because there's a bigger motive than you think."

"What's that?"

"Well—our grandmother told us, when we were kids, that we were descended from polygamists. And she said that polygamy is like incest, and that the children of any one wife, or of the descendants of any one wife, could have something, you know, *awful* wrong with them, just like when brothers and sisters marry. She said it was like when a purebred girl dog mates with a stray it can hurt all the future litters as well as the litter from that mating."

"But that's not even true," I pointed out. "Only the one litter is affected. And the royal families of ancient Egypt and of ancient Peru practiced brother-and-sister marriage all the time and they didn't have very many two-headed children that I ever heard of. Of course if one of the wives had some STD the other wives would probably catch it, and back then there was no cure for syphilis or gonorrhea, and newborns could catch it from their parents, so several generations of perfectly monogamous people could have it and pass it on, but still—"

"Oh, I know all that. But Lucinda believed everything Grandmother said. And when Arnie was born with his problems she was so angry, she kept screaming that it couldn't be her fault, it couldn't be her husband's fault, that some ancestor had done something awful to cause Arnie to be, you know, retarded. I kept telling her it

· · · · ·

didn't have to be anybody's fault; these things just happen some-times, but she was so angry and so hysterical. So I'm thinking—when she found out that Grandmother was right that we were de-scended from polygamy . . ."

"You're saying she could kill the messenger out of rage about the message."

"Yes. Like she could change it, make it not true, by killing the messenger. She—even back when we were kids, she always seemed to have this idea that if you could get rid of all the evidence you could, like, *unhappen* something. Like one time she had cheated on a test and got caught, this was clear back when we were in the fifth grade, and she sneaked back into the classroom during lunchtime and stole that entire batch of tests right out of the teacher's desk and tore them all up. So if she somehow thought that by killing the messenger she could get rid of the message, yes, I think she'd do it. If it was that important to her."

"I'll have to think about that, and I appreciate your telling me. That gives me some more to go on. Back to Arnie and the medical school—do you know what he does for them?"

"Cleaning, mainly, but sometimes they have him haul around cadavers. He's not superstitious; he's not sensitive; so it doesn't bother him at all where it might bother somebody else."

"Did he have a key to Mullins Brothers?"

"Oh, yes, until he lost the third one, and then they wouldn't issue him another and told him he'd just have to go there only when somebody else was there."

"Do you think she would have noticed the physical resemblance between Uncle George and Marvin Tutwiler and thought of switching the bodies?"

"That sounds *exactly* like something Lucinda would do," Dorinda said. "She reads all these weird books. She always has. I mean, *really* weird books. Like—you remember as a kid, did you read Nancy Drew and the Hardy Boys?"

"Oh, yes."

. . . . .

"So you remember all those crazy clues, like *The Clue of the Twisted Candles* and stuff like that? Well, she went right on reading adult versions of those. And—she had this book, I don't remember the name of it for sure, something like *The Anarchist's Cookbook* or *The Terrorist's Cookbook* or something like that, and she, when she was a kid she was always reading it. She's—ever since it started—she's been fascinated by that guy, the Unibomber or the Unabomer or whatever they call him, you know the one I mean, but she told me one time that he was going to get caught because he was stupid. She said anybody with good sense, he wouldn't ask for any publicity. And he wouldn't do it sequentially. He'd decide who he wanted to bomb and then he'd mail bombs to all of them, all at once, and then he'd vanish. She's always coming up with these crazy ideas. Then she pretends they were just jokes. She thinks she's so smart—I always told her if she ever did take to a life of crime she'd be caught in no time. But she insisted they'd never suspect her."

"So that's why she didn't use gloves?"

"Probably, because her fingerprints aren't—weren't, anyway—on file anywhere, and if nobody suspected her then they wouldn't know to fingerprint her and check. So you're asking if she'd dispose of bodies that way, yes, I think she would. It's exactly the kind of thing she'd think up. Anybody else, if they had a body they wanted to get rid of, they'd just go dump it in a field or maybe bury it."

"She might have tried first to bury it in Mrs. Keating's cellar."

"Garden-club Mrs. Keating? That woman with the boarding-house?"

"Yes."

"She always looked down on Mrs. Keating. She thinks she's much better than Mrs. Keating is."

"But you don't."

"No, I don't. Mrs. Keating works for a living, even if she does do her working at home. Lucinda married rich on purpose; she

· · · · ·

205

couldn't possibly have really *loved* her husband. And I'm not saying there's anything wrong with having money, we have some ourselves, and Uncle George was rolling—I'm just saying that making it your God is wrong, and that's what she did. He was sixty-three and she was twenty-three when they got married, and he was rich—a lot of oil money. I've always thought it might have been his age that caused Arnie's problems, though I might be wrong. I know the woman's age matters but the man's might not. I don't think she ever planned on having children anyway; I know she was surprised, after they got married, that he could still, you know, get it up. Sixty-three seemed ancient to her then, and I had the impression she was horribly disappointed when he lived to be eighty-one."

"I can imagine," I agreed.

"I mean, here she was, a woman in her forties is at the top of her sex drive, and her husband is eighty-one *and* too jealous to let go of the purse strings until he had both feet in the grave. I always thought—" She stopped suddenly.

"You always thought what?"

"Oh, I'm sorry, I don't mean to sound spiteful," she said, "I really don't, but—but—it's just the way she's always been. I really always thought she might have killed her husband. I mean, he was eighty-one, but he seemed perfectly healthy, and then the next day he was dead."

"Was there an autopsy?"

"No. Who wonders when somebody eighty-one dies? But she kind of looked like the cat that ate the canary. Oh, I'm talking too much, and I know I sound perfectly hateful, but I'm not, I'm just realistic. I know her. I grew up with her. And I—from what you said—your friend sounded so nice to me. I don't—want my sister to have killed her. And if you're right, if she hasn't yet, I don't want her to. So, anything I can do to help—is there anything else you need to know?"

"Do you really think she would commit deliberate murder?"

"I've answered that." She paused. "Yes, I do. I think she would. I think she did. But—I heard you and that inspector talking about that Tutwiler case, and that one sounds to me as if it might have been an accident."

"We think so too."

"But—she always would run right over anybody who got in her way. Anybody at all. Ever since she was born. So yes, those other ones you told me about, that poor woman, and that policeman, and your friend, yes, I'm sorry, I wish I didn't believe it but I do. I think she would have killed them on purpose. I think she *did* kill them on purpose. She—did I tell you she called me last night?"

"No, you didn't."

"She sounded—excited, a little *wild*. She asked me if she could come and live with us for a while. We told her no. I guess that sounds heartless, but you just don't know what living with her when I was a kid was like. When I left home I said I'd never live with her again if I had to live in a tent on the bank of the Trinity River. And I wouldn't. I'd be afraid to. Even before you told me what you think she did—and here I go babbling again. I'm sorry. Anything else you need now?"

"No, you've pretty well answered my questions. May I call back if there turns out to be anything else?"

"Yes, sure."

"Do you understand that we may have to subpoena you to testify on these matters?"

There was a long silence, before she said, unhappily, "Yes, I know. If I have to I will, but I hope you can get by without it. I mean, she *is* still my sister. And to be perfectly honest, I think I'd be afraid to testify against her, unless I was one hundred percent certain she'd be convicted and locked up for good. I guess I'm a sissy, but that's how I feel. And I—I'm sorry. I hope I didn't sound like a tattletale trying to get my sister in trouble. But as far as I'm concerned my sister got herself in trouble. Uncle George was a lot nicer than she ever was and it makes me sick that she'd treat his

. . . . .

body that way, even if she didn't do anything else. I guess she figured if he wasn't *her* uncle it didn't matter, but he was my husband's uncle and I loved him. And—I've pulled her irons out of the fire before. My mother, our mother, did it as long as she lived and then I took over. But murder—I'm not surprised she turned to murder but I never expected it. And I'm not going to pull that kind of iron out of the fire. Obviously I can't, but I wouldn't even if I could."

"I don't think anybody would expect you to. But I just realized, I do have a few more questions. What's Arnie's whole name?"

"Arnold Harrison Meredith."

"Does he live with her?"

"Oh, heavens, no, she can hardly stand to be around him. She had a nanny for him all the time while he was growing up, and then as soon as he was old enough she made him move into a shelter home. Let me get you the address. . . . It was rather a pity, actually, because he's always absolutely adored her. He'd do anything she asked him to without thinking twice."

"Including kill."

More silence. "I hope not that," Dorinda said, and then added, "I guess it sounds awful that I'd rather she be the killer than he, but she's responsible and he's really not. He's trainable but he—I don't know how to put it. It's like he doesn't know how to reason. When something looks like a good idea, he just goes and does it."

"I know a lot of people who aren't retarded who do that," I said. "Sometimes including me."

"Oh, I know, I do too, but not to the degree he does. All right, here's the address." She read it to me and I read it back to her, to make sure I had it right.

I thanked her again, she apologized again for her sister and for sounding like a tattletale, and I finally got off the telephone. Then I went out and found Captain Millner, to inform him that we were now also looking for a mortuary key that Arnie had lost and his mother, presumably, had found. He swore for a while before yelling, "Has anybody found any keys?"

. . . . .

Nobody answered.

He called the roll, everybody who was out there searching, and asked each one individually.

Nobody had found any keys.

"Well, if anybody does, show them to me," he said, and then went back to what he was doing, which was laboriously searching through every box, carton, and bag in an extremely full walk-in closet.

After that, I called the medical-school personnel department to find out where Arnie worked. "He's all over the school at different times," the woman told me. "I'm not sure anybody can locate him right now. Would you like me to try, and call you back?"

"I would appreciate it very much," I said, and gave her both callback numbers, the one at this house and the one at the police department.

Then I went on searching computer files.

Finding nothing further of interest in them except a draft of a new charter and membership form for the Daughters of the American Flag, which, interestingly enough, did *not* contain the clause about descendants of a plural marriage, I closed down the computer program, unplugged the computer (I always leave mine unplugged in case of thunderstorms, so I figured I ought to do Meredith the same courtesy even if her chances of ever touching it again were vanishingly small), and opened the top drawer of a four-drawer filing cabinet.

I looked at every file in that first drawer, and I was well into the second drawer before the woman from the personnel office called back and said, "Officer Ralston? I'm sorry, we've looked for Arnie, and the best anybody can tell, he never came to work at all today."

"Do you know whether he's been in any way involved with the body-farm project?"

"Yes, of course, he helped to move the cadavers. I thought I told you that was one of his jobs."

"Did he ever have a key to it?"

"Not that I know of," the woman said, sounding rather startled.

. . . . .

"There was no reason why he should, and we've kept that under high security."

"Well, look," I finally said, "if he shows up, if anybody sees him, please call the Fort Worth Police Department and ask the dispatcher to notify Detective Ralston at once. Tell them it's urgent."

"Is it okay to call nine-one-one for that?"

I assured her it was. Then I closed the filing-cabinet drawer with some relief and went to find Captain Millner.

Twelve

· · · · · ·

I WAS BEGINNING to feel like the end of that movie *Fatal Attraction,* when the witch-woman has been stabbed and drowned and you think everything's over with and then she sits straight up out of the water. You can't drown a witch. That's how I know she was a witch-woman. Good job by the writers and producers, I'd always thought, as well as by the actors.

But in real life, when every time I think I'm getting close to something, something else comes along to go wrong, I'm less pleased. In fact, I wasn't pleased at all.

But conscientiously, before leaving my fellow officers to continue to serve what had originally started out to be my search warrant, I went to tell Captain Millner why I was jumping ship.

Millner, who was trying to open a cedar chest without removing the stacks of magazines on top of it, hardly noticed when I told him I was going to try to find Arnie Meredith. But then he did a double take, gently lowered the lid, which he hadn't gotten that far up anyway, and stared at me. "Who the hell is Arnie Meredith?"

"Her son," I said. "Twenty-five years old. Trainably retarded. Worked for Mullins Brothers at one time, now works at the medical school."

If I hadn't been so worried, I'd have enjoyed the sensation that created. Not only Captain Millner, but three other nearby detectives also stopped what they were doing to stare at me. "How did you find that out?" Millner asked.

· · · · ·

"I looked in her computerized address book," I said, "and then I telephoned her sister in San Francisco."

"There," Millner practically crowed, "I *told* you learning about computers would do some good. Well, are you going to tell me the rest of it? What are you just standing there for?"

"Because you're talking," I said, "and we can't both talk at once." I proceeded to explain what I knew and how I knew it, and why I was now going to look for Arnie Meredith. "And if you don't want me to go alone," I said conscientiously, "you can send somebody with me."

"You might as well go alone to look for him," he said grudgingly, "but call somebody to help with the arrest."

"I didn't say I was going to make an arrest."

He glanced once more at me and then returned his attention to what he was doing. I went looking for Phelps, finding him in the living room, supervising Bob Castle to make sure that every piece of evidence collected was logged in properly and immediately, and that one person from Ident stayed in the living room and did nothing but log in evidence. He couldn't, of course, do the logging himself, as that would involve his having to testify, but he was determined that there be no possible questions later in court.

"I've got the male subject identified," I told him, "and I'm going out to look for him. But he's very severely retarded, and the best I can tell, he was just doing what his mama told him to do. Can you give me permission to promise him immunity if he leads us to Matilda and tells anything else he knows?"

"If he's that severely retarded, do you think he'll be any use?" Phelps inquired.

"I won't know till I find him. But I want to know what I can go in offering and what I can't."

Phelps stared thoughtfully at me. "I haven't worked with you before."

"That's true. You haven't."

"I understand you're emotionally involved with this case."

. . . . .

"We're all emotionally involved with this case," I said. "Remember that Bill Livingston is—was—a friend of everybody here except you, and you'd have liked him if you'd known him. But it's true that Matilda Greenwood is a close friend of mine."

He stared at me some more, rubbing his chin thoughtfully. Then, finally, he said, "If you want to make the promise, I'll back you up. And I have the authority."

"Thank you," I said, and headed for my car. My police car, that is, which was what I was driving. I'd arrived with two other detectives in it with me, but they could return to the office with somebody else.

In the car I tried to force my brain into full function. What first?

I'd called the medical school. Arnie hadn't shown up for work. Quite clearly he was not at, and had not been at, his mother's house. So the sensible thing for me to do first was to go to the shelter where he lived.

It wasn't far from downtown, and although on the outside it looked like a warehouse, indoors it was bright and airy, with shiny yellow vinyl floors, brightly painted walls with cheerful posters, a cafeteria, and individual bedrooms. Doubtless some charity funded this, and I wasn't too surprised to notice, on the donors' "honor roll" near the office, the name of my son-in-law Olead Baker.

I went on into the office and introduced myself, badge case out and displayed.

"I'm Ruby Latimer," said the woman at the desk, after I introduced myself. "What can I do for you, Mrs.—er—Officer Ralston? There's nothing wrong, is there?"

"Well, there might be, I'm afraid," I said, as diplomatically as possible. "I need to locate Arnold Meredith, and he didn't go to work today."

"Oh, that naughty boy," Mrs. Latimer said with some annoyance. "He didn't come home last night, either. Or the last two nights before that."

"Did you report him missing?" I asked. "I haven't seen a report on him, but then I could have missed it." Could nothing, I *would* have missed it. I rarely check Missing reports, unless they're likely to relate to what I'm doing. The number of Missing reports even the average-size city can generate in a week is truly astounding, although most of the missing tend to show up again within about forty-eight hours. The only time anybody gets really alarmed very early is if the person missing is a child or an elderly person.

But from what I'd heard about Arnie Meredith, he should be considered a child notwithstanding his size and age. Apparently Ruby Latimer agreed, because she added, "His mother called three days ago and said he would be spending a night or two with her. We did expect him back last night, but when he didn't arrive we just assumed he was staying over one more night. But I *should* have thought at least she would have gotten him to work, as difficult as it is for these children to find work and as important as it is for them to feel at least a little independent."

"Has he been here at all during those three days?"

She looked at me, lips trembling. "Tell me the truth," she said. "Is Arnie in trouble? Because he's such a sweet boy, and his mother is so hateful, I always worry when he's with her."

"I don't know whether he's in trouble," I said, "but I'm afraid he might be. Has he been—"

"Yes," she interrupted as if reading my mind, "he's been in and out several times."

Half to myself, I muttered, "I sure do need to see his room."

"I can let you do that," she said.

"I'm afraid you can't."

"I don't understand."

"This concerns a possible criminal case," I said. "You can't legally give me permission to search his room, because he's in control of that space. I have to have his permission, or else a search warrant. I have enough probable cause to get a search warrant, but I really hate to take the time. I wish—"

"But, dear, he's not competent to give permission."

. . . . .

214

"I know that. But his mother certainly wouldn't."

"His mother has no say in the matter."

"I beg your pardon?"

"His mother has no say in the matter." Mrs. Latimer's voice was grim; her expression was even more so. "I am his legal guardian. She did not want the responsibility. You really don't seem to understand, Officer; his mother dislikes him very much. When we agreed to take him—we normally do not accept residents who have living parents able to care for them, as our space is so limited, but his situation was really quite unfortunate, and she was willing to pay enough to help support several of our children. When we agreed to take him, she had her lawyers sign guardianship over to us. To me personally, because I am the director of this facility. So I believe that I should be able to give you permission to look in his room, if it will help you in any way."

"Hmmm," I said rather stupidly. "I think so too, but could I use your phone?"

Of course I'd written down Lucinda Meredith's telephone number. I dialed it now, and Bob Castle answered. "Let me speak to Phelps, please," I said.

"Phelps here."

"Can the legal guardian of a mentally incompetent adult sign a consent to search?" I demanded

"Are we still talking about Arnie?"

"Yes."

"Exactly how incompetent is he?"

"Just a minute." I turned to Mrs. Latimer. "I've got the assistant district attorney on the telephone. He wants to know exactly how incompetent Arnie is."

"Tell him that Arnie's IQ is approximately fifty, and the court has ruled him totally incompetent and in need of permanent guardianship."

I conveyed the message, and Phelps said, "Let her sign."

So I got into Arnie's room. It was large for one person, clean, with bright primary colors. The single bed was topped with a quilt, and here too attractive posters covered the walls. "This is really a nice place you have here," I told Mrs. Latimer.

"Thank you," she said. "We do the best we can, but we have space for so few people compared to the many who need our help. We feel that human dignity is important. Each of our charges has an individual room, and we don't order anything in bulk except for consumables, so that we can avoid that nasty institutional look. Each two rooms share a bathroom. Of course we do have a common cafeteria, Arnie couldn't possibly be trusted to cook for himself and neither could most of the other children, but—well, you don't want to hear this. Is there anything I can help you find?"

I was, by now, cautiously opening and shutting drawers, checking shelves. Clothing, a few toys: a G.I. Joe doll, a couple of Transformers, something that looked like it might have come from a Cracker Jack box, a very full ring of keys. "I don't think so," I said. "How much clothing did he take with him?"

She was looking over my shoulder. "That's funny," she said.

"What's funny?"

"The keys."

I glanced back down. The key ring was tightly packed with keys and key blanks of every description. "Haven't you seen them before?"

"Oh, yes, of course," she said. "But he always takes one ring with him everywhere he goes, and there used to be three rings. So I would expect to find two here. You asked about clothes. Well, he didn't take any at all. His mother originally planned to take him just for one day; I'm not really sure why she wanted him at all. She usually takes him only when she has some work for him to do like digging the flower beds—as much money as she has, catch her *paying* somebody for something like that—and then she called late that first night and said she would be keeping him longer." I pivoted slowly and stared at her, thinking furiously, as she added, "I suppose he must have some clothing at her house."

· · · · ·

But he didn't. . . . There was absolutely nothing at that house that would indicate that a man had ever lived there. What did that mean?

By now I had seen that there was no gun, no police walkie-talkie, and no evidence of first aid in his room. "When is the last time you saw him?" I asked.

"Oh, my, let me see, he dropped by for just a few minutes yesterday."

"Did he seem all right?"

"I think he must have been to a movie."

"What makes you say that?"

"Why, he was babbling about guns, and shooting—he even tried to tell me he'd been shot himself, but there he was up running around, and these children do get things so terribly confused." She followed me to the bathroom, where there was a shower stall, a toilet, and two widely separated sinks with cabinets above and below both sides. "This side is Arnie's."

I touched a dry toothbrush, a dry razor, and then opened the cabinet.

There was an open box of Band-Aids on the shelf.

I looked in the trash can, and found two of Matilda's towels—I recognized the color and pattern. And both of them were stained with blood.

Mrs. Latimer crept slowly closer, looking into the trash can herself. "Oh dear," she said thinly.

Going back through the bedroom after collecting the towels, I paused to pick up the ring of keys. "I'll give you a receipt for all this," I said.

"Do you know when trash pickup is on that street?" I asked Bob over the phone.

"No, I don't," he said. "When would I have had time to find out anything? I'm in here sitting on a stack of evidence and nobody will let me go anywhere."

"Let me speak to Captain Millner."

. . . . .

As I explained what I had seen and what I had heard, I could almost see Millner taking off his glasses and rubbing the bridge of his nose before he replied, "I'll detail some people to check trash cans all up and down the street. Where will you be?"

"In my car on the way to the medical school."

As I turned to go, Mrs. Latimer said, "What was that about? Who were you talking to? Please tell me the truth! Is something wrong with Arnie?"

"I think," I said bleakly, "that his mother may have killed him."

Millner reached me by radio before I was more than halfway to the medical school. "Dutch found two large garbage sacks full of men's clothing, shoes, toiletries, and so forth in a trash can a block and a half away. The resident says she's never seen any of it before."

"Ten-four," I said. "Thank you. I'll be ten-six at the medical school in a few minutes."

I didn't bother asking anybody to look again for Arnie. Arnie wasn't going to be there. I knew that, now. Instead, I hunted down Professor Lindstrom.

He was in his office, and Olead was in there with him; they were having an animated discussion about something of which the only words I could recognize were *and, the,* and *is.* Olead rose courteously when I came to the door. "Hi, Deb," he said in some surprise.

"I'm glad I caught you both here," I said. "I suppose you would have let me know if an extra body or two turned up in the compound again?"

Both of them stared at me as if I had lost my wits. Olead found his tongue first. "Yes, of course we would," he said.

"How many times a day is it checked?"

"Twice a day," Professor Lindstrom said. "I believe we told you that."

"You did, but I wondered if there had been any change. Has a key to the compound ever been lost?"

They looked at each other, and then Professor Lindstrom said, "Well, yes, as a matter of fact."

Olead glanced at him. "I didn't know that."

"No reason why you should know."

"Who lost it?" I asked.

"That orderly, Arnie whatever-his-name-is. We had him out there putting some cadavers in place. I had laid the key down, and—do you know Arnie?"

"I don't know him," I said, "but I know about him."

"Well, did anybody tell you that he's fascinated by keys? You can't leave a key in sight around him or he'll take it to play with. And I absentmindedly laid down the key to the compound—it's not on my key ring; I keep it on a separate key ring of its own—and I looked around and he was playing with it. Well, I didn't think much of it. How much harm can anybody do playing with a key? But then a few minutes later I asked for it and he had lost it."

"May I use your phone?" At the moment I was sorely envying all those fictional detectives who somehow contrive to get all their witnesses and all their suspects into one room, so that they can question them all at once. It seemed that everything anybody told me posed a question I needed to ask someone else immediately.

Ruby Latimer answered the phone. I told her who I was, and asked, "Does Arnie ever lie?"

"Oh, yes, of course, all the children lie, though I don't think of it myself as lying. They don't understand the concept, you see, and besides that they tend to be badly confused quite often. So they tell what they think happened, or what they wish happened, or what might have happened, or what they want you to think happened. I thought I had mentioned that, before—before you found those towels."

"Well, if Arnie said he lost a key, is it possible he could have hidden it in his pocket instead?"

"Oh, dear, yes. We've had to lock the keys here up, he's so fascinated by them. I think that his mother used to lock him in a room or even a closet sometimes when he was small, because he's frightened of closed doors, we can't *ever* get him to close his bedroom door or even the bathroom door when he's in there, and he's never happy unless he has keys to play with. Even when he's watching television he has to have his keys."

"Thank you." I turned to Professor Lindstrom. "We're going to the compound *now*. Will you give me a consent to search it, or will I need to get a warrant?"

"Oh, I'll consent, of course," he said, rising, "but I can't imagine what you expect to find there. If there had been anything there unusual, one of us would surely have noticed it."

"I know that," I said, "but I've got a hunch—I've just got a hunch—if she'd been right in her guess that they'd have a closed-coffin funeral in San Francisco she'd have gotten away with it. She knows that. So, if she tried the compound again—"

"Whoever she was, she didn't," Lindstrom said. "I assure you none of us would have failed to notice another extra corpse."

"Or an unlocked gate?" I asked.

"Of course we'd notice. But if it'll make you feel better to look again—shall we all go in my car?"

"No," I said, "the two of you go in your car. I'm driving a police car and I might need to leave before you do."

"Deb, I just don't know what you expect to see," Olead said. "I mean, there's not anything here that looks the least bit out of the ordinary."

"Then maybe what I'm looking for looks ordinary." I pointed to a small building. "What's that?"

"It's part of the test. And if we open it we're going to interfere with the test process."

"And if you don't open it you may find out you have a lot more realistic test than anybody ever wanted."

He looked at Professor Lindstrom, who shrugged, and then opened the door.

· · · · ·

The stench that came out was not pleasant, but then neither was anything else in the compound. I was glad the day was cold; I'm sure it would have been twice as bad if the weather had been hot.

I walked around, leaving few footprints on the hard-packed earth despite the recent rain and the thin, slick layer of mud. Several automobiles were in the compound; I could see a clothed cadaver under the back of one of them. In another, a cadaver was sitting upright, a plastic bag over its head.

I looked inside each automobile. There was nothing pleasant in any of them. But there was also nobody I recognized. "What about the trunks?" I asked.

Again the two exchanged glances, and then Olead opened the back of a twenty-year-old red Chevette. There wasn't room for anything back there, but a half-skeletonized cadaver was there anyway, wadded up like a pretzel.

He closed the back, walked past a station wagon. "No trunk," he said over his shoulder, and headed for the next, a dark blue Oldsmobile. "I don't know what you want to do after this," he said, looking at me as he swung the lid open.

"We won't need to look further," I said, running forward and fumbling for my pocketknife at the same time.

Matilda was lying on her left side with the top of her head toward the passenger's side. Her arms and legs were tied together behind her with duct tape, and a wide strip of duct tape covered her mouth. Her eyes were open, but they were moving. Moving. She was alive.

I slashed through the duct tape binding her limbs, and she snatched off the tape covering her mouth and began to breathe in great gulps of air despite the stench, until I was afraid she would start hyperventilating. Lindstrom and I together helped her out of the trunk, and she threw her arms around me, weeping wildly, as Olead bent over the brown-haired man who had been behind her.

Like Matilda, he wasn't wearing a jacket; Band-Aids inadequately covered a long bullet crease on his right arm, which was

. . . . .

221

incredibly swollen and red, with black streaks going up and down it. Like her, his arms and legs were tied together; like her, he had duct tape over his mouth.

His eyes were closed.

He, too, was alive. An untended corpse has open eyes.

The third person in the trunk was dead. He'd been dead a long time.

"This man's burning up," Olead shouted. "And gangrene—he's got, Professor, I've never seen gangrene before, but isn't this—?"

"That's exactly what it is," Professor Lindstrom said grimly. "I can't believe this—to lay him on top of a rotting corpse with an open wound like this." He looked over at me. "You have a radio," he said. "Get an ambulance—stat—"

"Just a minute, Matilda," I said, and spoke into the radio in my hand. "Get an ambulance out here ten-eighteen. Make that ten-thirty-nine. Two to transport, shock and exposure, one of them with a bullet wound and gangrene. And tell Captain Millner I've got them both, they're alive." Ten-eighteen is maximum reasonable speed; ten-thirty-nine means "floorboard it."

"I'm okay—I'm okay," Matilda gabbled, and then burst into tears again. She was shivering terribly, and I started to slip my jacket off to wrap around her, but Olead was there first with his.

"Mine's bigger," he said, smiling at me.

Then he turned sharply, at Professor Lindstrom's shout, and said, "Deb, you've got to come see this."

I looked over in that direction.

"No, you've got to come here."

I broke loose, for a moment, from Matilda, and walked toward the trunk again, Matilda following me closely. "What is it?"

"Look," Olead said.

Lying in the trunk, where they had been covered by Arnie's bulk, were a police radio, a nine-millimeter semiautomatic pistol, and a box of ammunition. And I might as well say right now that we never found the keys; my guess is that as soon as she locked up the compound she threw them in the river.

· · · · ·

"Deb, I've got to tell you . . ." Matilda began, still shivering.

"Let me get you something to drink first, I've got a Coke in the car."

"He cried so much, Arnie, he was so scared, even with the gag on he cried, and then he stopped crying, and he got hotter and hotter. He kept me warm, but something's bad wrong with him, he was like a furnace—Deb, I've got to tell you. . . ."

I put the Coke in her hand and she drank ravenously, pushed her tangled hair back with her left hand, and said, "Deb, I've got to tell you . . ."

"Whatever it is, you can tell me later."

"No I can't! I've got to tell you now!"

I could hear sirens in the distance already. "What is it, Matilda?"

"She's crazy, that awful woman, she's crazy, she's out of her mind, Deb, did she tell you we were here?"

"No, I guessed."

"Then you're a good guesser—Deb, she's crazy, her own son, after she had me all tied up and stuck here she told him to kill me and he wouldn't, he said, 'It's not nice to hit ladies,' he'd been trying to be as nice to me as he could get away with, he's terrified of her, but he slipped me food a couple of times. And she told him to kill me and he wouldn't, so then she told him—his *own mother* told him—to get in the trunk and he did. He was scared, she had a gun, but he was begging, he kept saying like, 'Don't close the door, Mommy, I'll be good,' and he was crying, and then she taped him up the same way she taped me, and he kept on crying and she just slammed the lid shut. She said, before she slammed it, she said, 'You can't yell and you can't kick. They'll find you. Someday. But they won't find enough to identify.' And then she just slammed the lid and walked off. Her own *son!*"

"Matilda—" I hardly looked around as Olead put into my hand a handkerchief he'd soaked in water from a spigot just outside the compound. I began to wipe her face with it, and she shoved my hand away.

. . . . .

"That's not what I needed to tell you, Deb, I think I'm sort of crazy."

"I think you're in shock. Whatever it is, can't it wait till you're in the hospital? Just let me wipe your face a little—"

"No! It might already be too late!"

Beside us, both Lindstrom and Olead were leaning over Arnie Meredith. They had him untied by now, ungagged, wrapped in a couple of blankets and a sleeping bag from Lindstrom's trunk, but he looked horrible, his face red with fever, his eyes—now open— sunken and semiglazed.

"Listen, she, Deb, she was doing something with computer disks, she had a bunch of computer disks, little disks, not like the big ones I use, and she had so many, I mean like hundreds, and she had this stuff like modeling clay and she made Arnie and me cut the end out of the computer disks and put this stuff in them, and before that she put each disk in her computer and loaded some kind of program on it, and then she had us cut the end out of it, there's an end that's got metal on it and the other end just looks like plastic, it was like a—you know that thing I use to notch my disks so I can use them double-sided?"

I nodded. Matilda uses 5¼-inch disks, and like many people who do, she buys single-sided disks and then notches them herself rather than put out the extra money for double-sided. Obviously what she was talking about was the 3½-inch disks most people use now.

She was still talking feverishly. "And she had us put this clay stuff in place of what we cut out, and then she put it in some kind of mold thing and—the clay stuff, it was gray, and when she got through and the stuff hardened it looked just like a regular disk, and she put a label over where the plastic was so you couldn't see it had been cut, and then she had us put them in disk mailers with let- ters—she used a letter-folder, she didn't let me see the letters—and she was putting labels on the mailers, and postage, a lot of postage, probably more than the mailers needed. She was mailing them a lot

. . . . .

of places, and she'd printed address labels for her computer—but she told me if nobody knew it didn't matter. I don't know what she was talking about, but she said all the files it was in, she'd get rid of them, and the people who knew—she said it, whatever it was, I don't know what she was talking about, but she said it was in some-body's Bible, she said Tutwiler told her whose Bible it was, and she'd get rid of that person and burn the Bible and get rid of all the records it would have been in and then it wouldn't ever have hap-pened. Deb, I think the clay stuff was some kind of homemade plastique."

And at that moment I saw the whole thing, clear in my mind. That computer inside my skull took what Matilda had said just now, and what Dorinda had said about *The Anarchist's Cookbook* or whatever it was and what she said Lucinda had said about the Una-bomber, and what Aunt Brume had and hadn't said about geneal-ogy, and the addresses of just about every genealogical library in the world all in Lucinda's computer, and when I put it all together, I knew what Lucinda Meredith had done and I didn't know how long I had to stop it from happening. Because it didn't matter, now, that she was in jail. Her plan was already in motion. And Matilda was right, she was crazy to think it would work. It wouldn't—was she fool enough to think she could blow up the granite vault the Church has cut into the side of a mountain? But if there had been that many disks, the results of her attempts would be disastrous if a lot of people weren't notified fast.

"Thank you, Matilda, I'm going to go take care of it right now," I said. "Olead, I've got to go. Take care of Matilda."

"I'm all right," she said, and fainted into the mud, and Olead left Arnie to run toward her.

I couldn't wait even to help lift her out of the mud. I grabbed the sheltered phone at the compound, called Millie, and said, "Get somebody from the FBI and the Postal Inspection Service into my office in half an hour. Tell them it's very, very urgent, and if they can't make it, the Unabomber may look like a pussycat by comparison to what's happening now. And call somebody at that search scene, the Meredith house, and have them print out that *genlib* file and get it to the office ten-eighteen."

"You want me to tell them what this is about?" Millie asked.

"I don't have time to explain. Just tell them to hurry. I've got to get some other information first."

I ran for my car. I don't use my siren often; an unmarked car is hard for people to spot on the highway, and they may get in the way more than they get out of it. But I put the flashing blue strobe up on my dash and turned it on, hit the switch that made my headlights alternate, one side high, one side low, back and forth, back and forth, and then I hit the siren switch. I fairly flew over the bumpy dirt road from the compound to the highway, hitting my head once in the process despite my seat belt.

If I was wrong, a lot of people were going to be mad at me. But if I was right, a lot of people were going to be dead—real soon. The FBI and the ATF might not take Matilda's word, with her in shock and babbling as she was, but I knew I could take her word no matter what condition she was in, and I knew they would take my word.

Now all I had to do was find the missing piece, and I had to find it myself, because I was a relative and relatives can—sometimes—get away with things other cops couldn't in the same situation.

It took exactly twelve minutes to reach Aunt Brume's house. If it had been anybody else, I would have called or sent the closest officer. But there's nobody who can put up more obstacles to answering simple questions than Aunt Brume can. I pounded on her door. She opened it, said, "I thought I told you never to come here again," and tried to close it.

I stuck my knee in the way. "Oh no you don't!" I yelled. "I'm here on police business. Who owns the Bible that Amos Gridley's marriages are recorded in?"

"I don't know what you're talking about. And *what* is that *hideous* stench on you—get it out of here!" She wasn't just running her mouth about that; she was starting to gag.

· · · · ·

"It's mortality, Aunt, and we all come to it sooner or later. And you do know what I'm talking about. Oh yes you do. You gave it to me by accident, I've no doubt, but you gave it to me all the same. Who owns that Bible?"

"I don't have to tell you anything. Get out of my house!" She straightened the lace of her collar and tried again to close the door.

"The hell you don't!" I yelled, blocking the door again. "Look, that maniac Lucinda Meredith has sent a mail bomb to the owner of that Bible, and if you don't want murder on your conscience you'll tell me *right now* where that bomb is going!"

"Are you out of your mind?" she screamed. "Unlike you, Lucinda Meredith is a lady."

"Well, that *lady* has murdered a few people and is trying to murder a whole lot more. I can find most of the others, I know where she stored their addresses, but I have to know whose Bible that is. Now, who is its present owner?"

She stared at me. Apparently it finally penetrated even her thick skull that I wasn't playing games, because she put her hand to her mouth briefly, and then muttered, "Your mother."

I shoved past her and ran to the telephone. I have never been so relieved in my life as I was to hear my mother's cheery answer. "Mom," I said, "has your mail come?"

"Why, yes, I was just beginning to open it, why?"

"Thank you, God," I muttered, and then said, "Was there a computer disk mailer in it?"

"Yes, there was, and a nice letter with it. I've been asked to test some new software. But I can't imagine why they would have picked me. You know I don't even have a computer—"

"Mom, this is police business. Please do *exactly* as I say and don't ask why. Leave that disk and disk mailer exactly where they are. Get out of the house. Do not start the car.

"Do not slam the door. Get out of the house as quickly and as quietly as you can and go to the house across the street and wait for me there. Do you understand me?"

"Yes, but what on Earth—"

· · · · ·

"Don't ask. I'll be there as fast as I can."

I pressed the switchhook, dialed again. "This is Detective Ralston. Get hold of the Bomb Squad *fast* and have them meet me . . ." I gave my mother's address.

"As a chemist, she was a real good computer programmer," Bruce Franklin said.

"You mean it wouldn't have gone off?" I asked. The FBI agents and postal inspectors I'd asked for, along with a couple of people from ATF who had wandered in when they heard what was going on, were all crowded around. One of the FBI agents, and one of the ATF agents, had been assisting Franklin.

Franklin shook his head, continuing to put away the portable spectrometry unit he had spent the last half hour working with. "I see what she was trying to do, but—let's say she didn't follow the recipe right. Fortunately. Now, the program is real smart."

After determining that the plastic, whatever it was, was nonexplosive, he'd calmly—at least far more calmly than I would have, probably because I don't understand spectrometry—put the disk into his computer to read what was written on it. "If she'd had real plastique and anybody had booted up, they'd have been scattered over about four blocks. But, like I said, she didn't follow the recipe right." He slammed the locker door, locked it with a key, and turned to me with a grin.

"So it doesn't matter if we don't get to all of them right away."

"No," he said. "It's not going to blow up. It's not going to blow up in the mail, and it's not going to blow up in anybody's computer. I can see what she was trying to do. If she'd been just a little smarter it would have worked. But she wasn't as smart as she thought she was."

A nearby FBI agent wiped imaginary sweat off his forehead and grinned, and a couple of postal inspectors visibly relaxed.

"I think I'm going home," I said.

Epilogue
· · · · · · · ·

"BUT I WAS sorry they couldn't save Arnie," Matilda said. "He was—I know he had problems. But he was kind to me."

"Good," Olead said. "Now how about letting somebody else be kind to you? Look, Matilda, this isn't charity. I'm offering you a deal."

She looked at him stubbornly.

"If Arnie was alive you'd do it."

"Maybe I would," she said. "But—I don't know. I have the most horrible nightmares now, and I'm able to understand what's going on, but he wasn't. And he was at least between me and the corpse, but he was lying right on top of it. Maybe—maybe it's better he did die. I don't know if anybody would ever be able to get him through that kind of trauma. I don't even know if—if I'll ever . . ."

She turned her head to the side, pressed her fist to her mouth.

"Listen to me," Olead said not very patiently. "You don't have to go on living like you've been living. I know that you started that Sister Eagle Feather thing out of the best intentions in the world. You told Deb why you did it. You told me why you did it. *But it didn't work.* You did everything you could to make it work and it didn't work. You have a good education. You have skills that are very badly needed. I'm offering you the opportunity to use those skills. I'll set you up in an office, advance you the money to live on

· · · · ·

while you get started. If you like, I'll set you up in a big house that you can use as both residence and office. Give one-quarter time to the shelter. Those—children, as Ruby calls them, need help. I'm paying a counselor to work with them but he's not getting along with them very well. You will. You cared about Arnie. Now, what about it?"

There was a long silence.

"I just don't see why you're doing it," Matilda said.

"Call it an investment."

"An investment in what? Because I don't know if I'll ever be able to pay you back."

"Matilda," he said, "paybacks don't have to come in money. Don't you understand? I have more money than I'll ever need. But it's no good to me or anybody else if I don't do good things with it. You think I'm trying to help you? Think again. I'm asking you to help me."

She stared at him and then, slowly, she nodded. "But if I do it at all, I want to do it the way I want to do it."

"Okay, how do you want to do it?"

"I want—will you buy that house? The Meredith house?"

"You mean you want to live *there*?"

"Yes," she said. "I do. And I want—how many bedrooms? I think there are four. I'll take one to live in and one for my office. The other two—Ruby Latimer has all the people she has room for. She's hardly making a dent in the need. I won't either. But— two—I'll have room for two. Two who need a stable place to live. Women, I think. Maybe Native Americans."

Olead began to grin. "You've got it, Matilda."

So I will never again enter the building where Bill Livingston died. Olead had it razed. He's building a community center in its place and donating it to the community.

And I'm not going to join the DAF. Even though Aunt Brume and Aunt Darla both swallowed their prejudices enough to invite

· · · · ·

230

me and offer to sponsor me, I'm still not eligible. Aunt Brume isn't either, but she's still in it all the same.

But I just don't think I would be happy in an organization one of the founders of which is doing life plus ninety-nine years, thanks to me.

. . . . .